TIMELESS *Regency* COLLECTION

Autumn Masquerade

TIMELESS *Regency* COLLECTION

Autumn Masquerade

Josi S. Kilpack
Donna Hatch
Nancy Campbell Allen

Mirror Press

Copyright © 2016 Mirror Press
Print edition
All rights reserved

No part of this book may be reproduced in any form whatsoever without prior written permission of the publisher, except in the case of brief passages embodied in critical reviews and articles. These novels are works of fiction. The characters, names, incidents, places, and dialog are products of the author's imagination and are not to be construed as real.

Interior Design by Rachael Anderson
Edited by Donna Hatch, Heather B. Moore, Jennie Stevens, and Lisa Shepherd
Cover design by Rachael Anderson

Cover Photo Credit: Dress photo, hair, make-up and gown courtesy of Matti's Millinery & Costumes of www.mattionline.com
Cover Photo Copyright: Matti's Millinery & Costumes

Published by Mirror Press, LLC
ISBN-10: 1-941145-75-2
ISBN-13: 978-1-941145-75-3

TABLE OF CONTENTS

A Merry Dance 1
by Josi S. Kilpack

Unmasking the Duke 99
by Donna Hatch

What's in a Name? 213
by Nancy Campbell Allen

OTHER TIMELESS REGENCY COLLECTIONS

A Midwinter Ball
Spring in Hyde Park
Summer House Party

A Merry Dance

Josi S. Kilpack

OTHER WORKS BY JOSI S. KILPACK

The Sadie Hoffmiller Culinary Mystery Series
The Newport Ladies Book Club series
A Timeless Romance Anthology: All Regency Collection
Timeless Regency Collection: A Country Christmas
Her Good Name
Unsung Lullaby
Sheep's Clothing
A Heart Revealed
Lord Fenton's Folly
Forever and Forever

One

At the far end of the study was a desk set against a corner where, if a girl were overly curious and perpetually bored—as Lila was—she could hide away and entertain herself with both the thrill of being unseen and the snippets of information she was not entitled to otherwise. Lila had discovered the hidden corner when she was first deposited at Franklyn Farm, her uncle's estate in South Shropshire. In an unfamiliar place with unfamiliar people, young Lila often disappeared into *her* corner when she needed to feel in control of her space, albeit a small one. At six years old, finding respite there was reasonable, perhaps even endearing. At nineteen, it was ridiculous, but her uncle would never guess she still found herself there somewhat regularly. She was trying to reflect the good manners her uncle had worked hard to instill within her, but the time had not yet come to give up her hiding place. Maybe next month.

Today Lila sat in her triangle of space with her back against one wall and her knees bent while she crocheted the second of a pair of socks. The typical English girl embroidered, and a few knew how to knit, but the governess hired to care for Lila when she was nine had recognized her excess energy and taught her the unconventional skill of crocheting so she would always have something with minimal equipment—a single hook. "Busy hands create a calm mind," Miss Lowry had said.

Lila had complained at first, but in fact her mind did calm as row after row of stitches melted from her hook. And it was practically silent—perfect to do when hiding in the corner of Uncle Peter's study. Lila crocheted blankets, doilies, shawls, purses, and countless caps, but mostly she crocheted socks. She could make a pair in just a few hours, and the servants, as well as the vicar, who would distribute them to the poor, were always in need of such practical items.

Today she was crocheting socks for Neville, her cousin—and Uncle Peter's only son—who was coming home from an extended tour to America in just a few weeks. During the two years he'd been gone, their easy friendship seemed to have turned into something more, until the idea that Neville was the love of her life had grown in to an absolute. Just a month ago he had promised he would be home in time to have the first dance at the Marchetts' annual Autumn Masquerade. Their blooming romance would be the stuff of novels—heir to a profitable estate finding love with his penniless cousin raised above the unfortunate circumstance of her birth. They had known one another most of their lives—though Neville had been at school a great deal of the time—and it made sense they would spend the rest of their lives together, as well.

A Merry Dance

As it was the second Tuesday of the month, Uncle Peter had been meeting with his solicitor, Mr. Jeppson, much of the morning. Lila loved to closet herself away on the second Tuesday of the month if she could manage it. She liked knowing things like the price of corn that season or when the next sheep exchange was scheduled, and the conversations often ended with some masculine gossip regarding mutual friends. One day Neville would run Franklyn Farm and Lila felt sure a wife who had been privy to more than a decade of the estate's financial climate could only be a help for him. She was so comfortable with the official talk that she could listen with half an ear while she crocheted and thought about the afternoon she would spend with her good friend Eloise. They had been working on their masquerade costumes for weeks but were going to pick bilberries today. Franklyn's cook had already promised to bake a pie for each family if they would do the gathering. With the change of season, there would not be fresh berries for long.

". . . the son of an old friend looking to settle here now that he's sold his commission. He shall arrive the first of next week. I did so admire his father and am flattered that he asked for my help."

Lila slowed the pace of her looping and hooking and turned all her attention to the conversation.

"Will he be settling in High Ercall permanently, then?" the solicitor asked. The sound of rustling paper informed Lila he was likely gathering up his records in preparation to leave. She hoped he would stay long enough to extend this topic. Uncle Peter had told her nothing of the son of a friend relocating to this part of the county. Why would he not have told her?

"Or somewhere hereabouts," Uncle Peter said, his chair creaking—likely he was leaning back to stretch his back after so many hours of sitting. He was an active man and often went for a walk or rode his horse after his morning meetings. This was fortuitous for anyone hiding in his office in that they could expect that shortly after his meeting, he would leave the estate for his constitution and give a miscreant the chance to easily crawl from her corner without discovery. "I do so hope he takes a liking to Lila. She needs a steady sort of man."

Lila stopped crocheting completely.

"He had a military career, you say?"

"Nearly two decades. He entered at fifteen, I believe."

The solicitor was silent, and Lila suspected he, like her, was doing the math in his head.

"How old is he, then?" the solicitor said.

"Thirty and three."

Lila felt her eyes go wide. *Thirty-three?* Fourteen years older than she was, and an ex-soldier? She was confused, or at least she wished she was confused. In truth, however, she understood too well what was happening.

"Rather older than Miss Lila, then," the solicitor said diplomatically.

"We are not in a position to be too particular," Uncle Peter said while Lila stared at the last row of stitches she had placed. "When Mortimer—I suppose I shall need to call him Mr. Luthford—contacted me of his hopes to come to High Ercall after his discharge, I told him of Lila and her circumstance. I did not want to mislead him, but he had said he was in search of an estate and a wife, so I saw little reason to be coy. To my delight, he was not dissuaded by her situation, and his status would secure Lila quite well. For my part, it would be a relief to see her settled, and I will be glad if Lila remains close to Franklyn Farm. This may be the very thing for her."

A Merry Dance

"Indeed it sounds as though it will be a good fit," Mr. Jeppson said. "I hope Miss Lila will be as easily entreated by the idea."

Uncle Peter let out a heavy sigh. "There is the rub," he said. "I love her like a daughter, and daresay, after I lost Gaylene, she has been my greatest comfort. She does not feel the fear for her future that I feel, however."

"Love is tricky business," Mr. Jeppson said. Lila could hear movement as he stood from the chair. Uncle Peter's chair creaked as well, and the two men's footsteps moved away from her. "I wish you the best," Mr. Jeppson said.

"Thank you," Uncle Peter said. "I fear I shall need all the luck I can find."

The footsteps exited the room, and Lila sat with her past and future stripped naked before her. It was not Lila's fault she was born on the wrong side of the blanket or sent to live with Uncle Peter a year before Lila's mother died in some London rookery. Mama had never been able to rise above her poor choices, but hoped Lila would not suffer the same fate. And she hadn't. Lila had been living in High Ercall as the niece of a well-respected man for nearly as long as she could remember. She wasn't equal in status to her uncle, however, even though she was accepted into his social circle here. She would not have a London season—she would too easily become a source of gossip—and while her uncle had offered a generous dowry, that it came from him and not her own parents was damning. The growing realization of her situation was part of why she felt so sure Neville was her destiny—yet Uncle Peter had not seemed to consider the match at all likely. Instead, he was bringing a man to Franklyn Farm in hopes that he might capture Lila's interest, and her his.

Was she considered an inappropriate match for Neville?

She pushed away the question. She was *perfect* for Neville. This other man—with the stodgy name of Mortimer, no less—could never be as perfect for her as Neville was, and though she felt somewhat raw regarding what she'd overheard just now, she would not let it distract her from what she knew was not only right but her very best chance for happiness. Once she was married to Neville, her beginnings would not be testimony against her. She would not be a baseborn byfly niece saved through Christian charity, but a respected wife of a respected man. She longed for that kind of resolution, and she was already comfortable with Neville. The choice was such an obvious one in her mind. Why was her uncle so obtuse?

Two

"Thirty-three years old?" Eloise looked at Lila across the bilberry bushes between them. Her blue eyes were wide in her round face. "That is nearly the age of my *mother*."

"I know!" Lila agreed completely with her friend's shock. "I am repulsed by the idea of such an old man." She shuddered as she envisioned a shiny pate and weather-worn skin the color of leather.

"And your uncle made no mention of Neville?"

"None!" Lila let out an exaggerated breath. "I had assumed Uncle harbored hope that Neville and I would make a happy match. It is not as though he has pushed me toward other men, and I was not *out* when Neville left." She made no mention of her inferior birth and the part it might play. That no one spoke of her history often led her to believe they did not know or did not care. After this morning, however, she felt conspicuous and exposed by the reminder that all was not forgotten or forgiven, despite the fact that she had nothing to do with the circumstances of her birth. "Uncle

Peter did say some very kind things about his regard for me," she said. "That eased the sting some." He had specifically said he hoped she would remain nearby, but apparently not at Franklyn Farm.

"Everyone knows your uncle adores you," Eloise said, smiling as she pushed a tendril of blonde hair from her face. She wore a bonnet with an extra wide brim to protect her fair skin from the September sun. Eloise would be presented in London next spring, something Lila had to continually suppress her envy toward. "Will Neville still return in time for the masquerade?" Eloise asked.

"According to his last letter to me, yes. But *Mortimer* will be here next week, nearly a fortnight before I can expect Neville." She made a face and picked more berries. "I must admit to being a little bit impressed that Uncle kept this Mortimer's coming from my attention for so long; he's not one who keeps secrets very well. At least not from me."

"Because you hide in his study," Eloise said with a smirk, though she didn't look up from her berry picking. "And then trick him in to telling you what you already know."

"The end justifies the means." Lila lifted her chin. "I have no regrets."

"I am well aware of that." Eloise rolled her eyes at her friend and then moved behind a thick portion of foliage that hid her from Lila's view. "What shall you do about Mr. Mortimer, then?"

Mortimer, Lila repeated in her mind. How could she ever love a man with such a name? Really, did her uncle know her at all? "Perhaps he will not like me and everything will come to naught."

"Which would be an easier hope to nurture if you were not so lovely, charming, and well-spoken." The laugh in

A Merry Dance

Eloise's voice, though she was hidden by the bilberry bush, gave appropriate humor to her statement.

"Very true," Lila sighed dramatically. "It is such a trial to be so very appealing. A curse, really." In truth she was very pretty, and gentlemen had always been attentive to her, but only to a certain extent. They were careful, it seemed, not to appear too interested but Lila had never been terribly vexed by this because of Neville's presence in her heart.

"No doubt Mr. Mortimer will fall madly in love with you from the start," Eloise continued, "and then you shall really be in the soup."

Lila laughed at the outrageous conversation, but then stopped abruptly and hurried around the thicket. "That's it," she said as what felt like pure wisdom seemed to pour into her mind from heaven itself.

"What?" Eloise said, pulling her eyebrows together.

"I cannot leave it to chance," Lila said. "I must make sure he does not fall in love with me from the very beginning."

"How will you do that?" Eloise cocked her head to the side. "We have already reviewed your multiple charms."

"I do not know," Lila said, already doubting herself since this man knew of her situation and was not dissuaded by it. "I cannot be rude to him—he's Uncle's guest—and I wouldn't want to offend him. Even an old man with an unfortunate name does not deserve to be made to feel poorly." She began pacing, swinging her half-filled basket back and forth as she contemplated. "What I must do is make it seem like his idea."

"*Not* falling in love with you?" Eloise sounded confused.

"Exactly," Lila said. "I must find a way to make myself . . . unattractive. He's already expressed interest, or at least willingness, in meeting me, so he has positive expectations. If I can present myself as different than he expects, he might feel disappointed but pardoned at the same time—glad to not have had any existing obligation to me he would be expected to fulfill."

"Yes," Eloise said, catching the spirit of Lila's plan, which was forming one straw at a time. "If done correctly he'll feel badly for not liking you, rather than feeling disliked for himself."

"His confidence will not be damaged," Lila added. "And neither will his relationship with Uncle Peter."

Eloise grimaced slightly. "Your uncle will still be disappointed."

"Yes, he will be." Lila frowned, wishing that part weren't necessary. A smile shortly broke free. "But then *Neville* and I shall make such a happy match that Uncle will forget all about the hopes he pinned on Mr. Mortimer Luthford, and, in time, he too will be grateful." She pursed her lips. "All we need to do is determine how to make me unappealing."

Eloise feigned an innocent expression. "Perhaps you could act arrogant and prideful. I think all sorts of people are turned off from that sort of behavior."

"You think you are teasing me," Lila said, narrowing her eyes. "But that is *exactly* the type of thing I need to do. What would make a man disinterested in me without embarrassing my uncle?"

The young women stared at one another a few moments, then went back to their berry picking until Eloise made a little squeak. Lila turned to see Eloise's eyes wide again. She put a hand on Lila's arm. "I've thought of something," she said, speaking fast. "There was an article a few months back in *The Ladies' Expositor* about how to impress a gentleman—it had a list of what men like and what they don't like in young ladies. If you had a list like that and then did the opposite . . ."

"Yes!" Lila's enthusiasm for this brilliant plan was growing by the minute. "That's exactly it. Do you still have the periodical?"

"Oh yes, I keep them all under the bed so that Mama doesn't throw them out. She thinks they are silly things."

"Well, they are silly things," Lila agreed, turning back to the bush and picking twice as fast as she had before. She glanced sideways at her friend. "Yet you're squirreling them away? I had no idea you were interested in such flippancy."

Eloise also turned back to the bilberry bush and shrugged as though her cheeks weren't suddenly bright as cherries. "I like to have something to read on nights I can't sleep."

"Of course," Lila said with a smile, choosing not to comment on the extensive library at Eloise's home that would be far more approved material in her mother's eyes.

"But anyway, I'm sure I still have that edition. Once we finish here and get these berries to Cook, we can find that article."

"Perfect," Lila said, popping a just-picked berry into her mouth. "I have a very good feeling about this, Eloise. A very good feeling indeed!"

How to Impress a Gentleman Caller, by Lady Ivy Carlisle

Finding a proper husband is the single most important responsibility of the gentle-bred woman, and one to be undertaken with utmost care and consideration. Beyond fine manners and etiquette, which are expected in all situations, there are some specific points that warrant additional attention when one interacts with members of the opposite sex. The following is a list of the most important aspects of meeting eligible men:

Gentlemen prefer the smell of roses to lavender. Consider such when you shall be close enough in proximity for him to catch a gentle whiff of your perfume.

A lady should defer to a gentleman in regard to any decisions, such as whether to walk or ride for an afternoon.

Gentlemen prefer to tell of their exploits and accomplishments rather than listen to those of women beyond some mention of embroidery and watercolor.

A lady should always compliment a man's horse.

Gentlemen prefer a woman who does not prattle or gossip.

A lady should never share her opinion regarding politics or business, assuming she bothers to have one at all.

Gentlemen prefer a young woman to eat but little, showing consideration toward the preservation of a youthful figure.

A lady should never, under any circumstance, gamble or drink, especially in a gentleman's presence.

Three

For the next three days Lila made sure she was hiding in the corner of Uncle's office each morning and was rewarded with additional details regarding Mr. Mortimer Luthford's arrival as Uncle communicated with a variety of servants and workmen regarding the preparation of the dowager cottage, where Mr. Luthford would be staying. He would arrive Monday morning and stay at Franklyn Farm for however long it took for him to secure his situation. He would dine with them every night and be included within invitations extended to the household as a matter of course.

During all this time—three entire days filled with incredible tension and anticipation on Lila's part—Uncle did not say one word to her about their guest. On Friday evening, after their guests—Mr. Riding and his young daughter, who Lila got on with quite well—had left, Lila turned to her uncle and smiled her most innocent smile. "What a lovely evening," she said. "I do so like the Riding family. It was a pleasure to have them join us."

"Quite," Uncle said, already lighting his pipe. He didn't smoke when company was about. According to proper etiquette he should not smoke in front of her either, but they were on far more comfortable terms and Lila did not mind. He puffed as the tobacco caught, and Lila inhaled the smoky-sweet scent that would forever remind her of this kind man . . . who was even now in the process of deceiving her. She retrieved her crochet basket from beside the fire and settled into her chair, certain Uncle Peter would tell her of Mr. Luthford now that they were alone, but a full ten minutes passed with Uncle doing nothing more than staring into the fire while her tension increased.

Finally, when she could stand it no longer, Lila cleared her throat. Uncle did not look her way, apparently quite lost in thought. She cleared her throat again, louder and not very ladylike. He turned to her, and she put the innocent smile back into play.

"I took a walk down the front lane this afternoon," she said with feigned casualness. "I had not realized you were renovating the dowager cottage." In truth she had looked in every window, assessing what was being done, and then interrogated a painter.

"Oh, just taking off the covers and such."

"I am quite sure I smelled paint."

"Well, yes, to repair a water stain in one of the bedrooms. I fixed the roof years ago but hadn't gotten to the damage left behind."

"I'd have been happy to help manage such things," Lila said, looking at her crocheting as though feeling a bit left out. Which she did, only not in the way she was presenting.

"I certainly meant no offense," Uncle said.

She gave him a small but grateful smile and held his eyes with determined intent. She could feel his resolve cracking. Shifting. Until . . .

"There *is* something I've been meaning to tell you, however," Uncle began.

Here it is, Lila thought. She lifted her eyebrows expectantly.

"I've a guest coming to stay in the cottage for a time," he waved his pipe through the air. "Mortimer Luthford is the son of an old friend, looking to settle here in Shropshire. I offered him the cottage until he could firm up his own situation."

"Oh really," Lila said evenly. "Is he from Shropshire originally?"

"No, no, grew up in Essex, but doesn't have a great deal of connection there. He's had a career in the military but is now returned to England and looking to settle in. I think you might very much enjoy his stories; I know how such things appeal to your adventurous spirit."

Lila wanted to refute her interest in stories of travel and even war, but that very night she had plumbed Mr. Riding for more details of the time he spent in Spain following the battle of Trafalgar. Maybe her desire for adventure was because, despite the fact that Franklyn Farm was her home, she had always known she was a visitor, though a welcome one. Since having determined herself in love with Neville, however, she had tried harder than ever to talk herself out of such exotic interest in things outside of England, or even Shropshire. Once she and Neville married she would spend the rest of her life in High Ercall. The pang she felt at the reminder was quickly quashed. In time she fully expected not to feel the pang at all. "But Mr. Luthford is not in the military any longer? Did he lose a leg or some such thing?"

"Nothing like that," Uncle said. "Only, he is prepared to make a home and family after so many years abroad."

"*Many* years?" she asked.

"Well, not *so* many," Uncle said, a bit flustered. "But he is dignified and well-bred. I quite admire his level of responsibility in determining to settle down."

"After so many years eating off a tin plate he's probably ready to be waited on a bit," Lila said. "Do you know, I wonder if he might take a liking to Mrs. Mason. She's been widowed for, what, two years now and has the most conciliatory nature. Perhaps we could have her over one night after he arrives."

"Perhaps," Uncle said, but he did not seem to like the idea.

"And when does Mr. Luthford arrive? Next month?" She was attempting to make the point that it would be reasonable to have told Lila of his coming with far more notice than this.

"He'll, uh, arrive on Monday."

Lila lifted her eyebrows and widened her eyes. "Monday? Why, Uncle, that is but three days away. Why did you not tell me?"

"Oh, well," Uncle said, pulling at his waistcoat and taking a draw on his pipe. "I suppose I just did not think it through."

It was exactly what she'd hoped to hear as it gave her the chance to say what she had hoped very much to say. She softened her expression into a smile. "I understand," she said. "He is likely so much older than me, and rather backwoods after so many years in the army." She smiled wider at the confused expression that came upon her uncle's face. "I hope you will not worry that I might insert myself too much. I would not want to dissuade any women closer to his age from taking an interest."

"Well, I don't mean to discourage you from—"

"Not at all," Lila said, rising to her feet and winding up her crochet—a scarf now that she'd finished Neville's socks—

A Merry Dance

while smiling indulgently at her uncle. "I admire very much you helping your friend's son, and Mr. Luthford will only benefit from your recommendation to High Ercall and your willingness to put him up for a time." She crossed to Uncle Peter's chair and planted a quick kiss on the top of his head. "What a kind, understanding man you are, Uncle. I do believe I shall go on up to bed now. However, do not worry about me overstepping my bounds. I shall be certain to give Mr. Luthford a wide berth once he arrives. Good night."

It was a few seconds before Uncle responded with his own, rather flattened, "Good night." Lila continued to her room with a satisfied smile on her face. Were she keeping score, she would give herself ten points for her success this evening. Uncle might still be in the lead, but she was not far behind and intended to catch up quickly once Mr. Luthford arrived.

Four

On Sunday, Lila made sure to find Widow Mason and ask her to dinner Tuesday evening. Mrs. Mason was surprised—she'd never dined at Franklyn Farm before—but graciously accepted the offer. Beyond that, Lila made sure to tell everyone about their upcoming guest. By the time Lila and Uncle Peter began the walk home, every unattached, church-going, middle-aged woman in the village was aware of Mr. Luthford's status and recommendation. If one of these women caught his eye, and he theirs, Lila may have worried for nothing. The idea was almost disappointing; it could have been a bit of fun to see if she could un-attract Mr. Luthford. But she may very well have to make herself content with wishing him happy. Perhaps she would get a new dress for Mr. Luthford's winter wedding.

Monday morning Lila awoke early, dressed in her least flattering morning dress—the color of mashed pumpkin with a high ruffled neck and wrist-length sleeves—and asked Katherine, her maid, to do her hair in a simple bun.

A Merry Dance

"Are you sure you would not like something a bit more . . . elaborate?" Katherine asked. Lila preferred a full twist, with some hair left to frame her face. Or she would wear her hair down around her shoulders with only the very front caught up on the top of her head.

"I am most certainly not in the mood for anything elaborate," Lila said. "I would like to see how my face looks without anything to encumber it."

When Katherine finished, Lila looked at herself with a critical eye. She had hoped the removal of all the softness of her hair, along with the dress she did not feel set her off to any advantage, would make her look unappealing and plain. Instead, the heart shape of her face was more apparent, her cheekbones were shown at an advantage, and her eyes looked large and luminous. The dress was still awful, however.

"I can change it, miss," Katherine said eagerly.

"It is just right," Lila said, turning her head to admire the graceful curve of her neck. "Thank you."

"Do you wish to change into a day dress before luncheon?" Katherine said, running her eye over the dress when Lila stood. "I could set out the sprig muslin."

The sprig muslin was one of the Lila's favorites to be sure—Uncle had ordered it from a dressmaker all the way in Shrewsbury—but it was far too flattering. "No, I shall keep this one. I woke up a bit chilled." That was a lie; in fact, the day promised to be rather warm for September. But her comfort was not the focus, and wearing a morning gown all day was something Uncle Peter would never notice in her attempts to put herself at a disadvantage.

Lila didn't dare hide in Uncle's office today since Mr. Luthford's arrival was a change from the usual schedule. Instead, she spent some time pasting bright green feathers to the mask she would wear to the masquerade—she was attending in costume as a peacock—and then went to the garden, admired the chrysanthemums taking center stage this time of year, and picked a bouquet of wildflowers she would put in her room. There would soon be only hothouse flowers to brighten the house, though she liked those too. Since the garden was on the opposite side of the house from the front drive, and she did not expect Mr. Luthford before noon, Lila did not hear the carriage that arrived a full hour early. She entered the house from a side door and was taken aback by the timbre of male voices. She moved toward the voices and came to a stop in the doorway of the parlor when the men turned to face her. The stranger who must be Mr. Luthford was dressed in rather dull grey trousers and a navy blue coat. His black waistcoat was unadorned, and his necktie tied in a simple knot that would never do in London drawing rooms . . . or so she supposed. Lila had expected Mr. Luthford to be old but was immediately disappointed. Of course he *was* old; only, he didn't *look* as old as she'd hoped he would. His hair was dark, and though there was some peppering of grey at the temples, and a rather rugged look to his face, he did not look aged, really. But he was *not* particularly handsome, and that made her feel better. His nose was rather small, his face long, and his brow heavy, giving him a somewhat broody look. His was *nothing* to Neville's good looks, she was pleased to note.

"Lila," Uncle said, stepping forward to meet her at the doorway with a smile. "This is Mr. Mortimer Luthford, the son of my friend I was telling you about, who shall be staying in the cottage for a time." He led her into the room until she was a few feet from Mr. Luthford. "Luthford, this is my niece, Lila Grange."

"Miss Grange," Mr. Luthford said, bowing toward her but not taking her hand since she had put them behind her back. "It is a pleasure to meet you."

A Merry Dance

She smiled and gave a minimal curtsy. "And I you," she said softly. In a usual situation she would ask after his journey, confirm those details she knew about him in order to make conversation, and inquire after his impressions of High Ercall thus far. But she was not to be on her usual behavior and needed to therefore hold back her natural interest in people.

After a few moments of silence she battled with herself not to fill, Uncle Peter came to the rescue. "Luthford arrived a bit earlier than expected, and I have some matters of correspondence I need to complete before I am free." He looked at Lila. "Would you be so kind, my dear, to show him the stables so that he might know where to find his mount?"

Lila lifted her eyebrows in response to the bold request—her uncle was inviting her to walk alone with a man after less than five minutes of acquaintance?

"I don't want to interrupt the household's schedule," Mr. Luthford said. "I'm sure I can find my way to the stable and remain occupied until my trunks and my man arrive in the hired chaise."

"Lila would be happy to show you about, wouldn't you, Lila?" Uncle said, looking at her with expectation.

No, I would not, she wanted to say, but she didn't. She couldn't. "Certainly," she said, smiling politely. "Only, let me fetch my bonnet."

She went to her room and reached for the straw hat that would best coordinate with her dress, but then hesitated and instead took hold of the purple velvet. It matched a pelisse she only wore in winter and would look hideous with her orange dress. With Uncle Peter behaving bolder than she had ever known him to do, she had no time to waste in giving Mr. Luthford a poor impression. She met Mr. Luthford in the foyer while she was still tying the ribbons and although she searched his face for some type of reaction regarding her uncoordinated presentation, he gave no indication of notice.

She smiled and then led him through the front door a footman opened for them.

"It is lovely country here," Mr. Luthford said once they reached the gravel road that skirted the house and led to the outbuildings.

Lila had to think hard of her objectives before determining she could answer him without going against them. "Yes, it is quite lovely." She bit back a question about where he was from, where his regiment had last been before he left the army, and if he'd been to London after arriving in England or come straight here. Stifling her natural curiosity was difficult, but the sacrifice would be worthwhile once Neville returned.

Gentlemen prefer a woman who does not prattle or gossip.

It was time to begin.

"Just the other day I went into the countryside with my dear friend, Eloise Capener—her father is the magistrate here in town, you know, and we have been friends all our lives. We picked bilberries and though our fingers were rather stained by the time we finished, it was a diverting afternoon nonetheless."

She was quite pleased with herself. She'd made no mention of watercolor or embroidery and not asked a single question about him.

"Ah, bilberries," Mr. Luthford said with longing. "Were the berries for scones or for a pie?"

"A pie," Lila said, walking beside him with her hands clasped behind her back, worried that if she did not take such a posture he would put out his arm for her. That would be altogether too familiar. "Two pies actually—one for Eloise's family and one for my uncle and me."

"Was the finished product worthy of the excursion?"

She turned to smile at him. "It was perfectly delicious," she said, wondering when Mr. Luthford had last had bilberry pie. She imagined something so fine was difficult to come by when one was rusticating at some military post. If only she could ask. The questions were building up like water behind a dammed up stream.

"Do you often go into the woods for berry picking?" he asked.

"When they are in season," she said. "It gives purpose to what would only be wanderings through the woods without a task otherwise."

"And do you object to wandering through the woods *without* purpose?"

She gave him a sidelong look, surprised that he was asking so many questions. The article had implied that gentlemen preferred to talk about themselves, yet Mr. Luthford had not said anything of his own interests. "Well, I'm not sure I have thought much about it, but now that you suggest the idea, I would say that I generally prefer to have a purpose in the things I do. While I don't mind a walk in the woods, I prefer to be going somewhere or having the walk as part of some other accomplishment."

He said nothing, prompting her to turn her head to look at him. He smiled back at her, first with one side of his mouth and then the other. She had the strangest feeling in her chest and looked ahead once again while reminding herself why this man was objectionable. He was old. He was . . . not handsome. He was strangely interested in what she had to say.

"Here is the carriage house," she said, though they were still some distance from the building. "Uncle Peter has a traveling coach, a barouche, and a gig."

"And a wagon, I see," Mr. Luthford said, walking toward the basic farm wagon outside the carriage house. He took hold of the side and shook it, causing Lila to give him a curious look when he met her eye once again. "I admire quality," he said by way of explanation. "For instance, this wagon has planks nearly four inches thick, and the wheels." He moved down the wagon and crouched to inspect the wheel more closely. "The spokes are only three inches apart, which would be necessary due to the extra weight of the construction."

Lila could not help herself as she moved forward, looking at what he saw. "What is the benefit of a heavy wagon if it requires additional structure?"

"Longevity," Mr. Luthford said, looking up at her. She took a step back, not realizing how close she was to him. He turned back to the wagon and continued to talk about the construction—something Lila would never have guessed to be interesting but somehow was. She'd never thought about nails versus wooden pegs, or the thickness of the rim fit to the wheel itself.

"I'd have done almost anything for a wagon of this quality when I was in Spain," he said as his explanation came to an end. "We had little choice but to make the most of broken down conveyances that were often a liability to our entire regiment." He slapped the side of wagon. "I shall have to ask your uncle where I might find such a wagon."

"Will you be in a need of a wagon?" Lila asked.

"It seems that farming is my future," Mr. Luthford said with a touch of resolution. "I am determined to do it well." He met her eyes and lifted one shoulder. "Like you, I prefer to have purpose to my actions, and I believe the purpose left to me is to raise crops and sheep and find my way within such industry."

Purpose left to me? What did he mean by that? Instead of asking the question, however, she simply smiled and turned toward the stable. "I assume you rode your own mount and that is why you sent your trunks by hired chaise?"

"I did," Mr. Luthford said, hurrying his steps to catch up to her. She reached the corral fence, and her gaze landed on the only unfamiliar animal in the paddock, even though it did not look like anything a gentleman would ride. The horse was thickly built, like a stock horse, with a short neck, dull grey coat, and dark mane. She would expect such an animal to pull a plow.

A lady should always compliment a man's horse.

Insulting his horse would be an easy task to complete.

"Is that your horse?" she asked, nodding toward the decrepit looking thing.

"Ah yes," Mr. Luthford said, a smile in his voice. "That there is Gordon."

"Gordon?" she said, turning to look at him with her nose wrinkled.

He raised his eyebrows as though surprised, but his half smile told her he was not. "You don't like the name?"

She focused on the horse again. "Perhaps it fits him," she said, cocking her head to the side. "A strange name for a very strange horse."

She had meant to offend Mr. Luthford, but he laughed instead.

"Indeed," he said. "Only, it's not a him, it's a her."

She looked at him again. "You named a mare Gordon?"

He shrugged a shoulder. "Everyone has these horses with names like Thunder and Prince and Ragtail's Promise. I thought the least I could do for an animal I trust with my life every time I throw myself into the saddle is give it a name of respect."

"Then why not Elizabeth or Lady Mary for a mare?"

He scrunched up his face and looked at the horse as though for the first time. "I think she'd have been embarrassed by such a title as that," he said. "But a name like Gordon, steady and sure, but not flouncy in any way, seemed just the thing for such a nag as her."

It was Lila's turn to laugh. He'd called his own horse a nag! As soon as she realized what she'd done, however, she cut off the laugh and faced forward again. This was going horribly, terribly wrong! She had meant to talk only of herself, and yet he had made her an expert on wagon construction, and now she had intended to insult his horse only to find his response clever. She searched the paddock until she found Neville's faithful stallion, Wind Runner—a name that suddenly seemed very silly. He was a beautiful chocolate colored gelding with white socks and a star upon his forehead. Wind Runner was a thing of beauty—a grand horse for a great man. The man she was going to marry. The man she *must* marry.

"Miss Grange?" Mr. Luthford said after several awkwardly silent seconds. "Is everything all right?"

"Of course," she said with polite indifference she hoped he could hear. She was already suffering from the heat of this gown, which perhaps she should be grateful for, as the physical discomfort made it easier for her to be unpleasant. "I only wonder that you rode this animal all the way here. She looks scarce able to make it to the next village over with a man upon her back. Do your feet touch the ground when you're astride?"

He laughed and shook his head. "I might appear a bit awkward, but she is as steady a mount as any have ever known." He moved forward to rest his arms on the top rail of the fence. Gordon saw him and whinnied as she lumbered toward them and then pushed her nose into Mr. Luthford's hand like a dog might do.

"No apples today, old girl," Mr. Luthford said, scratching her behind the ear, to which she nickered once again. He turned to look at Lila with soft eyes. "She saw me through Spain," he explained. "Wasn't more than a filly when I first obtained her, and then she followed me around like a loyal puppy, truth be told. When I realized I had to give up my commission, I went to great expense to bring her with me. She's not the fastest, and she's certainly not the most beautiful specimen of horseflesh you'll ever see, but I have never known a horse of greater stamina and loyalty than my Gordon."

Lila was touched—but she didn't want to be. A trickle of sweat moved down her back, making her shiver.

"Well, I think it a very stupid name for a very ugly horse." The words came out much harsher than she meant them to. She swallowed and looked away when Mr. Luthford's head turned toward her. She could feel the hurt and surprise from him, even without seeing the emotions play across his face. She wanted him to not like her, but she hated that he likely thought her horrid. "But I suppose beauty is in the eye of the beholder."

"Indeed," Mr. Luthford said evenly, turning back to his horse and scratching her behind the ears with both hands now. Lila watched him without turning her head, then took a step back toward the house. "Well, I should check on luncheon—we have a small meal around noon. I assume you've already seen the cottage?"

"I believe I passed it on the way up the drive."

She should show him the cottage, but then he had already turned back to his horse and she didn't dare risk further intimacy.

"Very well," she said, smiling politely. "I'll see you at luncheon. Good day, Mr. Luthford."

"Good day, Miss Grange," he said, turning toward her and bowing. "And thank you for the tour and hospitality."

There was no edge to his voice, no censure or dismay—though she certainly deserved such things. She swallowed, smiled, and then turned back to the house, moving as quickly as she could. The only consolation she could dig out of the experience—though it did not bring her much joy to note it—was that making herself unattractive was not nearly as hard as she thought it would be.

Five

Lila recounted meeting Mr. Luthford while pacing back and forth in Eloise's parlor. They were visiting under the guise of tea and putting the finishing touches on the capes they had both made to go with their masquerade costumes. Both cups had gone cold, and each cape remained folded in their sewing baskets. Lila hadn't even eaten a roly-poly pudding Eloise's cook had put on the tray. Lila always ate as many roly-poly puddings as she could when they were offered. But she had no appetite today.

"And then how was luncheon after you said such things to him?" Eloise asked when Lila came to the end of the conversation outside the corral.

"Fine," Lila said, turning to her and throwing up her arms in exasperation. "He was polite and told the most fascinating story about a storm his ship was caught in on his very first crossing. It was all I could do not to pepper him with questions about it. How does a ship remain afloat when the masts are broken and it is thrown so severely from side to side that the men have to tie themselves into their hammocks? I did not ask a single question, and it nearly killed me. I ate twice what I would have normally just to keep my mouth occupied, which I can only hope he noted and was disgusted by. It was one of the aspects in that article, not eating too much."

She huffed and continued her pacing.

"I'm not sure I understand why you are so frustrated," Eloise said. "It seems that everything is going according to plan. You are not presenting yourself well, just as you planned, and he is not seeking your company, just as you hoped. He could have insisted you show him the cottage, for instance, but he did not argue the point."

"Everything *is* going as planned. Only, it feels wrong." *Wrong?* Was that really what she meant? Did it feel wrong?

"Perhaps you should reconsider your plan. It sounds as though maybe you would like to know him better."

"I can't reconsider," Lila said, though she did ponder the idea. "He is still fourteen years my senior, he is not handsome—at least not in a dashing kind of way—and most of all he is not Neville." She stopped and closed her eyes, bringing Neville's sparkling eyes and chiseled jaw to her mind's eye to fortify her belief that he was the only man she could ever love. "Surely Mr. Luthford is the very devil come to prevent me from the true man of my dreams. Only, I am not so strong as I thought I was, and he is more interesting than I expected. *That* is the trouble!"

She resumed her pacing.

"I think you like him," Eloise said.

"I do *not* like him," Lila said with complete sincerity, though something prickled in her chest that only served to annoy her further. "I had envisioned a certain smoothness in my own actions that is lacking, as well as a sense of accomplishment I simply do not feel. I insulted his horse for heaven's sake, yet at luncheon he was as polite as he'd been when we were first introduced."

"Well, you are not used to being unkind, even if it is for a very good reason. That is surely why you feel so unsettled."

Lila finally sat down. "Yes, that is true. Being unkind goes against my character. I am used to behaving much better than this."

"And you do love to talk to interesting people."

Lila sighed. "And he may have some of the most interesting stories I have ever heard."

"But you cannot forget that the reason he has so many stories is because he is very old."

"*So* old," Lila confirmed, keeping to herself that he didn't look very old.

"And you are in love with Neville."

Lila closed her eyes and raised her hands to her temples. Surely she was developing a headache from all this anxiety. "So help me, I am." Beautiful Neville. Wonderful Neville.

"Giving in to your curiosity about Mr. Luthford's experiences and risking his increased interest in you would pose significant difficulty in the reunion with Neville, which will take place in less than two weeks."

"*Significant* difficulty."

"Then there is nothing more to do but stay the course," Eloise said. She put down her cold cup and saucer and looked strongly at Lila. "You have always been a woman of strength who does not back down in the face of adversity. This may very well be exactly what you said, a test of your love for Neville, and therefore you must triumph. Remember that you are not being unkind—though perhaps the commentary about his horse was overzealous—but you are instead *helping* Mr. Luthford. The sooner he determines you are not the woman he wants to base a future around, the sooner he will look at other women who are better suited for him." She scooted forward on her chair. "You must not give up, Lila, and you must see this through."

Lila's confidence was improved with Eloise's encouragement. "You're right," she said. "I must hold firm." She stood.

Eloise stood and made a fist of solidarity. "Hold firm!"

"I shall not give up," Lila said, straightening and lifting her chin.

"Not give up!" Eloise repeated. She smiled.

Lila smiled back.

Eloise stopped smiling. "I do have one further question, though?"

Lila lifted her eyebrows expectantly.

"Why are you wearing that horrible dress?"

Lila looked down at the smashed pumpkin dress—a morning dress that she was wearing well into the afternoon and not even within the walls of her own home. She had, at least, worn the straw chip for the walk to Eloise's rather than the purple velvet. "I was trying to look unattractive." She raised a hand to her hair. "I tried to do the same with my hair."

"Oh, the hair is fantastic," Eloise said admiringly. "It sets your face off very well, indeed. But the dress." She frowned. "I don't think you need to try so hard to look poorly. Someone else may have seen you in that dress, you know. Remember your ambitions and stay the course without too many differences someone else might notice."

Lila was relieved by the sound advice. "Tomorrow I shall wear the sprig muslin then, but will offset it with talk of politics, a foul stomach, and perhaps I shall drink some brandy in his presence."

A Merry Dance

"Have you ever drunk brandy—or any strong drink for that matter? Perhaps start with something like elderberry wine or ratafia."

"Only, will a lady's drink put him off enough?"

"Coupled with talk of politics and foul stomachs, I think you could drink lemonade and still make progress toward your goals."

Lila nodded. "Very good. I am renewed and prepared to face Mr. Luthford at the dinner table tonight."

"Only, change out of the dress before you do," Eloise reminded. "It really is quite hideous."

Six

Dinner, like lunch, was filled with even more fascinating stories of India, France, and Spain. At first Lila had to keep her mouth full of food again to keep from barraging Mr. Luthford with questions. Eventually she found her plate empty, but by then she was content to simply listen to him talk. He had a way with words and had so many remarkable experiences that, although she would have liked to ask questions, she realized she did not really need to.

The men lingered only a short while over their port and joined Lila in the drawing room where she crocheted by the fire. After only a few minutes Mr. Luthford begged off; he was worn out from his travel this morning and getting settled once his trunks arrived in the afternoon. Tomorrow Uncle Peter would be giving him a tour of the village.

"Why don't you join us, Lila?" Uncle Peter said.

"Oh, I do believe I have an . . . uh, obligation with Eloise tomorrow."

A Merry Dance

"Surely it can wait. How often do we have a guest unfamiliar with our wonderful hamlet?"

"If Miss Grange is otherwise engaged—" Mr. Luthford said.

"Nonsense," Uncle Peter said, waving away any resistance. "She sees Eloise nearly every day; she can make arrangements." He gave Lila a strong look, and Lila finally smiled politely and nodded her agreement.

"Eleven o'clock," Uncle Peter said, pushing up from his chair. "We'll meet in the foyer and make an afternoon of it. Perhaps we will take lunch at Burns & Patter so that he might see what High Ercall used to be. I'll send them a note to reserve a table."

The next morning Lila came down the stairs at five to eleven, having spent the morning making up for yesterday's dowdiness by putting extra attention to today's toilet. She was not trying to impress Mr. Luthford, but she *was* secretly relieved not to have to work at being unattractive today. With Uncle there she couldn't behave in the contrary way she might if it were only she and Mr. Luthford. The most she could do was not be too interested in Mr. Luthford's stories. If only thoughts of his dinner narrations had not left her yearning for a few clarifications. Why were there only cats to eat in northern Spain that winter, and how, exactly, did one cook a cat?

Not asking was as hard to do as not putting her best self forward, but all must be endured in the name of Neville.

Lila was reminding herself of all these things when Wilhite, the butler, came upon her and reached a paper toward her. "A note from Master Franklyn, miss."

She took the note and unfolded it.

Lila,

My deepest regrets for being unable to join today's escort, but there was a dispute between two tenants and I've been called in to help resolve the matter. Please give Luthford my apologies. I have made arrangements for the two of you to take lunch at Burns & Patter. They are expecting you at 12:15.

Additionally, Mrs. Mason sent round a note accepting the invitation to dinner I believe you extended without appraising me. Please be so good as to keep me informed of such things in the future. I have issued a further invitation to Mr. And Mrs. Marchett to extend the numbers.

Have a lovely afternoon,
Uncle P

Lila couldn't believe that for the second time in two days her uncle was fairly throwing her into the arms of a man she barely knew! A carriage ride with him alone? It would have to be an open carriage for matters of respectability, of course, but then the whole village would see her and Mr. Luthford together. What would they think when Neville returned in just over a week and she rode in an open carriage with *him*? She expected more from her uncle and would find a way to tell him as much . . . just as soon as she figured out how she would handle the next two hours with Mr. Luthford.

"I believe the carriage is ready," Wilhite said.

"I need a moment," Lila said, turning to hurry back up the stairs.

She could not let the chance to be alone with Mr. Luthford go to waste. Once in her room she went to her desk and removed the list so she might review it.

"Politics," she muttered under her breath. "Foul stomach." Was there anything else?

Gentlemen prefer the smell of roses to lavender. Consider such when you shall be close enough in proximity for him to catch a gentle whiff of your perfume.

Lila had already splashed rose water upon her neck, as she did every morning. But that was playing directly into the theory of the article rather than opposing it. So she must remedy the inadvertent mistake with lavender. After a moment's consideration she hurried toward her wardrobe. For Christmas two years earlier Eloise had given Lila a bottle of lavender oil and a small pillow. Every few months Lila would put a few drops of the oil on the pillow, then place the pillow in her wardrobe to keep the moths away and the fabrics smelling fresh. The oil was far more concentrated than perfume.

Lila found the oil and pulled out the cork, then turned over one wrist and let a single drop of the oil drip onto her skin. With the fingers of her other hand she rubbed the oil in, then raised it to her face. Strong, but perhaps not strong enough. She placed another drop on her other wrist and rubbed both wrists together, but still worried it was not strong enough. Knowing time was short—Mr. Luthford was likely waiting for her even now—she lifted the skirt of her dress and let a drip fall onto the petticoat underneath where she would not have to worry about an oil stain. She let another drop fall, and then another. She put a drop behind each ear, one at the base of her neck, and still another on the cords of her reticule before putting some oil on her fingers and running her hands through her hair left down today. She paused in her application to assess the level of scent and took a deep inhale. Her lungs seized, and she coughed several times as tears came to her eyes. The oil was certainly pungent, but that was exactly what she needed. She replaced the stopper and put the bottle back into the wardrobe, then walked regally out of her room and down the stairs, rather proud of her quick thinking.

The faithful butler had been waiting for her and opened the door as she reached the main level.

"Mr. Luthford is awaiting you out front. Have a very good afternoon." His voice increased in pitch toward the end, and he quickly lifted a hand to cover a cough.

Lila pretended not to notice but felt the misgivings. "Thank you, Wilhite," she said with a stiff smile while rapidly blinking her eyes in hopes to clear them. She hoped it did not look as though she were crying, but she began to worry she'd overdone things. Mr. Luthford was standing next to the carriage, waiting for her. He smiled and, so help her, she smiled back.

"Good day, Mr. Luthford," she said as she descended the porch steps, watching the stairs carefully so her blurred vision didn't lead her to disaster.

"Good day, Miss Grange," he said when she reached him. He put out his hand to help her into the carriage but as he was handing her up, he paused, his hand still holding hers and enveloping her fingers in a warmth that made Lila very uncomfortable in a very comfortable sort of way. His brow furrowed slightly, and she braced herself for him to ask why she smelled so strongly of a scent gentlemen did not prefer.

"Are you well, Miss Grange?" he asked instead.

She blinked rapidly. "Yes, I am very well." The stench of lavender was choking her.

"Are you certain? If we should postpone this tour, I can wait for your uncle to escort me."

Was he trying to get out of the tour because she smelled so badly? She could not waste this opportunity. "No, I am happy to be your guide," she said, watching his eyes closely. She coughed behind her free hand.

His eyes did not seem to be affected, and he had not coughed even once. When he spoke, his voice was all kindness and sincerity. "Are you very certain?"

"I am very certain," she repeated with a smile she was surprised to realize she meant—a little bit at least. She *did* want to be with him, but she convinced herself it was because she would surely turn him away once and for all with this ride. Once in the carriage she took the seat facing forward— as a woman always did when riding alone with a gentleman. Mr. Luthford stepped in behind her, taking his place behind the driver. The carriage moved forward, and Lila realized, too late, that with her sitting here and him sitting there, she would be downwind. If their places were reversed, the movement of air around the carriage would keep him in a veritable cloud of the stink, but etiquette prevented that from happening, and so he would remain unaffected and she would have to fight the urge to cover her nose—or vomit. What's more, Mr. Luthford had not seemed to even notice the wretched smell. How could that be?

"You look very well, Miss Grange," Mr. Luthford said as the carriage began toward the heart of the village.

"Thank you," she said, catching herself just in time before she complimented him in return. He did not dress flamboyantly, but there was a quality of his dress she found appealing—masculine and confident without attempts to distract from the man himself.

"Are you sure you feel up to this tour?" he said, looking at her with concern.

"I am very well, Mr. Luthford," she said, wishing he would stop asking. "Only, I am a bit concerned over the political climate of our nation after this last session of Parliament."

Mr. Luthford smiled—a true, sincere, and interested smile. "I'm afraid I haven't followed British politics very closely these last years. I would be grateful if you might fill me in, so that should a discussion at some event or another turn to that topic I won't make a complete cake of myself."

Seven

"Oh my goodness," Eloise said as she helped Lila out of her dress later that afternoon. "I can barely breathe."

"I understand," Lila said, trying to help. "I have felt just the same for the last three hours!"

Lila could have asked Katherine for help, but was too humiliated to admit what she'd done. So while taking lunch at Burns & Patter, she had sent a note to Eloise, asking her to meet at Franklyn Farm at two o'clock. She then made certain Mr. Luthford returned her in time to meet her friend, who she whisked up to her room. While Eloise undid the straps and ties from behind, Lila gave her an overview of the afternoon.

"You'd have thought I smelled of nothing for all the notice he paid to it, and then, toward the end, he mentioned that he'd fallen from his horse once, a few years into his training—not Gordon, a different, difficult horse—and that his sense of smell had been affected by the injury." Lila shook her head, grateful to wriggle out of the dress and petticoat that stunk to high heaven. "The entire escapade was completely wasted!"

She stepped out of the fabric pooled at her feet, still dressed in her shift and high stays, and picked up both items from the floor, wrinkling her nose. "I didn't put any oil directly on the dress, but it smells as if I did. I hope I haven't ruined it."

"Set it over the windowsill," Eloise said, hurrying to open the window. "Perhaps we can air it out before you have to explain to Katherine what happened, though I suppose you could tell her you spilled the oil."

"I could tell her that," Lila said after arranging the clothing over the windowsill. Then she moved to her bed and fell face down on the coverlet. The landing was not a soft one, but she deserved every moment of discomfort. She turned her head to the side to look at Eloise. "Then I can be a liar as well as a complete dolt." She closed her eyes, overwhelmed by the day, and rolled onto her back. "Oh, Eloise, I have never felt so ridiculous in my life. At Burns & Patter, everyone was trying to determine what the smell was until realizing it was from *our* table. I'm certain my face was bright red every minute we were there, and my food even *tasted* like lavender. It was nothing but sheer stubbornness that kept me from retching." She placed a hand on her stomach, which was still queasy, and raised her other arm up to cover her eyes. The movement brought with it the continued smell of the blasted lavender rubbed into her wrist, and she sat up, bracing herself on her elbows. "What if I can't get the smell out?"

"Of the dress?" Eloise asked, glancing toward the dress and petticoat now hanging half in and half out of the window.

"Of my *skin*," Lila said. "I rubbed it into my wrists, my neck, hair, behind my ears."

"I think you will have to take a bath with copious amounts of soap," Eloise said with a frown. "And I don't believe I can be much assistance with that. Shall I call your maid?"

Lila closed her eyes, then nodded in surrender. A bath in the middle of the day—how ridiculous.

Eloise pulled the cord, then came to sit on the bench at the foot of the bed. "Besides the unfortunate lavender portion, what was the rest of the afternoon like?"

"Fine," she said, then reconsidered and gave Eloise a look of surrender. "Quite lovely, actually. Because of the list, I introduced the topic of politics in hope to put him off, and he wanted to hear *more*. I was never so grateful for having read the morning papers and listening to Uncle's conversations as I was today. When I couldn't eat another bite of food, I explained that my stomach was sour, and he was not repulsed, only concerned. When we left Burns & Patter, he had me wait in the carriage long enough for him to slip into a sweet shop and buy me a peppermint to ease my discomfort—which I certainly needed by that point. I did my best to educate him about the village and its people to the point of sharing gossip I'm embarrassed to have repeated, but he was quite interested to know the comings and goings of people, so it didn't feel like gossip at all, only introducing him to the ways of our community. He ended up talking about his time in India—where he was first posted—and I couldn't help but ask questions, which he answered with such detail that I am now quite sure my life will never be complete if I do not see an elephant in real life." She paused and shook her head. "Can you imagine seeing an elephant, Eloise, in its own habitat? And dark-skinned people who chant their prayers to a different God than we worship in church each Sunday?"

"You were supposed to only talk about yourself."

"I know!" Lila threw up her hands. "I tried, so help me, I did, but it is yet one more way in which I failed. He was so very attentive, so interested in what I did have to say, and then so generous with his own tales that if not for the stinking lavender oil I'd have forgotten my objective completely. I have bungled this entire ordeal."

There was a light knock at the door before Katherine entered. She took three steps into the room and stopped. Whether her surprise was to find Lila dressed only in her corset and chemise with Eloise right there, or the skirts of Lila's dress and petticoat hanging down from the windowsill, or the fact that the room smelled like a field of lavender, Lila would never know. Probably all three things had her confused. Lila rose from the bed and smiled as best she could though she felt humiliated all over again. "I am so sorry, Katherine, and I know you have other tasks to accomplish at this time of day, but I am in desperate need of a bath, and I'm afraid I might need to soak my dress for a week in hopes it can recover."

"Recover from what, miss?"

"Recover from my own stupidity," she said with a sigh. Lila turned to Eloise. "I best let you return home, Eloise, but thank you for helping me."

"Of course," Eloise said. She turned to the door but then turned back. "Have you reconsidered pursuing this course, Lila?"

Lila took a breath while Katherine began to work on the stays that, even though they had been untouched by the oil, had managed to soak up the scent—as had every other item Lila wore. "Honestly, Eloise, I don't know what to do. I am madly in love with Neville, yet I find Mr. Luthford increasingly intriguing. Never mind my attempts to discourage his interest have not seemed to have worked in the least. He's asked me to go riding tomorrow—to prove to me Gordon's appeal."

"Did you agree?"

Katherine hesitated to remove the stay, what with Eloise right there, but Lila tugged at it enough that the maid finally removed it, leaving Lila in only her chemise. She frowned. "I agreed to meet him right after breakfast, and I don't think I can gamble or drink or any of those terrible things I haven't done yet." Katherine inhaled sharply, but Lila ignored it. "Eloise," she said as though confessing something deep and terrible. "I want him to think well of me. I want his good opinion."

"What of his age?"

"Should it matter so much?" Lila lifted her arms as Katherine helped her put on her dressing gown, which Lila wrapped around herself. "I find myself thinking of other marriages with such discrepancies, and they do not seem any worse for it. I believe Uncle Peter was nearly ten years older than Aunt Gaylene, and they got on beautifully. I wonder why I didn't think on that before."

Katherine cleared her throat. "I shall get the water heated and return with the basin."

"Thank you, Katherine," Lila said as the maid left the room.

"Could you love a man who is not handsome?" Eloise asked when they were alone again.

"He *is* handsome," Lila said. "Just in a different sort of way than I imagined; he does not even appear as brooding as I initially thought he did. And the way he looks at me as though I alone hold every bit of his attention . . . and the way he smiles with half his mouth." Remembering it sent a shiver through her. "I am a failure in this design, Eloise."

"Perhaps you should simply be at ease with this, then,"

Eloise suggested. "Maybe he is not a demon set to beguile you away from Neville, but is here to show you a better place for your affections."

"The idea of not loving Neville makes me feel cut in half," Lila said, crossing her arms. "But playing this game with Mr. Luthford is beginning to feel exactly the same way. I don't know what to do."

Eloise gave her a sympathetic smile. "Perhaps it is times like this that we give ourselves up to fate and simply let be whatever will be. It is never a good idea to ignore the stirrings of one's heart."

Lila let out a sigh, but with it went a great deal of fear and reservation. Give up the plan she had made to thwart Mr. Luthford's attention and simply be herself? Be free to ask questions about his time abroad and enjoy his company with her whole heart? The idea was so overwhelmingly appealing she knew she could take no other course. But it was not a course without risk. "What if he falls in love with me after all?"

"I beg your pardon, Lila," Eloise said with a raised eyebrow. "But I think you need to give equal consideration to what will happen if *you* fall in love with *him*."

Eight

Lila scrubbed each place on her body where she'd put the oil until she feared she would take the skin right off. She washed her hair twice, and Katherine took the dress and petticoat to the kitchen where she said she would soak them in vinegar overnight before laundering in hopes to save the items.

By the time dinner was announced, Lila could still smell the lavender, but it was no longer making her ill. She dressed in a navy blue dinner dress and had Katherine be extra attentive to her hair in hopes of making up for the spectacle she'd been that afternoon. Not that Mr. Luthford had noticed, seeing as how his nose did not work right. The odds of such a thing! If nothing else, she needed to give the extra attention to make herself feel worthy of his company. Perhaps he would not know she was trying to repair her deficit, but she would and she hoped presenting her best self would ease her fractured opinion of herself.

She did not remember that they had dinner guests until she entered the parlor to find Mrs. Mason with Mr. and Mrs. Marchett and their youngest daughter, Jenny. The Marchetts were dear family friends and the hosts of next week's masquerade ball—an event that had become less important to Lila as Mr. Luthford had overtaken her thoughts. The very man of those thoughts, dressed in a black evening coat and shiny black breeches that looked as fine as anything she'd ever seen before, was there too, and she smiled at him. Not having to keep to her wretched plan put her at greater ease with herself and his company, which was a relief.

Uncle Peter joined them just before they went to the dining room. Mrs. Mason was seated beside Mr. Luthford on the opposite end of the table, and Lila tried not to look their direction too often. Though she could not hear what they said, Mrs. Mason smiled a great deal, and Mr. Luthford seemed as easy with her as he'd ever been with Lila. By the end of the meal she was only too happy to get Mrs. Mason away from the table. When the men joined them, Jenny entertained them at the pianoforte while the adults conversed about the room. Mr. Marchett was aware of some property in Longdon, and the men began discussing how Mr. Luthford might best go about seeing it. This left the women to talk amongst themselves, which they did with the ease of women who had known each other all their lives. At one point the men moved into Uncle's study to consult a county map, and though Lila had resisted the temptation to pry when the women had been alone earlier, she could no longer hold back her questions for Mrs. Mason.

"What do you think of Mr. Luthford?"

"He seems kind," Mrs. Mason said with a smile. "And a very good conversationalist."

"Yes, he has so many exciting stories," Lila agreed,

though she hated that he'd shared those stories with Mrs. Mason, who seemed very undeserving of the attention. Never mind it was Lila's idea to invite the attractive widow.

"Only . . ." Mrs. Mason said, letting her voice drift off as though thinking better of what she was about to say.

"Only what?" Lila said, hiding her eagerness to hear the answer.

"Only, I sense a certain restlessness in him," she said. "As though he is resigned to this change in his circumstance but not fully glad for it."

"Really?" Mrs. Marchett said. "Did he not give up his commission of his own volition?"

"That is what he said," Mrs. Mason confirmed. "But he said it with such necessary acceptance. Why, I had the impression he would prefer to remain abroad."

"Surely he could, if that is what he wished," Mrs. Marchett said. "Many military men marry, and their wives either follow the drum or set up in some port city nearby. Why, my brother's wife traveled with him for a great many years. She lived on a ship for six months and in a grass hut for almost nine."

"What a wonderful adventure that would be," Lila said, seduced by the image of such a life. It took a moment to realize the other women were looking at her in confusion. "Do you not sometimes long to experience a life different than the one you live?"

"No," Mrs. Mason said with a shake of her head. "I have no desire for any life outside of Shropshire, though I would not mind an extra pound or two to use toward extra comforts. That is as different as I care to be."

Mrs. Marchett laughed and Lila smiled politely, but as the conversation moved toward comings and goings of mutual friends, Lila reviewed the time she had spent with Mr.

Luthford and some things he'd said that had her wondering at his possible wanderlust. Was he sad to leave the life he'd lived for so long? If so, why had he left it? Even if he were determined to marry, why not find a wife that might go with him?

"Lila?"

Lila blinked, having been inattentive to the conversation. "I'm sorry, do repeat the question."

"I asked how your costume was coming for the masquerade."

"It is nearly finished," Lila said, wondering how it was that the enthusiasm she'd felt for the ball last week was so different now. She would dance the first dance with Neville, but might she dance another dance with Mr. Luthford? With such thoughts, it did not take long for her enthusiasm for the ball to return. Thinking of both men gave her a queer feeling, as though she were being untrue to one or both of them. She reminded herself she had made no promise to anyone, and, like Eloise said, to ignore the stirrings of her heart did not seem like a very wise undertaking.

The conversation seemed to drag on for hours until finally Lila and Uncle Peter said good night to their guests—with Mrs. Mason and the Marchetts leaving via the Marchetts' carriage, and Mr. Luthford walking down the lane to the gravel drive, despite a light rain that was beginning to fall. When the door to the house was shut behind them, Lila made the expected compliments on the night and turned toward the stairs.

"Before you go, Lila," Uncle said. She turned in time to see him motioning to Wilhite, who was apparently prepared. "Neville wrote to me this afternoon and included a note he asked I give you."

"Neville," Lila said, but his name did not bring with it

the warmth of sunshine or the giddiness of kittens. She took the letter—still sealed—from Wilhite, but she looked at her uncle. "He comes home soon," she said.

"Yes. It seems he's been writing to you more privately these last months than he did when first he left us."

"It does seem to be that way," Lila said noncommittally.

He looked at her another moment, the line between his brows rather pronounced, but then it softened. "Ah, well, good night, my dear." He gave her a quick kiss on the forehead and headed to his study where he would end the day with a final glass of brandy.

Lila went upstairs to her room and sat at her desk before breaking the seal on the note, eager to read what was written there. She wondered if perhaps Neville's writing would rekindle the flame that seemed to be fading these last days.

Dearest Lila,

It is with a heavy heart that I write you with the news that I will not be returned to High Ercall in time for the Autumn Masquerade on Friday next. We have arrived in Liverpool, but there is business both here and in London that I must attend to before I return. I am very sorry for it, as I have looked forward to taking you to the floor that night, but will instead anticipate the delight in seeing you as soon as I can conclude my business.

I promise to make up for the disappointment.

With much affection,
Neville

Lila did not read the letter a second time, as she once might have. Instead, she lowered the paper into her lap and felt another level of burden removed from her shoulders. Neville would not come back next week. And he would not be at the ball. Some part of her wished he were not bowing out, but another part was not disappointed at all. She had just been given the chance to further explore these strange new feelings she had toward Mr. Luthford, and she would make the most of it.

Nine

At ten o'clock in the morning, Lila took a final look in the mirror and then turned and left her bedchamber. She wore her riding skirt—the train draped over one arm so it wouldn't drag on the ground—and boots, a wool coat cut like a man's with gold buttons and braid, and a jaunty, wide-brimmed hat pinned at a slight angle. She loved the look of her riding habit—adventurous and rugged compared to the typical pastel dresses of daily life. Truth be told she preferred to ride astride—the excessive skirts, shown off to advantage on a side saddle—were cumbersome until actually on the horse, and while she was quite good on a ladies saddle, she often thought she could be even better if she could distribute her weight more equally. For some time she'd been trying to convince Uncle Peter to allow her to ride with a regular saddle, but he was as yet unconvinced it was appropriate. Rather than argue she simply did her best to improve her form on the sidesaddle. One day she would be a married woman and surely, if she could prove her mastery of the ladies' version, her future husband would allow her greater margin than her uncle. The thought brought her to a stop just inside the back door of the estate. *Her husband.*

For some time the title of "her future husband" and Neville's name had been one and the same. This morning, however, Neville had not been part of the equation. Rather the expectation of her future husband was now a neutral one, based on title only but without a man attached to the position. The change was somewhat worrisome, like finding an object once loved and not feeling the same joy with it you once did. If Mr. Luthford were not waiting for her at the stable, perhaps she would have explored the change with greater attention. Or perhaps she would not have. Thinking of Mr. Luthford, talking of Mr. Luthford, and mostly, talking *with* Mr. Luthford had created a kind of veil between her automatic expectations of just a week ago and the now vague and smoky expectations of possibility. She did not want to ponder on the change too much—such things could be fragile—so she quieted the thoughts and focused her mind on the present.

She arrived at the stable to find Gordon and her uncle's horse, Braystorm, already saddled at the far side of the paddock. She had specifically told Mr. Luthford that she had a horse of her own; she had never ridden Braystorm and was unsure that a sidesaddle had ever graced the fine animal's back. Had Mr. Luthford been confused? The stable hands would not have made the mistake. The sound of footsteps from behind caused Lila to turn, and then Mr. Luthford's smile—first one side and then the other—filled her with sunshine.

"Good morning, Miss Grange," he said, inclining his head as he approached. He was dressed in buff breeches and tall riding boots with a riding coat that hung nearly to his knees. "You look the very picture of a horsewoman."

"I do like to ride," Lila said, surprised at the sudden shyness she felt as he approached. "And I wish you would call me Lila."

His smile grew even more. "Then you must call me Mortimer—or rather Mory, if you would." He paused a moment. "Do you know that there are likely only three people left in all the world who call me that?"

"Really?" she asked, raising her eyebrows.

"Other men call me Luthford, and in the military I was Lieutenant or Sir. With both my parents gone now, only my sisters call me by my Christian name. I had not thought of that until this very moment. What a strange thing to have so few people call me by the one name that is mine alone."

The sentiment made Lila feel special, selected to have a level of intimacy and trust with this man that she would only share with a handful of other people. "It would be an honor to be part of such an exclusive group, Mory." Had she once thought the name stuffy? Mory was better, of course, but even Mortimer no longer seemed so bad.

He smiled back in humor. "I am very glad you think so, Lila." He held her eyes a moment longer and then turned toward the corral. "I hope you will forgive me for taking a liberty with our mounts today."

She turned to look at the horses too and only then realized that it was *Gordon* with the sidesaddle, not Braystorm. Mory didn't say anything, apparently letting her absorb the situation for herself.

Finally she turned to look at him. "*I* am to ride Gordon?"

"If you are rabidly opposed, I can have the groom prepare your horse instead, but if you are willing to take a chance, I think you would find Gordon a very pleasing bit of horse flesh, though she does not have the bloodline that would recommend her in polite circles."

Lila cocked her head to the side and narrowed her eyes in a playful way. "Have you arranged this because I insulted her?"

"I agreed that she was not much to look at," he conceded. "But ten to one you will fall in love with her as I have once you experience her charm for yourself."

While they'd talked, Gordon moved toward them and, as she had the first time Lila was introduced, nuzzled her master's hand.

"It seems the two of you have made a very happy match with one another," Lila said.

Mortimer laughed. "A man could do worse in his female company, I dare say."

"She is trained with a sidesaddle?"

"Or no saddle, a broken saddle, a cart, wagon—she is a horse of all trades. In Spain there were times when she was needed for some commander's wife, so she is familiar with the different weight distribution."

"And you don't mind my riding her?" Most men were rather protective of their mounts.

"Not at all. I asked your uncle for a recommendation I might ride in her place, and he offered up Braystorm, which was very generous." He was still stroking Gordon's nose and turned to look at Lila. "Are you ready?"

Lila grinned. "Indeed I am."

They started down Shrewsbury Lane, then turned onto Cotswall, talking of the weather and some properties in and around High Ercall that Mory would be visiting in a few more days.

"What brought you to Shropshire? Uncle Peter said you grew up in Essex."

A Merry Dance

"That was where my parents lived, yes, but I went away to school when I was very young and then joined the military at fifteen after my parents could not afford my schooling. The land was sold off bit by bit as we had several bad years, and then when my father died my mother sold the home in order to secure dowries for my sisters. One of my sisters lives in Birmingham now, and another in Wales. Shropshire seemed a good place to plant myself between them."

"That is a good reason, then. You will be farming?"

He gave her a sidelong look. "Are you going to lecture me on the importance of retaining my level?"

"No," she said with a laugh. "We do not stand on so much ceremony here."

"I miss the physical toil of my military career; in fact, I avoided some promotions for fear they would put me behind a desk. To grow fat and useless is a fate I hope to avoid at all costs. An active farm seems the best way to maintain myself. I believe if my father had been willing to learn the management, he'd have done better than he did when he was determined not to work."

"That is an unusual perspective," Lila said. "Especially amid a society that prides itself in not having to work with one's hands."

He smiled, but there was a sadness in it. "I find it harder to fit in with this society than I ever did with that of India or Spain."

"Do you really?" she asked. "You don't seem to have any trouble making friends and conversation."

He shrugged but said nothing. She thought of the conversation she had with Mrs. Mason the night before, regarding Mory having resigned himself to this lifestyle.

"Do you regret leaving the military?"

He seemed to ponder this and then let out a heavy breath. "More often than I thought I would," he said. "I always knew I wanted to return to England and have a family—I have planned this course for quite some time—and yet the actual fulfillment of that goal has been a difficult adjustment." He glanced at her and forced his smile bigger. "Purchasing my own estate will be a great help in the transition, I believe, and I hope to set up a household and nursery soon. I have great faith that not too far into the future I shall no longer miss the activity of my military career and be glad for having made the decision to begin a new life here."

"Are there not any number of married soldiers?" Lila said, saddened by the idea that he had to give up one dream to take hold of another.

"It is hard on them, especially the wives," he said. "Not so much when they are unencumbered by children and can follow their husbands from post to post, but when they have a family, the wives often stay in British settlements while the men move with their assignments. They can go months, years even, without any interaction. Too often the children barely know their fathers, and the wives and husbands settle into an arrangement rather than the kind of union I hope to have."

"Are there no *happy* military marriages, then?"

"There are some," Mory said. "But the odds are against it, and I wanted to strengthen my potential. English women prefer English society, manners, climate, and ritual, and while there are British settlements formed around those ideals, it is a hard life—one that few women are truly capable of finding contentment within. I believe I will prefer a happy home over exotic locations; that is what it came down to for me." He glanced her way again. "Do not feel sorry for me, Lila. I am content with my place and, if I dare say, intrigued by my prospects here."

A Merry Dance

She felt the heat in her cheeks—the second time today—and looked at Gordon's mane, which did not shine. She reached forward anyway and stroked the back of the mare's neck. "I must confess Gordon is a very smooth ride. I am not overly pitched to either side, nor do I feel much impact from her steps."

"I knew you would see things my way."

Lila laughed and patted the horse's neck again. Her mind was still very much focused on the prior topic of conversation, however. "I read an article not long ago about women taken to India each spring in search of military husbands. They were often older, or perhaps not as highly bred as a typical debutante here in England. Did you see much of that?"

"Ah yes, the fishing fleet," he said with a grin. "A hundred or so women sent out to settlements with a thousand men. It is a reasonable idea, and for many men—and women—it has worked well, but I believe most of those women came because they had no other choice. Many never find the contentment they hoped for, and a fair amount left as soon as they were able, married or not."

She was trying to think of something more to say when he began to talk again.

"I would not usually discuss matters of business with a woman, but from our prior conversations I deduce that you are not to be put off by it."

"Not at all," she said, perhaps too eagerly. She evened out her tone. "I have a wide variety of interests."

He must have decided to take her at her word. "When I was first stationed in India, another soldier and I went in on an investment. Many military men do so in hopes of making a fortune they can then take back to England one day."

Lila nodded. This type of thing was common knowledge, and she had supposed he made exactly this kind of investment since he was now in the market for a farm of his own. That he was taking her into his confidence, however, was far more than she'd hoped for. Many married women did not fully understand the extent of their husband's holdings. Most did not want to know. In yet one more way Lila was reminded that she was not like most English women. What surprised her was that, in this moment, she did not want to be.

"This partner and I purchased a tea plantation and over the years improved and expanded it as we could spare the time and expense. When he retired five years ago, he took over the management of the farm, which has only increased its success, but for each year he manages the plantation, he gets two percent of my ownership."

"So he now has ten percent of what you once held."

"Exactly," Mory said, pleased with her attentiveness. "We began as fifty-fifty partners, but we are now sixty-forty, with him holding the majority. In February we shall be sixty-two and thirty-eight."

"It seems a fair arrangement," Lila said. "Other than the fact that in twenty years you will have no ownership at all."

"Yes, but the profits continue to increase, and so it is not a poor arrangement for either one of us. At least not so far. There was a time I considered retiring to India as well, or perhaps my partner and I would trade off—a year in England and a year in India. I would retain my percentage, and we would both have the chance to reconnect with family and society of our homeland."

"Why did you not pursue that course?" Lila asked when he did not offer additional information.

"We would need a joint holding here to accommodate our time in England," Mortimer said. "And he has never expressed an interest to come to England. He married after retirement to a widow who had lived in Bombay for more than a decade. She is well suited to the lifestyle, and I did not want to seem ungrateful for all they have done for the plantation thus far. And, once again, such a thing would require a great deal of the woman I should marry. It seems a much simpler matter to set up a holding of my own in England from the profits of the plantation this last decade and offset my decrease in India with an increase here. Basic economics, really, and without the difficulty of convincing a woman to leave everything she knows."

I would do it, Lila thought to herself, genuinely intrigued by the idea. She had Uncle Peter, of course, and would miss the comforts of English life, but adventure of exotic lands and new cultures seemed a fair trade. But then, she had Neville here too. Thinking of him caused her to swallow with discomfort. How was it she could forget about him so easily? And it was not as though Mory had made her an offer. But what if he did? And what if she told him she would go to India and live on that plantation? Would she be happy there? Could she live without familiar things and people? She couldn't guarantee her own success at making such adaptations, of course, but she would be eager to do her best.

"Where does this road lead?" Mory asked, interrupting her thoughts that were rather embarrassing to have been so lost within.

She turned to look in the direction Mory was pointing. "Toward some ruins," Lila said. "They are a few miles up that road, though the road narrows some, the farther you go in."

"A few miles might be too far a distance," he said. "I took the liberty of asking the cook to have luncheon ready for us at noon."

"If time is the determining factor," Lila said, easing Gordon to the side of the road in case Mr. Luthford took her up on her suggestion. "I do know a shortcut." The part of her character that craved experiences and intensity was fairly screaming at her to be shown to him—a man who could certainly appreciate such wild bits of character.

He raised his eyebrows.

"Through the meadow there," she said, pointing to the western field with her chin. "At the tree line there is a path that winds through the wood. That part is a bit perilous if you become inattentive, but it is beautiful. Then we have to go over a rather significant rise, but once we do that the ruins are just before us. Half the distance of the road, I would guess."

"And you are not intimidated by perils and rises?" he asked.

In reply she smiled, leaned forward and slightly right to balance herself, and gave Gordon a snap of the reins. She did not expect such a quick jump forward but was able to retain herself as Gordon broke into a run Lila did not think such a thick horse capable of. She leaned down and wove her fingers through Gordon's mane. "Don't lose me, girl," she said against the wind as the meadow grass flew beneath Gordon's legs. A flick of Gordon's ear felt like a promise that if Lila did her part, they would both enjoy this ride very much.

Lila didn't dare look behind her for reasons of balance, but she didn't need to. Soon enough Braystorm's nose came into peripheral view, and moments later Lila and Mory were side by side, skimming over the meadow as though they were rocks skipping upon the surface of a pond. Lila had only ever ridden thus when she was alone and, while she couldn't be sure what possessed her to share this part of herself now, she had no regrets. The wind in her face, Gordon's solid strength

A Merry Dance

beneath her, and an increasingly interesting man at her side seemed to be an analogy of the life and freedom she wanted to hold with the same tightness as the reins in her hands.

Ten

"You look lovely," Katherine said as she stepped back from her charge.

Lila turned to face the full-length mirror and lifted her arms as high as the dress would allow, which was not quite to her shoulders. Tiny straps attached the edges of the modified cape to her wrists, causing the cape to spread like wings. The mask of dark green feathers framed her eyes, and her hair was left long and free, cascading over her shoulders in mahogany waves set off by the rich emerald of the gown. The back of her cape was embroidered with peacock plumes—detailed work that had taken Lila weeks to complete, but with which she was quite pleased. She had sewn every stitch thinking Neville would be the man to admire it. That morning she had received a note from Mory, formally requesting the first dance of the night—a dance that had once belonged to Neville. She had responded with equal formality that she would be honored to lead the evening with him. His response—received just a few hours ago—was a single yellow rose that now stood in a vase on her dressing table.

"Thank you for your help, Katherine," Lila said, a bit awed by the final result of so much work. "Will you tell my uncle I shall be downstairs shortly?"

"Certainly, miss," Katherine said before leaving the room.

Once alone, Lila turned slowly in front of the mirror, hands outstretched so she might see the complete effect of the costume. She felt beautiful in such a rich color and wondered what Mory would think when he saw her. A shiver washed through her at the anticipation of his reaction, and a smile drew up the sides of her mouth.

Uncle Peter was indeed waiting in the foyer, his red and black feathered mask that he wore each year held at his side. He would wear it as they entered but eventually find his way to the card room and remove it so that he might better focus on his game. He went to the Marchetts' ball because everyone in the parish went to the Marchetts' ball. He was not one to much enjoy social events beyond small dinner parties.

Lila was gratified by the look on his face as she descended the stairs. He asked her to turn and present the full costume for him to see. "You have outdone yourself, and I could not be more proud to escort such a lovely young woman."

"Thank you, Uncle," she said, feeling conspicuous and yet very pleased with his compliments. He put out his arm, and she took it, allowing him to lead her to the carriage and feeling as though nothing in the world could be more perfect than this.

Torches lined the staircase and outer wall of the Marchetts' sprawling estate made of local stone, with turrets on both ends. Only half as many torches had been used than would be lit for a typical ball, so as to keep a mysterious ambiance about the whole affair. There was no announcement when they entered the dimly lit ballroom—only masked foot men who instructed men to go one direction and women to go another. The sexes would mingle on the far side of the room once they navigated the edges. Uncle Peter kissed Lila's hand before releasing her. Lila made her way through the masked women, stopping every few feet to guess someone's identity. Some women wore only a ball gown and coordinating mask, while others, like Lila, wore fuller costumes reflective of a theme. It was surprising how many people did not recognize Lila. Once they realized who she was, the words they used were "enchanting" and "fantastic." Lila's confidence grew as she made her way to the end of the ballroom.

"Lila?"

She turned and smiled as wide as she had all night to see Eloise dressed head to toe in pink. She had chosen to dress as a flamingo, an exotic bird they had only ever seen in picture books. "You look amazing," Lila said, standing back and taking in the full effect of Eloise's costume. "I am so pleased with how well your costume came together."

"As am I," Eloise said. "I look forward to this night all year long."

"So do I," Lila said. She looked past Eloise to the mixing of men and women at the far end.

Eloise laughed. "I shall not detain you any longer. Shall we join our gallant companions?" Eloise moved to Lila's side and took her arm. Lila put her other hand over Eloise's and gave it a squeeze, her stomach a fit of butterflies and eager anticipation. They walked together, still exchanging greetings with other guests but not stopping to engage conversation. Instead, their intent was upon the gathering crowd at the far end of the room, where men and women were now weaving in and out of one another, guessing identities, sharing whispered conversations behind fans, and enjoying the intimacy of covered faces and flickering candlelight.

Lila and Eloise were still several steps away from the crowd when the orchestra paused and a scale was played on the pianoforte to indicate the first dance would soon begin. Lila had not realized she'd spent so much time greeting the women and scanned the group of people before her with greater detail. When she saw the man dressed all in black, but holding another single yellow rose in his hands and staring straight at her, she caught her breath. Mory. He was somehow standing apart in the crowd, and she was as struck by his presentation as she was by the fact that he knew it was her. She had just interacted with any number of women she had known for years who had not recognized her, but somehow Mory had. He'd seen through the costume and seen *her* inside it. The sense of connection and belonging made her dizzy.

"Is that him?" Eloise whispered.

Lila could only nod, her eyes locked on to Mory's and her heart thrilling. Without moving, the distance between them seemed to become smaller and narrower. For a moment Lila felt as though it was only the two of them in the ballroom, alone with this tether drawing them closer in a way she had never felt before. The shadows created by the low light became sharper, and the whispered conversations became part of the music. She took a step forward but was brought up short when someone stepped into her line of sight, blocking Mory and breaking the spell. She blinked and tried to look around this interloper, but he did not continue upon whatever course had created the interference. Eloise's hand tightened on Lila's arm. Lila looked at Eloise, who stared at the man before them, her eyes wide behind her mask. Lila then looked into the man's face, as well.

"Neville?" Eloise said, vocalizing the recognition that had fallen like a stone into Lila's mind. Eloise took a step forward. "Is it really you?"

Eleven

Neville! Handsome Neville who Lila had pinned all her hopes on stood before her. He was dressed in blue and grey, with a simple fabric mask tied over his eyes. His hair had darkened to an amber color that fairly glowed beneath the light of the candles. If anything, he was more handsome now than he'd been when he left.

"Dance with me, Lila," he said in that voice so familiar, so known, so missed for so long. Couples were taking the floor and before Lila uttered a single word, Neville was leading her to join the dance. They took their places, and her tongue was finally loosed.

"You've returned," she said softly. "I can't believe you've returned . . . here . . . tonight."

"Are you surprised?" he asked with his merry grin. "I promised you I would be home in time to have the first dance at the Autumn Masquerade and, if nothing else, I am a man of my word."

"But you said you were not coming," she said. "I did not expect you."

"Precisely," he said with a nod. "That is why my arrival is such a fine surprise. I didn't even tell Father for fear he would give me up."

Mory!

Lila turned her head and scanned the crowd until her eyes locked on Mory's. He was standing on the edge of the floor, watching her with his expression hidden behind his mask, and Eloise not far away, certainly trying to determine what she could do to help. The yellow rose that had been a beacon meant to lead her to Mory was now at his side, the bloom facing the floor and reminding her of a glass tipped over and relieved of its contents. Her heart, already racing, now seemed to spin within her chest.

Mory watched her. Waiting. Wondering.

"I am promised to another for this dance, Neville," she said, turning back to look at him.

His smile dropped immediately. "You have only just arrived," he said. "How could you be promised to another?"

"I did not know you were coming. You said you would not be here."

"You said you were waiting for me," Neville said. "I believe the words you used were 'on bated breath.'"

She did not know what to do. She *had* said those words, in the last letter she'd sent to him when he was in America—sent before she'd met Mory. But Neville had withdrawn his promise, and she had made a new one. To leave the floor was ill-mannered, but Mory was the one to whom she had given her word. Or had she given it to Neville when he had said he would arrive back in time to take her to this ball?

But Mory.

The rose.

A Merry Dance

The magic of the moment when their eyes had met.

She took a step out of formation, but Neville's hand shot out and took her arm. "You will not leave me standing here," he said softly, with embarrassment rather than anger.

"I promised another," Lila said, pleading. Torn. Horrified.

Neville did not remove his hand, but the dance would be starting at any moment. "This is not how I imagined our reunion."

The dancers on either side of them began the first steps. It was too late to leave.

Years of etiquette training set Lila's feet to move as well, but her heart was thumping, and as the dance commenced she continued to look for Mory, wishing she did not have her mask so that he might see how sorry she was things had happened as they had. *Stay,* she said in her mind and heart in hopes he might somehow hear it. *Wait. Let me explain.* For some time Mory remained in place, and then Lila could not find him there. Eloise was where she'd been standing all along, but again the mask prevented Lila from sending her a questioning look. Had Mory left? Had she angered or embarrassed him so drastically that he could not bear to stay?

She missed a step and was in the process of regaining her place when suddenly Neville's hand was at her elbow, and he was propelling her from the floor. A slight hush fell over the crowd as he pushed her through them, and Lila's neck caught fire with an embarrassment and fear she had never felt in Neville's presence before.

"Neville," she whispered desperately.

"You have spent the entire dance looking for someone else," he whispered in her ear. "I need to know the whole of it before I embarrass myself further. Do you not realize the effort I made to be here tonight?"

Lila felt someone behind her and looked over her shoulder to make eye contact with Eloise—dear Eloise—just before Neville pulled Lila through one of the open side doors that led to the covered terrace. There was a bonfire in the middle of the wide porch, and several people stood near it to remain warm in the chilly evening. Neville led her away from the people and away from the warmth. Her skin prickled in the cool air, and the heaviness of confrontation fell upon her when they came to a darkened corner, tangled in shadow. As soon as Neville stopped, Lila wrenched her arm from his grasp and pulled away. Eloise hurried to her side, and Lila gripped her hands as they stood shoulder to shoulder, facing Neville with their backs against the balustrade.

Lila saw Neville's hurt and thought of what pains he must have gone through to surprise her tonight and how horribly wrong it had gone. The regret was cutting. This was *Neville*, the cousin that she loved in each way someone could love another. Only she no longer understood exactly how she loved him *now*. Were the feelings she had always felt for him only that of a dearest cousin? Had the fact that she had known no other kind of love led her to believe her feelings were more than they had truly been? Until meeting Mory, she'd had nothing to compare her feelings with. Now she did. And yet she found herself confused and unsure of what she felt for whom. She had known Neville most of her life. She had known Mory for a handful of days. She felt love and tenderness and affection for Neville. She felt heat and intrigue and depth for Mory. Which was love? Which was more powerful than the other?

"What has happened during my absence?" Neville asked. "What have you done?"

The accusation of his words shocked her. Years of shame regarding her mother's own recklessness had left Lila with the

A Merry Dance

fear that she was her mother's daughter in ways she did not want to consider. This fear was why Lila was trying to improve her behavior, why she saw marriage to Neville as a kind of proof she had outlived her mother's reputation. To hear him question her ability to rise above was staggering.

"She has done nothing untoward, Neville," Eloise said when Lila began to curl into herself. "Surely you are not accusing her of such."

Neville's face softened. "I was not trying to accuse," he said. "Only, I don't understand what's happened. A month ago I received a letter rich with excitement for my return, and now you are looking for another man in the crowd rather than glad to see me. I am taken off my guard, to be sure."

"I *am* glad to see you, Neville," Lila said, finding strength in Eloise. "But I promised another man the first dance. Had I known you were returning this evening, it would have been very different."

"Would you have danced the first dance with me?" Neville asked.

"Of course," Lila said, attempting to defend her character. "I had pinned all my hopes upon it."

"She has been so fiercely devoted to you, Neville," Eloise said. Blessed Eloise.

"Has been," Neville repeated. He looked sharply at Lila. "Are you in love with someone else?"

"I . . ." Lila did not know what to say. Was she in *love* with Mortimer? Could she take ownership of such a feeling when not long ago she was so certain she was in love with Neville? "I do love you, Neville. You are as dear to me as anyone." She paused, wishing she could explain beyond her own ability to articulate. "But I *have* met another and . . ." It was coming out all wrong. Where were the right words she needed to speak her heart and her mind and the truth and the feeling?

"And now you love us both?" Neville supplied.

"No," she said, thinking of her mother again. The shame of her loving too many, too much. Lila let go of Eloise's hand in order to reach up and untie the ribbon that kept her mask in place. He needed to see her face. He needed to know—without barriers—that she meant what she said. A moment later the green feathered mask hung from her fingers at her side. "What I mean is, I tried very hard not to even *like* him. He is nothing of the sort of man I have ever wanted."

"It is true," Eloise said. "When we learned of Mr. Luthford's coming, we came up with a plan to thwart his interest from the start—all manner of manipulations meant to keep him from falling in love with her. Only, it didn't work."

"Why is he the sort of man you did not want?"

"He was not you," Eloise said in Lila's place. "And he is old."

Lila nodded, but her stomach was as hot as coals because Mory's age no longer vexed her. By agreeing with Eloise in hopes of easing Neville's feelings, she was betraying Mory. But she had to explain herself. "I was not on the hunt, Neville. I was not looking to soothe myself with some flirtation." *Not as my mother did.* "I did not want his attention." *But I want it now,* she thought. *Where had Mory gone?*

Neville stared at her and said nothing.

She looked back at him, and tears came to her eyes. Was it because she'd hurt Neville or because she'd said unkind things about Mory?

"She has missed you every day you have been gone, Neville," Eloise said.

"Until the last few, it seems." His expression lost its tightness and showed only his unfulfilled expectation of what could have been a lovely surprise.

"I'm sorry," Lila whispered. "I never meant for this to happen, and now you are here, and . . . I . . . I am very confused, Neville."

A woman at the fire laughed, loud enough to distract the trio and cause them to look toward the laughter, which was finished by the time it caught their attention. It was the need for relief from the chains of discomfort and strain, more than anything else, that made them eager to look that way, and then a sense of regret that there was not something more dramatic to offer them further respite.

Lila turned to look back at Neville, praying for the strength to say the words that needed to be said. "Neville," she said as she caught his eyes again. But then a yellow rose lying on the edge of the darkest shadow behind him caught her eye. She stared at it, then hurried to where it lay on the stone terrace. It had not been there when they arrived for this discussion. She looked into the shadows around them, the dark corners where someone could have been standing, dressed all in black—a silent audience to a confession that would burn and twist.

With tender hands Lila reached for the rose and picked it up, aware but unaware of Eloise and Neville watching her. Mory had brought that rose for her. It was to lead her to him, yet now it seemed to speak in silent accusation. What she'd said and what she hadn't said pinched and pressed within her memory. At one point she had felt as though she were betraying Mory with her account, now she *knew* she had.

She stood and turned. Neville and Eloise watched her.

"I am not in love with you, Neville," she said with a tender tone. "I love you, but not in a way a woman should love a man, and I only know this because I met a man who turned my mind and pricks my heart in ways you do not." Neville's nostrils flared slightly. "I don't say it to hurt you. I hate that I am causing you embarrassment, and I would give anything to have this play out differently than it has, but I would be doing no kindness to lead you on and . . ." She paused and swallowed the growing regret she felt. "I have already caused great pain to someone who did not deserve it."

She met Eloise's eye for only a moment before her eyes filled with tears that blurred her vision. "I am sorry," she said to them both, to the shadows, to the ears that she knew were not there to hear it.

Twelve

Lila stood at the paddock fence Monday morning trying to regain her confidence. Gordon looked her way, flicked an ear, and went back to the grass at the far side of the corral. Lila reached into her pocket and extracted the small apple she had stolen from the kitchen. When Gordon looked up a moment later, she paused, chewed, and then lumbered her way across the corral. She plucked the apple from Lila's hand and proceeded to make a very loud process of enjoying the treat.

"I am making all kinds of apologies this morning, Gordon, but I thought I would start with you." The horse turned to look at her and then walked away. Lila let out a heavy breath, hoping the horse's dismissal was not a portent of things to come. She watched until Gordon resumed her place on the far side of the corral before pushing away from the fence and turning toward the front of Franklyn Farm.

With each step toward the dowager cottage, Lila's heart beat faster and her stomach felt tighter, but she was determined to handle this with integrity. She owed both Mory, and herself, that much.

She could hear movement within the cottage as soon as she came to a stop on the porch and knew he was leaving. He had not yet decided upon an estate, as far as she knew, but he would not stay at Franklyn Farm now. Not after he heard her confession and not with Neville here. That was why she had to do this now, just two days after the ball. She could not risk waiting until she felt ready. If she had been less concerned about herself and more concerned about doing the right thing, she wouldn't be in this situation in the first place. She raised a hand and knocked. Fast, heavy footsteps moved toward the door. When it swung open, Mory was looking over his shoulder at something inside.

"I'm grateful you came early, Clemens. If you'd just . . . Oh." His entire body stopped moving when he saw her, and she attempted a smile in hopes it might soften the tension. "Miss Grange," he said, reverting to the formal address. "Good morning."

"Good morning, Mory," she said, maintaining the familiar. "I would like to talk to you."

He looked past her, perhaps hoping this Clemens man would save him from what could not be anything less than an awkward discussion.

"Well, my hired man should be here at any time, but I have until then. I would invite you in, but I think that would not be appropriate under the circumstances."

That was her fault, his standing on ceremony and keeping her at a distance. She cleared her throat. "I wanted to explain my actions Saturday night."

"That is not necessary, Miss Grange. I understand the situation and bear you no ill will."

His dismissal hurt at least as much as his rage would. "I

thank you for that," Lila said. "But I fear you did not hear the full account."

"I heard enough," he said evenly. "I will not bother you again." He began to close the door.

"That is not what I want," she blurted out, then swallowed and took a breath. "What I want is for you to know the truth—all of it."

"Answer me this, Miss Grange," he said when she paused for another breath. "Is the truth for my benefit or your own? If it is simply your conscience you wish to clear, I would prefer that you keep whatever explanation you feel so possessed to share to yourself. I do not need it, nor do I want the burden of such a thing. As I said, I bear you no ill will but would like to continue without discomfort between us, which, at this time, I feel capable of doing but cannot guarantee should you add to the weight of what has already taken place."

"Oh," Lila said, considering her motivation.

"I have no thirst for chaos and no interest in proving myself. Pursue the path you were on; I shall not interfere."

She swallowed the shame she felt, but pushed through. "I have behaved very badly toward you, Mory. I wish I could say it was accidental or that I acted without thought, but in fact I had quite a solid plan in place before you and I even met—a plan I felt sure would secure my destiny." His brow furrowed enough to prove his interest in hearing what it was she had to say. And so she told him of her pining for Neville, of the plan she made with Eloise to discourage the attention of an old military veteran, and the article she used as a guide. She told him how hard she tried to be everything he could never want, and how he surprised her at every turn by not being put off by her behavior. She then explained how she gave up on the game when she felt something for him that she had never felt before. "I believed my heart had changed, but when Neville surprised me at the ball, the fantasy I had petted and nurtured for him left me paralyzed, unsure of my own feelings. When I tried to explain what I myself did not fully understand, I said it badly. After I found your rose, I realized what I'd done and I told him what I hadn't said the first time."

"And he rejected you so you've come to me?" Mory said, lifting one eyebrow. "Forgive me if I'm not flattered."

"He did not reject me," Lila said. "But we have spoken and determined we are ill-suited."

"And so he rejected you and you've come to me," Mory repeated.

She felt her neck heat up and knew that equally hot tears would soon betray her. She took a step back and looked at Mory's boots instead of his face. "I am not here to present myself a viable option to you, Mr. Luthford. I have accepted that door to be closed. I am here because I have behaved badly, and my immature and impulsive nature has hurt people I care for, including you. I have many failings, of which you have seen far more than I would wish, but I understand my accountability." Once again words were failing her. "I will not take more of your time, but I hope that your relationship with my uncle will not be damaged because of my outrageous behavior. I hope that your interactions within this community and your attempts to set up your own living are not affected by my ill treatment of you these last weeks. I hope, more than anything, that you will not look poorly upon High Ercall because of my mistakes. I regret so very much what I have done and wish for you to know that I am very, *very* sorry for it." She barely got the last word out without her voice shaking, then turned and fled down the porch and to the front door of Franklyn Farm. She did not know if Mr. Luthford stayed on the porch until she disappeared or if he pushed aside her apology as soon as she uttered it and went back to whatever task he'd been involved in when she arrived. She didn't know, because she didn't look back. Wouldn't look back. Couldn't look back. She feared very much that Mr. Luthford was an opportunity she would never have again and that she had ruined her one chance to be truly happy.

Thirteen

A week passed, and the easy recovery between Neville and Lila seemed proof that whatever their feelings had seemed to be during his absence was not the true state of things. Lila hoped for the same change to take place regarding her feelings for Mory, but those were proving harder to forget. She thought about him all the time, wondering if she would see him again and, if she did, how they would act toward one another. She imagined he would be polite, and it would nearly kill her. Over and over again she replayed their final conversation, trying to accuse him of being unbending or cruel, but none of those accusations fit. Not really. It was her vanity that had driven her actions, and she could not fault any man for not wanting to pursue such recklessness. It seemed her nature was not so easily changed after all. In dark moments she wondered if it were the same matters of personality that had led her mother to such extremes. And yet even such fear of blighted character did not keep her from the corner of

Uncle's study. It was the second Tuesday, after all, and she was curious as to whether the sheep had fetched the price Uncle Peter was hoping for at the auction. That she felt unfit for company and in need of time apart while she licked her wounds gave her another reason to hide with her crochet and listen in on matters far more interesting than the state of her thoughts and conscience. Neville had gone hunting, and so she had no one to miss her presence this morning.

The sheep did fetch a good price at the auction, and Uncle was considering investing in a coal mine now that the industry was flourishing in this part of the country. The men were concluding their business about the same time Lila finished a shawl she would give to Eloise on her birthday next month. She couldn't snip the yarn without risking being heard, so she bundled up her craft and silently replaced it in the basket, then settled against her corner to wait for the business to end. She leaned her head against the wall and closed her eyes, drawing her knees up to her chest. If it were not so cold, she might be able to fall asleep. Rest had not come easily these last nights.

There was a knock at the study door. She did not open her eyes.

"Mr. Luthford to see you, sir."

Her eyes popped open, and she sat up, turning toward that portion of the room even though it was blocked from her. Mory had moved to a boarding house a few villages over and she had missed him terribly. Why was he returned? And why did she know nothing of it?

"Yes, thank you, Wilhite," Uncle Peter said casually, as though Mory's arrival was not unexpected. "Please excuse me for cutting our meeting short, Mr. Jeppson."

Lila didn't realize she'd stopped breathing until she had heard the men stand, move toward the door, and then Uncle wish Mr. Jeppson a good day. She carefully filled her lungs so that her head might be right upon her shoulders again.

"Good morning, Luthford," Uncle said. "Please do come in and take a chair."

"Thank you," Mory said. "I appreciate you seeing me."

His words washed over her, and finally she could exhale, though she did it slowly, so as not to make a sound. She should not be here, she knew it, and yet even if there were a way to leave now, she would not go. Though she was ashamed of herself for it, she would not give up this chance to hear his voice and know what he'd come to discuss with her uncle.

"Not at all," Uncle said. His chair creaked, indicating that he had sat down again. "What can I help you with? Have you found a place?"

"There is one that looks appealing," Mory said. "But it is not what I've come to speak with you about."

"Oh?"

"No, at least, not the only thing. I spent much of the last week pondering my situation and evaluating my future. As you know I gave up my military career to be the Englishman my parents always wanted me to be, though they were unable to prepare me for that future as well as they would have liked."

"I do understand that, Mory. For what it's worth, I know it was the regret of your father's life that things were not managed better for your sake."

"I bear them no ill will," Mory said. Lila smiled sadly, her heart softened by the fact that he didn't seem to bear anyone ill will. He was such a good man, and yet she had destroyed her chances of being in his life. "I am grateful for the opportunity I have been given, only, I am having a harder time picturing myself in this place than I thought I would."

"Understandable, considering the extent of changes that have taken place for you. You are not second guessing your decision to settle here, are you?"

"Perhaps a little," Mory said. He shifted in his chair, and Lila wished she could see him as well as hear his voice. He was so close. Then again, he would not speak so openly if she were in his company. "I do not regret leaving the military. Without a war there is little to do but run drills, but I have wondered if the reason I have not felt particularly drawn to any of the properties I have explored is because my future does not lie in Shropshire after all, perhaps not even in England."

Lila closed her eyes and dropped her chin to her chest. He was leaving because of her. She had given such a poor impression of English society that he could not find a desire to be a part of it. The shame and guilt was excruciating.

"I am very sorry to hear that," Uncle said. He let out a heavy breath. "I had hoped that you would feel welcome here."

"It is certainly not upon your shoulders that I have not felt at home. You have been everything kind and inviting. But you know that I came with the intent to find a living and a wife."

"I hope it not too bold to mention I had hoped you would find both here. I can only suppose you have instead found neither."

"Not . . . necessarily."

Lila's breath caught in her throat, and she now wished, more than she had ever wished for anything in her life, that she had not hidden in this corner. Hearing that Mory had found another woman, one who pleased him more than such an addle-headed child like Lila would cut her in two. She would then die behind this desk—here and now. She clenched her eyes together and was tempted to cover her ears, except some twisted part of her wanted to hear. Who had she lost Mory to? Who would take the place she had only begun to imagine could be hers before she had ruined everything?

"But that is why I am here today. When first you wrote me about Lila..."

Lila's eyes popped open.

Mory continued, "You expressed your deep affection for her and hoped that, along with settling in High Ercall, I might consider her. As I have explored my thoughts and hopes and ideals, I have considered that I might find greater happiness abroad, if, that is, I had the right sort of wife who might find that happiness with me."

Lila could not breathe once again. He couldn't mean...

"I am persuaded to think Lila might be the very type of woman able to endure the lifestyle required when one lives outside of England," Mory said. "She is smart, curious, enthusiastic, and energetic."

"She is also impulsive and young." Uncle's voice was no longer so casual.

"Such things would not work against her in India. For instance, impulsiveness, when properly directed, can lead to willingness to try new things and experience new society. Such abilities are essential to living differently than one has done."

"Lila has made no mention of this to me," Uncle said. "She has been moping about the place in your absence, but I was unaware of a connection between you. It is not like her to keep such secrets."

"I have not spoken to her," Mory said. "And I will not without your consent. I am not ignorant of the cost such an arrangement would be for you, sir, and after the good will you have extended toward me, I will not pursue this course without your blessing."

Uncle let out a heavy breath. "I never imagined Lila going far," he said with such sorrow that tears came to Lila's eyes. "I have always known her prospects would be different than if she were my daughter, but I have taken comfort in the fact that she would likely marry someone from this county and therefore remain near me."

"I understand," Mory said. Was that surrender in his voice? "And that is why I wanted to speak to you. I would not wish to cause myself unnecessary expectation. I thank you for—"

"I am not finished," Uncle said. "I would miss her terribly, but I would never deny my Lila the desires of her heart. I cannot guess what her answer might be, but if you would allow me to speak with her—"

Lila could be silent no longer. "Wait!" she shouted, then scrambled out from behind the desk on her hands and knees.

Mory saw her first and sprung from his chair, either because of surprise or good manners or both. "Lila?"

She jumped to her feet, but stayed rooted on that piece of floor, facing off with Mory across the room. Uncle Peter stood and rounded the desk.

"What on earth are you doing, Lila?" he said, grey eyebrows drawn together as he looked her over. He looked past her at the desk, and his eyes went wide. "Have you been eavesdropping?"

"Yes, Uncle," she said with a pained expression. "A few times a week I crawl into that childish hiding place and listen to every conversation that takes place."

"Goodness gracious, child." He closed his eyes and lifted a hand to his forehead in a weary gesture.

"Don't shame me, Uncle," she said in a pleading voice. "I

only want to hear of your sheep. Men always talk of more interesting topics than women are allowed to discuss."

She glanced at Mory, fearing that he would be equally scandalized, but instead he had his lips pressed together while his eyes danced, as though he were holding back laughter. His reaction emboldened her that much more.

"I am the most aggravating person, Mory," she said, giving him a pleading look. "I am curious to a fault, terribly independent, and—"

"Exactly the kind of woman I could live a full life with," Mory cut in. He crossed to her and took both of her hands in his. "I have wished that there were a woman, somewhere in England, who might have an adventurous spirit to match my own. A woman who had the confidence to leave the familiar and embrace the unknown, who might have the curiosity and determination a life abroad would require."

The sound of Uncle Peter clearing his throat reminded Lila they were not alone. She looked past Mory to see her uncle standing a few feet behind him. He smiled at her, a soft and loving smile. "I believe I should leave you two alone," he said. "I shall call for tea and meet you in the parlor when you are ready." He bowed slightly and left the room.

With the sound of the door closing, Lila looked up into Mory's face again, her whole body tingling like it did whenever she stepped from the bath on a winter day. "I have replayed my attempt at an explanation and wish there were better words to say it."

He crooked a smile. "Oh, I think you said it well enough."

"I do not believe I could ever say it well enough," she said, shaking her head. "The days since you left have been the darkest of my entire life. I thought I would never see you again, but . . . you came to speak with my uncle?"

Mory smiled and took another step closer, until she could smell the scent of salt upon his skin—never mind that he hadn't been at sea. "I was convinced I could have India or I could have a wife and family—not both. I chose the latter and felt sure the right woman would make everything right. And then I met you—a woman different than any I had expected to find in an English drawing room." He reached up to run his thumb along the curve of her jaw. "After leaving Franklyn Farm, I began to wonder: what if I found a woman who wanted to see the world beyond Britain?"

"I am that woman." Lila nodded so fast his face blurred for a moment—his beautifully imperfect face. "And I can promise that I shall never behave so badly again. I shall not insult your horse, and I shan't prattle on about politics or gossip or talk about those things that are unseemly for a woman to discuss. You shall make the decisions and—"

His look of disappointment brought her up short. "Ah, but that would be a shame," he said.

She blinked, completely confused.

"I would, of course, prefer that you do not behave in ways you believe I would dislike, but I can't think why a woman should have less interest in politics than a man would, and a woman ought to have more interests than embroidery and watercolor." He paused to smile. "I am not here today because I want to make you into the kind of woman some silly magazine would tell you to be. I'm here because of the woman you are. A woman with a sharp mind, quick wit, and willingness to go after what she wants, and then apologize to a man's face when she realizes she's behaved badly. I cannot think of another woman in the world with as much gumption as I have seen in you, Lila."

"It has been the trial of my uncle's life," she said.

"But not yours."

She could not withhold a smile. "I have only ever regretted my boldness when I thought it kept me from you."

He smiled widely. "On the contrary, it is exactly what drew me *to* you," he whispered. He put his hands on either side of her face and cocked his head slightly to the side. "I cannot promise you great wealth, fancy dresses, or even comfort at all times, but I can promise you my heart and the adventure of a lifetime if you will agree to be my wife and come away with me."

"I could never want for more," she whispered, raising her chin half an inch higher. Then she pulled back. "Only, I would want to come back and see my uncle now and again."

Mory nodded. "Any other demands?"

"Only one," she said, rising up on her toes so they were almost eye level with one another. "You see, I have never been kissed, but when I have imagined such a thing—I really am a very wicked girl—I hoped it would be something I would feel from my head to my—"

The sensation of his lips upon her own stunned her, but she did not pull away. His hands moved from her face to her waist and pulled her closer in a quick motion that took her feet off the floor. He then wrapped his arms around her back, holding her against him and awakening senses she had only ever read about in novels her uncle did not know she read.

Epilogue

The cicadas sang outside the screened windows as the evening breeze picked up, carrying away the heavy heat and inviting in the best time of day in Assam, India. To avoid the heat, the household often stayed up late through the night and early morning hours, then slept past noon. They then only had to endure a few hours of the extreme temperatures before evening set in. It seemed as though the entire household sighed a breath of relief this time of day. Mortimer bent his head with greater attention to the accounting for the plantation, recently expanded in an effort to support two households with two men working at the management.

The men had agreed that next year Mortimer's partner would go to England—he had not been back since taking over the management—then return and for a year they would manage in tandem before Mortimer and his dear Lila—and whoever else might have joined their family by then—would take their turn in England.

Soft footfalls distracted him from his work yet again, and he looked up to see Lila enter the room. They had arrived in Bombay in time for the monsoon season, which he felt sure would weaken her resolve, but she simply shed the unnecessary layers of undergarments—as many English women were loath to do—and updated her wardrobe with the lighter linens and silks of the native country. Neither of them minded the missing layers, and the increased comfort on Lila's part seemed to spare her the regret he so feared she would have one day. Mortimer leaned back in his chair and reached out a hand to her. "Good evening, my dear."

"Good evening," she said, coming to him and sliding onto his lap. He put a hand around her waist and kissed her when she bent down to do so. "I've a letter from Eloise," she said. "And I had to share it with you."

"By all means." He leaned back slightly as she read the letter from her friend word-for-word. There were portions Eloise would certainly have left out if she thought Mortimer would be an audience—things only women would write to one another—but Lila had no compunction, and he liked that she wanted to share every detail with him. When she finished, she let out a contented sigh and leaned back against his shoulder.

"I'm so glad she and Neville are happy together," she said in romantic tones.

"You miss her a great deal," Mortimer said, watching her face.

She smiled somewhat sadly and refolded the letter. "Of course," she said. "But I do feel it best that I am here and she is there. I had no idea the feelings she had for Neville all that time—feelings she kept locked up tight so as not to hurt me. I fear that had we stayed, she would have felt awkward being courted by him." She shook her head, then brightened her smile. She was never one to dwell on unhappiness. "Besides, she has always been the more traditional one, and I think she is perfectly content with her situation."

"As content as you are with yours?"

She narrowed her eyes at him playfully. "Must you always require I stroke your ego by telling you how over-the-moon happy I am with the life I get to live?"

Mortimer smiled. "It was a fear nearly twenty years in the making, and I shall need your constant help in overcoming it."

She leaned down so that their foreheads touched. "I am blissfully happy to be the wife of Nabob Luthford, living in a cement house in the wilds of India without corsets or neighbors but with more servants than anyone in England could imagine." She kissed the tip of his nose. "I have no regrets."

"I am glad," he said. "But I may need you tell me again tomorrow." He nodded toward the letter still in her hand. "From the sound of her letter, they are very, very happy together," Mortimer said, trailing his fingers down Lila's back in a way he knew would make her shiver. Which it did. "Do you share such intimate details of our life with her, as well?"

"Never you mind," Lila said, straightening and making to stand. He pulled her back down and nuzzled her neck. She laughed but did not pull away again. "Though if you continue, I may have a very delicious story to tell; her cheeks will burn for days from it."

He laughed and reluctantly released her as she stood again—it was too hot to explore the feeling she gave such easy rise to with more ardor. In a few more hours, however, when the early morning breezes picked up and the house was quiet—

"Cook is making that delightful curry for dinner," Lila

said, interrupting his growing expectations. "It really is a shame you can't smell it." She frowned, but then smiled again. "And then I should like to go for a ride since the moon is full tonight."

"Gordon does love those midnight canters," Mortimer said with a wink.

Lila made a pouting face. "Are you certain you don't mind that I have deemed her my horse now?" She had given up sidesaddle as soon as they arrived and was perhaps the best horsewoman this side of Bombay.

"I am still working it through," he said, pouting equally. "But the gelding from your uncle as a wedding gift has helped ease the sting." He was the finest bit of horse flesh Mortimer had ever had, leaving few regrets over losing Gordon to Lila.

Lila smiled and stood. "Cook will ring the bell at nine," she said as she moved out of the room. "I shall work on a response to Eloise's letter until it is ready."

Mortimer smiled and watched her go, then turned in his chair and looked over the lush forests of the surrounding country. Out of his view were rows and rows of tea plants that had made him rich, but the scrappy girl who once insulted his horse and tried very hard not to love him was by far the greatest fortune he'd ever made.

ABOUT JOSI S. KILPACK

Josi S. Kilpack is the author of more than twenty novels, which include women's fiction, romance, mystery, and suspense. *Wedding Cake*, the final book in her Sadie Hoffmiller culinary mystery series, was released in December 2014, and her Regency romance novels *A Heart Revealed* and *Lord Fenton's Folly* were released in 2015.

Josi and her husband, Lee, are the parents of four children and live in Northern Utah. In addition to writing, Josi loves to read, bake, and travel. She's completed six half marathons to date, but may never run another because right now she hates running and does hot yoga instead.

Josi's website: JosiSKilpack.com
Blog: JosiKilpack.blogspot.com
Twitter: @JosiSKilpack

Unmasking the Duke

Donna Hatch

OTHER WORKS BY DONNA HATCH

The Stranger She Married
The Guise of a Gentleman
A Perfect Secret
The Suspect's Daughter
Queen in Exile
Mistletoe Magic
Constant Hearts
Regency Hearts
A Timeless Romance Anthology: Winter Collection
Timeless Regency Collection: Summer House Party

One

Birthdays were overrated. People really ought to stop celebrating them after the age of sixteen. Snuggled into the featherbed of her sister's country estate, Hannah Palmer toyed with a croissant. This evening she might very well die of humiliation. Or worse, embarrass her sister and brother-in-law, the Earl and Countess of Tarrington.

Alicia practically bounced into the room. "Happy birthday, Sis!"

Hannah smiled wryly. "I think you're happier about it than I am."

At odds with her rank as a countess, Alicia grinned and climbed into bed with Hannah, holding her tightly. "I am happy about it. How often does a girl get to wish her favorite sister happy eighteenth birthday?"

Hannah gave her a wry smile. "I'm so relieved to learn I'm your favorite, since I have no competition."

Alicia laughed. "It would be sad if I claimed another for

that auspicious honor." She wound a strand of Hannah's blond hair around her finger.

"You're more energetic than usual today."

"Little Nicholas actually slept all night long." A maternal tenderness crept into Alicia's expression as it always did when she spoke of her infant son.

When the time came—if it came—Hannah planned to keep her baby in her room, rather than follow the convention of letting a nursemaid care for her child during the night hours. She vowed to be the devoted, loving mother her sister had already proved to be. Of course, she might never realize the sweet dream of motherhood.

Alicia twisted around in bed and fixed her amber gaze on Hannah. "And I'm so happy that you're finally letting me throw a ball in your honor."

Hannah winced. "Yes, I just love big parties filled with rooms of people I don't know."

"I know how you feel about it, dearest," Alicia said soothingly. "But this will be a good practice for you before you go to London next Season. When I'm finished with you, society will toast you as the New Incomparable."

"I'll be a clumsy, tongue-tied idiot, just like always."

"You're only clumsy when you're nervous. More practice at social events will help you not be nervous."

Not be nervous in public? Hardly likely.

Alicia tapped her on the nose. "You are a beautiful and accomplished daughter of a respected gentleman, and the sister of a countess. No need to fear."

"I hear blonds aren't fashionable at present."

"The only ones who say blond hair isn't in fashion are those who are jealous. Just keep your head high and smile as if you know an embarrassing secret about everyone."

Hannah stared into the flames writhing in the hearth. "It's not that simple."

"It is that simple." Alicia put an arm around her. "If you say next to nothing, everyone will think you are mysterious and will be all the more fascinated with you. Besides, you'll wear a mask tonight. Surely anonymity will lend you courage."

"I hope you're right."

Spending the evening alone with Alicia and her charming husband, Cole, would be preferable to a room full of strangers. But perhaps Alicia was right; a costume mask might help Hannah find some courage buried deep inside.

Hannah put a large spoonful of lumpy brown sugar into her chocolate, followed by a dash of cream. While Alicia rhapsodized about the ball, Hannah stirred absently before wrapping her hands around the china to warm her fingers.

Alicia ended on a sigh. "Maybe you'll meet *him* tonight."

"Him?" Hannah sipped the chocolate and snuggled into her pillows to drink the hot liquid turned decadent by the addition of the sugar and cream. Why most people chose to drink chocolate in its bitter form remained a mystery.

"Him," Alicia repeated. "The man of your dreams. Your future husband."

Hannah said dryly enough to be impertinent had she been speaking to a lady of rank who was not her sister, "Yes, meeting *him* at a ball would be convenient. I am persuaded that one must have a bit of cliché in one's life to obtain a measure of happiness."

"Only if you think marrying a wonderful man is cliché."

Chuckling, Hannah shook her head. "You know very well I speak of meeting at a ball." After setting aside her tray, she threw back the counterpane and stood. "I believe after breakfast, I'll go for a walk, maybe pick some flowers.'

Alicia's brow furrowed. "Oh dear. Are you sure that's

wise? I wouldn't want you to suffer from one of your sick headaches."

As she tied her dressing robe around her waist, Hannah exhaled a groan. "I'm not a fragile doll."

"No, but the sunlight does seem to bring on those dreadful headaches. And with your frail health, you ought to be careful."

It was all she could do not to snap at her sister. "My health isn't frail; I merely get occasional headaches."

Alicia gentled her voice. "Hannah, people don't normally get the kind of headaches where they must be shut up in a dark room with no noise for two days."

"Some do; the doctor has seen them in other patients. And I haven't been truly ill for years. Honestly I'm tired of everyone treating me like an invalid."

"I'm sorry, dearest. I just don't want anything to interfere with your enjoyment tonight."

Hannah drew a long breath, releasing her agitation but not entirely pushing back her fear that she *was* sickly and might not be healthy enough to have children or even properly manage a household. "I know."

She headed toward her dressing room but stumbled over something in her path. After sending a glare at the slippers that had tripped her, she shook her head. She must have missed the day the Almighty handed out gracefulness.

"There you are." Cole's voice boomed from the doorway.

Halting, Hannah wrapped her arms around herself and backed up slowly. Though Cole was her brother-in-law, a man in her room while she was in a state of *dishabille* pushed propriety. But she needn't have fretted; Cole's eyes focused solely on Alicia. Though he and her sister had been married almost three years, and Hannah had spent much time in his presence, such a powerful gentleman still sometimes left Hannah little better than speechless. Alicia hoped Hannah would meet someone like Cole in London, but the idea of hosting the type of guests a peer would entertain in his home left Hannah with the urge to hide—preferably in the library with a good book.

Surely she could find a country squire who sought little to no contact with society and all its games and demands, someone who would not require his wife to live in the center of the *beau monde*. Of course, any husband would expect children, which might be problematic.

"I have an appointment with the Duke of Suttenberg," Cole continued. "And then I am at your disposal for the rest of the day."

Hannah almost shuddered at the mention of an even more powerful man than Cole. Conveniently, the Duke of Suttenberg didn't appear to know Hannah existed.

Alicia crossed the room and took Cole's hand, smiling as he kissed her fingertips. "Thank you. I want this ball to be perfect."

"You've certainly planned it to the most minute detail." Cole's eyes crinkled as he gazed adoringly at Alicia, the hard edges around him softening.

What would that be like, to be loved so deeply? All the men of Hannah's acquaintance treated her either as if she were invisible or incapable of original thought.

As the couple stood in Hannah's room, absorbed in their private conversation, Hannah strode into her dressing room, shut the door, and began her morning toilette of bathing and dressing with her maid's assistance. By the time she emerged, her room stood vacant, but the couple joined her for breakfast, happily discussing details of the evening, asking for her input on occasion.

Alicia's eyes sparkled and her cheeks flushed in clear delight. Hannah smiled at the sight of her sister so happy; she and Alicia had not always enjoyed such bliss. Through heartache of losing their parents and brother, and all the financial troubles that had dogged them afterwards, Alicia had taken care of Hannah like a little mother. Alicia deserved to find happiness.

Alicia stood. "I'm going to spend a few minutes with Nicky before I check the progress of decorating the ballroom." She turned to Hannah. "Do you want to come? He's probably awake from his morning nap."

Hannah shook her head. "I'll visit the nursery this afternoon." Though she loved her tiny nephew, at the moment she couldn't bear to look at the sweet, torturous reminder of what she might never have of her own.

For now, she'd turn her energies to getting through the ball without embarrassing herself or her family. Later, she'd deal with her other shortcomings.

After donning her favorite old pelisse and straw hat, Hannah picked up a basket and went to the renowned Tarrington Castle Gardens. The air smelled fresh and rich, and the golden morning shadows played hide-and-seek with the birds. The trees adorned themselves in the halcyon rust, burgundy, and amber they only wore for autumn's brief reign before their inevitable surrender to winter.

Hannah scoured the area for the last summer roses. The maids would surely fill her room with roses from the hothouse if she requested, but she wanted to rescue the garden-grown blossoms before the frost damaged them. Too bad the lilacs had already gone for the year. Carefully selecting blooms, she snipped them and laid them in her basket. Serenity enfolded her in its matronly embrace, and by the time she turned toward Tarrington Castle, peace filled her soul.

Surely she'd do well tonight. She'd practiced conversing with Alicia's friends, entertained a few gentlemen callers, and spent hours with the dance master. Moreover, she'd be wearing a mask so if she tripped or trod on someone's toe, no one would know her identity.

Humming and swinging the basket, she strolled along a path skirting the main drive while birds flitted and twittered and fat bees buzzed. Hoofbeats clattered up to the front steps. A sudden breeze gusted, and Hannah reached for her hat to ensure it remained pinned to her hair. The rider, wearing a multi-caped coat, dismounted by the front steps. He paused, tugged his clothing into place, and tossed the reins to a stable hand who trotted to him.

Barely giving the stable hand a glance, the man said, "My visit will be brief."

The stable hand caught the reins and patted the lathering horse. "Yessir."

The visitor strode to the front steps. Hannah wrinkled her nose. Though his hat concealed most of his hair and shadowed his face, only the Duke of Suttenberg possessed such arrogant mastery, as if he viewed himself ruler of all the earth instead of only his own properties.

Though she'd planned to enter through a side door, Hannah followed him up the front stairs so she could better observe the full force of his snobbery. And if she were honest, catching a glimpse of his handsome face would be no hardship. As long as he didn't turn his intimidating stare her way, she ought to manage to hold on to her composure.

He glanced over his shoulder. Her breath stilled. Though she'd spent time in his company four times—yes, she'd kept track—she was never fully prepared for his masculine allure. She'd seen plenty of gentlemen, including her brother-in-law, Cole. But the Duke of Suttenberg's face never failed to turn her to a blithering pool of mush.

The duke cast a passing glance over her and intoned, "Inform your master I am arrived."

Hannah's mouth dropped open, and her face burned with one part humiliation and two parts anger. He didn't remember her. Worse, he'd mistaken her for some house girl, a servant.

The butler opened the front door, drawing the duke's attention. "Ah, Your Grace. My lord is expecting you."

The duke entered without casting a second look at Hannah. Arrogant, thoughtless cad! That he would forget someone whom he should recognize by now spoke volumes to his conceit. Clearly, he viewed her as too far beneath his notice to have gone to all the trouble of remembering her face. True, she didn't like being the center of attention, but neither did she want to be treated as if she were a patch of mud to be scraped off one's boots.

As she ascended the steps, Cole's and the duke's voices boomed through the main hall as they greeted each other. She entered the main hall as Cole bowed.

"Your Grace. Thank you for coming. I would have gladly come to you."

The duke waved away Cole's words with a graceful motion of his hands. As they crossed the great hall toward Cole's study, the Duke of Suttenberg removed his hat, revealing a glorious head of hair that bordered on black, and peeled off his gloves before handing them to the butler following him. "'Tis of no consequence," he said grandly, probably thinking himself so magnanimous as to condescend to call upon a peer of lower rank.

"May I offer you a drink?" Cole offered. The study door closed, shutting off their conversation.

Hannah nodded her thanks to the head butler, who closed the door behind her, and handed her basket to a passing maid. Just to prove she was not as thoughtless as the duke, she looked the maid in the eye. "Would you see that these are put into a vase of water and taken to my room, please... Mary, is it?"

"Yes, miss, but they call me Molly." The girl bobbed a curtsy and took the basket.

"Thank you, Molly."

A footman took her coat and hat and she thanked him. After firmly putting the arrogant duke out of her mind, Hannah busied herself with helping Alicia put the final touches on the ball. Noontime, as they sat at the breakfast table enjoying a cold lunch, Alicia sighed and glanced at the wall clock.

"Are you worried the ballroom won't be ready in time?" Hannah asked.

"No, it's well in hand. I only wonder when Cole will return. He went to the fields with the duke and hasn't returned yet."

"They went to the fields?"

"Apparently, the duke discovered methods to improve crop yield and has offered to help Cole with ours."

"Everyone seems to think the duke is some sort of expert on everything," Hannah grumbled.

Either Alicia failed to hear Hannah's ire or chose not to comment on it. "He is wise beyond his years and always does everything exactly as he ought."

Hannah made a face. "A true paragon."

Alicia smiled. "I know you find him arrogant, but I'm sure he can't help himself. I imagine any child who inherits the richest and most powerful title and property, second only to a royal duke, would grow up to be a man become accustomed to..."

"All the bowing and scraping?"

"A high level of deference," Alicia corrected. "Everyone admires and tries to emulate him. He takes his duties very responsibly and has uncommonly exacting standards for himself, which is why he excels at everything."

Hannah sniffed. "And views the rest of us as insects beneath his boots."

Her sister laughed softly. "Very well. I can see I cannot extol his virtues enough to change your opinion."

"No, and it doesn't signify; Cole was born heir to an earldom and manages not to be an insufferable bore."

"True." Alicia stood. "I believe I'll lie down now for a few minutes before I return to check progress in the ballroom. I want to be well-rested tonight. You probably should nap, too."

Hannah glanced sharply at her. But her sister seemed genuinely fatigued, so perhaps she meant the words sincerely rather than a prettily couched, overprotective statement about how Hannah ought to rest because "as we all know, you are rather delicate"—a statement that made Hannah fearful as a child, and frustrated as she grew.

Still, dancing until well after midnight would be fatiguing, not to mention keeping up with all the conversations and games that a large gathering required, so Hannah napped until her lady's maid woke her.

"My lady wishes you to join her in her front parlor for tea. There are some gentlemen callers, the Buchanan twins and Mr. Hill."

"Oh no. What next? I was careful not to encourage their attention."

"Not enough, it seems, miss."

She could dawdle long enough for the gentlemen callers to give up on her and leave. But no, Alicia was right; she needed to learn to overcome her shyness. Casting off the temptation to avoid the guests, Hannah dressed in an afternoon gown of white muslin with blue flowers, touched up her hair, and went to the main floor. As she headed to Alicia's back parlor, male voices and booted footsteps echoed in the main hall.

"Ah, Hannah," Cole called out to her. "Is Alicia having tea in her parlor?"

Hannah turned. Cole and the duke approached, both walking as if they owned the world. Hannah nodded as she lowered her eyes, her mouth drying.

Cole quirked a brow at the duke. "Care to join us for tea?"

"Thank you, no. I must return." The duke passed a brief glance over Hannah.

Cole made a loose gesture. "You remember my wife's sister, Hannah Palmer, of course."

The duke blinked before slowly replying. "Yes, of course. Good afternoon." He might as well have said, "No, I'm sure we've never met"; it would have been truthful.

In a single graceful motion, he swept off his hat, revealing midnight hair and that distinctive patch of blond on the left side that apparently marked members of his family for generations. He appeared to be proud of the unusual birthmark judging by the way he parted his hair in the middle of it. Briefly, he dipped his chin in a ducal version of a bow when greeting someone of low consequence.

Seething at his arrogance, Hannah sank into a very proper curtsy. In an act of uncommon boldness, fueled by ire, she offered a mischievous smile. "Delighted to see you again, Your Grace. I'm happy you've recovered from the strawberry incident." There. She'd made her point without revealing any hint of annoyance that he'd failed to remember her, and she'd even spoken without stammering.

His gray-green eyes opened wider, and his head jerked back ever so slightly in carefully controlled surprise. Was that a touch of blush on his finely chiseled cheekbones? Surely not. No one as perfect as the Duke of Suttenberg would do anything so boyish as blush.

"Strawberries. Yes. I'm careful not to give them the upper hand." His smooth baritone voice contained exactly the right amount of humor and arrogant *savoir faire*.

She might have been charmed by the almost chagrined smile now curving his beautifully formed lips if she weren't chewing on his admission that he refused to allow anyone, or anything, to best him. Not to mention that he still gave no hint of remembering her. He stood almost as tall as Cole, but where Cole had an intimidating breadth of shoulder, the duke had a lean, graceful build. But they stood with equally commanding postures inherent to peers who were lord of all they saw and knew it.

Saucily she tossed her head. "I wish you all success in your endeavors to submit all strawberries to your whim."

Cole glanced at her in surprise, as if he couldn't imagine what had possessed her to speak so boldly. She could hardly believe it herself.

The duke's gaze flicked over her face, still showing no sign of recognition, but every sign of unconcern, although he did seem to study her more closely. "Yes, well, a pleasure to see you . . . again." He turned away from her dismissively and focused on Cole. "Until this evening, it seems, Tarrington."

Hannah marched to the parlor without waiting to hear Cole's reply. That duke! Insufferable, rude, arrogant . . . perfect people at the top of the social pyramid never seemed to have any tolerance for mere humans, nor would they do anything as lowering as engage them in conversation.

Still in a pique, Hannah entered Alicia's parlor and tried

not to glare at the trio of men who leaped to their feet at her arrival.

"Miss Palmer, how kind of you to join us," Mr. Hill called out before the twins could say a word. The young widower bowed low, revealing a thinning spot on the crown of his head.

"How lovely you look, Miss Palmer," one of the Buchanan twins exclaimed.

"Of course, you always look lovely, Miss Palmer," the other rushed to say.

They bobbed alternating bows while Hannah tried to sort out which twin was Edmund and which was Eustace. There. Edmund's face was slightly more angular and his chin pointed more than his brother's. Eustace's hair curled a little more over his ears. Both had barely reached their majority and probably had only started shaving a year or two ago.

"Gentlemen." Hannah gave what would loosely pass as a curtsy and sat next to her sister. At least this time she'd managed not to trip like she had the last time guests had paid a call.

The callers perched on the edge of their seats. Alicia drank her tea, smiling as if enjoying a private joke.

"I was just telling Lady Tarrington how much I'm looking forward to the masque tonight," Mr. Hill said. "I hope you'll do me the honor of saving me the supper dance." He offered her a bland smile.

"I believe she is planning to save the supper dance for me," Edmund said.

Eustace cut in. "Surely you'd do me that honor, Miss Palmer."

From an assortment of pastries, Hannah selected an Eccles cake and bit into its buttery, crispy outside to the current-filled inside. Though her usual shyness had faded with each encounter with the sweet boys, she still found it difficult to converse with people outside her family. Unless she was angry at an arrogant duke, that is.

Chewing gave her a moment to formulate a reply to the twins. "Since we are to be in masquerade, it is highly unlikely any of you will know me, nor I you."

"I would know you," Eustace said with an adoring smile. "I only need to look for hair the color of morning sunlight to find you."

She smiled at his poetic turn of phrase but shook her head. "What if I wear a wig?"

Eustace deflated.

"I'd still know you." Edmund puffed out his chest. "I'd recognize your figure and your walk."

Hannah cocked her head to one side. "I might be wearing clothing from a different era, which would alter the appearance of my figure." She took another bite of the rich pastry.

Edmund stubbornly shook his head. "I'll still know you. And I plan to ask you for two dances. I wish it could be more."

Hannah smiled. That's all she needed—to dance more than two dances with one man in a single evening. People would think she was either "fast" or engaged to the man.

Next to her, Alicia shifted. "It sounds as if you all had better stand up with as many ladies as possible to be sure you have, indeed, danced with my sister."

"To be sure, I will dance with every lady present until I'm certain I've found you, Miss Palmer," Eustace said. "Well worth it."

Edmund looked thoughtful and unconvinced that he might not recognize her despite a costume and mask. "I will, as well."

Mr. Hill took out his snuff box. "Gladly, I shall. I enjoy dancing and conversation."

Hannah exchanged a knowing smile with her sister. Alicia had played that well. Now at least three gentlemen would dance with many partners in order to guarantee they'd found Hannah.

Mr. Hill carefully placed and sniffed his snuff. "I entertain a great deal, as you know. My late wife, God rest her soul, was a brilliant hostess. I'm sure you will be too, Miss Palmer."

Hannah held out her hands. "Ah, no. I prefer a quiet life."

"Nonsense," said Mr. Hill. "All pretty girls like you enjoy dinners and parties and balls."

Hannah stiffened but hoped her smile remained in place. She finished her pastry and sipped the last drop of her tea. She glanced at the gentlemen as she set her teacup on its saucer. She missed. It fell, landing with a thud on the carpet. Hannah cringed. At least the cup hadn't broken, and no tea spilled.

All three men leaped to their feet. Edmund got there first. Kneeling, he handed the cup to her.

"Thank you." Her face heated. Would she always be so clumsy in the company of others?

Then Edmund shot his brother a triumphant smile. Her embarrassment turned to annoyance. He didn't care to aid her; he only desired to beat out his brother for her favor. Were all gentlemen so competitive that they wanted to win, regardless of the prize?

And moreover, why did gentlemen either view her as a forgettable, possibly invisible, minor nuisance or a delicate flower without the strength to do anything more strenuous than lift a teacup? And heaven forbid she have likes and dislikes different from other "pretty girls" her age.

Cole entered, greeted everyone, and went to Alicia. He kissed her offered cheek and sat next to her, devouring tea and scones as if he'd missed luncheon.

Eustace glanced at the clock and stood. "We don't wish to overstay our welcome, Lady Tarrington. Thank you for seeing us. Miss Palmer, I look forward to seeing you tonight."

Edmund also stood. "Yes, thank you. I'm sure you'll be the loveliest two ladies at the ball."

Mr. Hill took the cue and stood as well. All the guests said their good-byes, leaving Hannah alone with Alicia and Cole. Tension left her as quickly as the guests. If only she could skip tonight's masque.

Leaning back against the seat, Hannah folded her arms and addressed her brother-in-law. "Did you enjoy balls when you were a bachelor?"

Cole nodded thoughtfully. "I did back when I was young and green and eager to meet girls. Especially because it meant shore leave and time away from the war, however brief. But balls and society games grew tiresome soon enough. Until I met your sister, of course." He put an arm around Alicia.

"The only time I stopped enjoying balls was when I had to hurry up and find a husband to save us from debtor's prison." She cast a pained expression toward Cole.

Hannah nodded. "But that worked out all right, in the end."

"And so it will tonight," Alicia said. "It will be magical. Just be yourself and let your costume lend you confidence."

If costumes could magically summon wit and grace and poise, tonight would be perfect.

Two

Bennett Arthur Partridge, the Fifteenth Duke of Suttenberg, bid farewell to the Earl of Tarrington, someone whom he would have called friend if he dared let down his guard enough to actually have friends, and rode to his brother's house. As the afternoon sun waned, he arrived at his younger brother's prosperous manor house. A flock of children playing on the lawn scampered up to him.

"Uncle!" shouted his three-year-old nephew.

Suttenberg dismounted and scooped up the child, swinging him into the air. Suttenberg groaned and staggered as if the child had suddenly grown too heavy to manage. "Good heavens," he teased. "Have you grown overnight? I do believe you are two stone heavier than yesterday!"

The lad squealed a laugh. "I big boy."

"Yes, I do believe you have promise of becoming a big boy someday."

"I big boy!"

"As you wish." Arguing with a child always proved pointless.

The other children danced around him, making more noise than a gaggle of geese. His nephew wiggled to get down. Suttenberg grinned at the happy cacophony around him. His nephew raced off with the other children, scattering a flock of chickens and splashing through an unsuspecting mud puddle.

"Be sure to get as dirty as possible!" Suttenberg called after them.

"I heard that," said a feminine voice.

Suttenberg grinned at his sister-in-law, Meredith, as she smiled at him through an open window to her parlor.

He strode in through the front door, handed his gloves, hat, and coat to the butler, and proceeded to the parlor where his grandmother, mother, and sister-in-law sat. Meredith bounced her baby, her second son, on her lap—the picture of maternal joy.

From where she sat on a settee, his mother, the Duchess of Suttenberg, looked up from a letter she held. Her lace cap set off dark hair and a pair of gray-green eyes exactly the color of his own.

"Good afternoon, Mother." He kissed her cheek tilted up to receive him.

"Is that my Bennett?" Grandmother called as if she were from across the room instead of in the next chair.

All attempts to encourage the dear old lady to call him by his title had, obviously, failed. Her use of his Christian name reduced him to a boy in danger of either getting a whipping or being drawn into her arms and kissed repeatedly. But it lent an intimacy that Your Grace and Suttenberg—titles that had replaced his name twenty-five years ago—never did. Those titles represented all he must do as a duke, including controlling the weakness in his bloodline; the name Bennett reminded him of who he was as a person.

"Yes, Mama, he's back," Suttenberg's mother said. Smiling, she glanced at Suttenberg. "How was your visit with Tarrington?"

"Satisfying." Suttenberg took a seat next to her near the window. "We found a solution to his drainage problem, and he seemed pleased. He challenged me to a fencing match Tuesday next."

He drew a contented breath. Helping a fellow peer solve a problem for what would probably become one of his most prosperous areas of farmland provided a satisfaction that serving in Parliament never quite provided. Oh, he did his duty, as always, but there was something truly meaningful about finding resolutions to complicated problems. And being the person with the answers, someone to whom others turned, added another layer to his present sense of pleasure.

His mother, whom he still often thought of as *the duchess*, indicated the letter in her hand. "Your sister has suffered yet another heartbreak."

"Oh dear," he murmured. Poor girl fell in love too quickly and never seemed to give her heart to the right fellow.

His mother's brow furrowed. "Apparently, he said he couldn't possibly live up to the Suttenberg standards, what with you as her brother."

Suttenberg paused, his contentment scattering like dry leaves in the wind. "Her favorite suitor dislikes the prospect of me as a brother-in-law?"

The duchess gave him a patently patient smile, as if he'd missed something painfully obvious. "He believes himself unworthy of you and a family connection to you."

Suttenberg winced. "Am I so insufferable?"

"No, son, but you have a rather unimpeachable reputation, you know."

"Good heavens. That's doing it rather too brown. I'm simply trying to live up to the family honor, not frighten off my sister's suitors."

"It nearly frightened me away," Meredith said from her corner of the room. She shrugged apologetically. "I'm sure you can't help it that everyone looks to you as the standard in dress and behavior, and, well, everything. People just naturally feel inferior in the face of such perfection."

Before Suttenberg could think of a reply to such a horrifyingly daunting and exaggerated statement, his grandmother cut in. "Did you find a wife yet, Bennett?" She looked in his direction, although her milky white eyes had gone blind years ago.

Suttenberg coughed. "No, Grandmama, I have not yet found a wife."

"A life?" She frowned. "I didn't ask about your life, boy; I asked about your wife!"

He chuckled. At thirty-two, he was hardly a boy. He replied more loudly, "I have not found a wife, Grandmama."

She thumped her cane on the floor. "Humph! You're dragging your feet, Bennett. Your brother already has two boys, and you aren't even married yet."

"Phillip was remarkably fortunate. It's not that simple for me. I have other—"

"Eh? Speak up."

He cleared his throat and enunciated, "It's not that simple."

"Pish." Grandmother waved her cane. "It's not so hard. Go find a suitable girl, and ask her father's permission."

He cast off all other possible retorts and settled with, "Yes, ma'am."

Smiling, the duchess nodded. "She's right, you know. You should spend more time actually seeking a wife. Of course, that might prove difficult for a man of your station and reputation."

Suttenberg cringed. He'd only tried to step into his father's shoes, but instead he seemed to have created a reputation that even he would never be able to uphold. If people really knew him, knew the passions that heated his blood and were the source of a fierce temper, they wouldn't believe this so-called image.

Still, perhaps his mother and grandmother were right; he should actively seek a wife instead of relying on chance meetings at balls and dinner parties. But finding a lady strong enough to take on the responsibilities and social pressures of a duchess, not to mention someone whose family, background, and accomplishments fit his family's definition of "suitable," created a herculean task. It would be truly refreshing to find someone genuine, someone who might truly love him, hidden flaws and all.

He cast a sideways glance at his sister-in-law. His brother had been fortunate indeed to have found a lady whom he loved. But love shouldn't figure into Suttenberg's needs for a wife. The pressures of maintaining the image of superior accomplishments, which taxed him heavily, now expanded to the area of family and progeny, which raised the stakes. Sometimes the weight threatened to crush him.

His brother, Phillip, strode in. "Is tea ready? I'm starved." He kissed Meredith and rubbed the fuzz on his youngest son's head.

As if on cue, the head housekeeper entered with the tea service, followed by a maid carrying a second tray of scones, Devonshire cream, lemon curd, and cheese. The nurse took the baby from Meredith and carried him away so the young mother could more fully enjoy her tea.

"Is your costume for tonight's ball ready, Meredith?" the duchess asked.

"It is." Meredith's eyes glowed. "I'm going as Queen Eleanor of Aquitaine."

"Should I be worried you'll plot an uprising with my sons against me?" Phillip teased.

She cocked her head to one side mischievously. "Only if you become a tyrannical king."

They exchanged loving glances that seemed too intimate for tea. Or maybe Suttenberg's desire for such simple joy as theirs tainted his judgment. He looked away.

Very well. He'd seek a wife. It might help stave off the brief moments of loneliness that had reared up lately. It would also have the additional advantage of getting his grandmother to stop harping on him to marry and produce an heir. While his family discussed the ball and their costumes, Suttenberg mulled over his newly realized goal.

How does one go about such an important task? Asking for his family's help was out of the question; they'd introduce him to a blinding array of ladies with practiced smiles designed to snare a peer. Chance meetings at balls and parties only cemented his fears that most women were calculating and insincere. He couldn't exactly place an advertisement in the paper the way he'd found his secretary. His parents' marriage had been arranged. Phillip met Meredith by capsizing her boat outside Vauxhall Gardens—not, obviously, something Suttenberg would do intentionally.

Hmm. This wife-hunting business presented a problem. Cole Amesbury, the Earl of Tarrington, had a famously happy marriage. Perhaps he would be a helpful resource. All Suttenberg had to do was find a way of asking for his help while not appearing to do so. Giving advice to others came easier than asking.

If only he could find a lady with a kind heart and a healthy dose of wit, plus all the other requirements for a duchess, of course. It would be just too easy to find such a lady tonight while wearing a mask. His thoughts stuttered to a halt. Tonight presented a unique situation. No one would know he was the Duke of Suttenberg. He could be his true self. And maybe, just maybe, he could find a lady who would see him as a man, rather than the Duke of Suttenberg, and treat him accordingly.

But if she saw the real him, would the flaws he so carefully hid from others deny him such a pure love?

Three

Hannah examined her Grecian-style white gown trimmed in gold. The flowing fabric draped around her in soft folds and caressed her skin. The gold, multi-chained necklace lay heavily against her collarbones, the perfect finishing touch. It was a lovely costume, but surely wouldn't save her from disaster. The front of her hair, swept up into an elaborate braid piled on top of her head and woven with gold threads, appeared ready to topple, and the long curls down her back would probably go limp before the evening's end. And worse, she'd no doubt trip or step on her partner's toes, despite hours with her dance master. With her stomach so twisted up in nerves, she surely wouldn't manage to utter an intelligent sentence. Oh, why did she let Alicia talk her into this ball?

She pushed back her fears. Tonight she was Aphrodite, the confident, provocative goddess of love—above reproach. She touched the mask concealing the upper half of her face, drew a bracing breath, and entered the ballroom. Though secretly Alicia had thrown this ball in Hannah's honor as a

Unmasking the Duke

birthday celebration, they'd chosen to make tonight a masquerade, so masks would stay on all night, unless guests chose to remove them for dinner. Hannah would leave hers firmly in place. Normally, Hannah would help Alicia and Cole greet their guests, but that would give away her identity, so she arrived in the ballroom like an invitee.

Fighting the urge to hang back, she stood with head high near the dance floor to watch the guests mingle. A man wearing the blue and silver tabard of a French Musketeer, complete with a plumed hat, stepped into her line of sight. His commanding bearing and the air of confidence enshrouded his lean form so completely that he might have been the prince Regent. In Hannah's limited experience with society, only Cole and the Duke of Suttenberg bore such wordless self-possession. But all lords probably had such a stance. He stood perfectly still, his masked face turned toward the dance floor. Hannah followed his line of sight. Cole and Alicia, dressed as beautifully as a duke and duchess from the Elizabethan Era, complete with white wigs, took the floor as head couple. Other dancers lined up behind them. The Musketeer next to Hannah appeared to search the crowd as if seeking someone. Perhaps the lady of his choice had revealed to him her costume and he desired to begin the evening with her.

The Musketeer's gaze made a wide circuit, turning her direction, and Hannah quickly looked away lest he catch her staring at him. She made a point of admiring the painting sweeping across the ceiling as if she'd never seen it. She was Aphrodite—confident and in control. She straightened her posture.

"My lady," the Musketeer said in a soft, husky voice.

She turned to him slowly, queenly, with all the confidence and poise of Aphrodite. "Sir?"

He extended a hand. "Would you do me the honor of standing up with me for the first dance?"

She inclined her head and placed her gloved hand in his. He led her to the line of dancers. Emboldened by her mask and the goddess attributes her costume lent her, she looked him in the face. Tall, lean, dark-haired, and with full lips, he arrested her gaze. Little else of his features were visible enough to reveal his identity to her, thanks to his costume, gold mask, and wide-brimmed hat. He returned her stare, but for once such focus did not leave her flustered and tongue-tied.

Cole and Alicia stood at the head of the line. The music began, an old-fashioned minuet. For a second, Hannah faltered. Did she remember the steps? Lessons with her dance master seemed long ago, and they hadn't spent much time on dances from a bygone era.

As she curtsied, her mind raced. What came next? Her partner took her hand and led her without hesitation, his touch firm and sure. As she moved with him, following his lead and bowing again, her panic faded. She could do this. Down the line a lady's steps faltered, and Hannah's heart went out to her. None of the dancers gave any indication they noticed the lady's misstep. Perhaps they all concentrated so hard on remembering such an outdated dance that no one noticed.

As the stately dance continued, her partner radiated supreme equanimity. There. He almost missed a step, but only the briefest tightening of his mouth betrayed the crack in his aplomb.

As he led her around in a little circle, she murmured, "I can't remember the last time I performed a minuet."

"It has been a while for me, as well," he admitted softly.

The sequence took them apart, and Hannah danced

with the lady diagonal from her before the steps took her back to her partner. Next she curtsied to the gentleman across from her and danced with him, counting the beat silently. As she returned to her partner, he again took her hand, leading her through the next portion, careful to keep the rapier at his side from getting in the way. She wondered if it were a real weapon or merely decorative.

He turned his head toward her. "I am trying to identify your costume. Are you a goddess?"

"I am."

"Which one?"

Uncharacteristically pert, thanks to her costume, no doubt, she tilted her head. "I believe I'll let you guess."

One corner of his mouth lifted. "A Greek or Roman goddess?"

"Greek."

He left her to the lady across from him, stepping in perfect time. When the steps brought him back to her side, they bowed and exchanged only the briefest glances before it was her turn to dance with the gentleman across from her. Clearly an older man, wearing the black-and-white domino of the previous century, he led her with ease through that portion of the sequence, no doubt comfortable with a minuet popular in his youth.

The ladies in their group of four began their promenade. One of them muttered, "Oh dear, oh dear," and waited to get her cues from the others. Hannah tried to give clues as to what came next to help the lady, and her features relaxed as she fell into step.

The minuet came to a close. They completed the final steps and bowed. As Hannah straightened, she lifted her gaze to her partner, who stared directly at her.

"I have narrowed down who you are," he stated.

"You have?" Alarmed that he might already have determined her name, she barely controlled the rising fear that threatened to strip away all her false confidence.

"You aren't Athena or Artemis because you have nothing of a warrior about you."

Relief left her almost weak in the knees. She scolded herself. He was, of course, speaking of her costume's identity. "No, not Athena nor Artemis."

"And you don't have anything earthy about you, so you aren't Rhea or Demeter. You are beautiful and regal, so unless you are one of the lesser goddesses, I believe you are Ernos, the goddess of dawn, or Aphrodite, goddess of love and beauty, or Hera, goddess of them all."

She studied him more closely, intrigued by his perceptiveness. "Which do you believe I am?"

As the dancers dispersed, he offered a hand again to lead her off the dance floor. "If I were to place a wager, it would be on Aphrodite."

"What if I remove my mask to reveal I'm not beautiful?"

He lowered his voice to a volume as to only be heard by her. "Of what I can see of you at this moment, you are beautiful—kind to your fellow dancers, you dance with uncommon grace, and comport yourself like a queen. Your skin, what I can see of it, is flawless, and your lips are shaped like a rose bud. Yes, you are beautiful. I have no doubt."

Hannah's mouth fell open slightly. She'd never in her life been paid such a lovely compliment. It took putting on a mask to earn such a rare gift. Yet surely only a practiced flirt would say such a thing. "You are kind to say so, but I suspect you are a smooth-tongued rogue who goes about charming women everywhere."

"I assure you, madam, I spoke with perfect sincerity."

She might never learn the truth. The mystery of his

identity and the meaning of his words sent a thrill racing down her spine. "Then I thank you. And I offer a compliment of my own: you dance beautifully, and I thank you for your skillful guidance."

"I am happy to be of service. May I bring you a drink? Lemonade?"

A gentleman dressed as a pirate, complete with a cutlass at his hip, appeared next to her. "Stand up with me, my lady, I beg you."

Hannah paused. That voice seemed familiar. Could it be Mr. Hill? Surely he hadn't discovered her so quickly.

The pirate gave her a crooked grin. "Dance with me, or I might be forced to carry you off to my pirate ship."

The voice seemed like his, but she couldn't believe he'd say such a thing . . . unless the mask tapped into another side of him, as well. Still, it was only a dance. Surely no harm would come from that.

She carefully lowered her voice to alto tones to protect her identity. "Very well, sir pirate. But as we are a great deal inland, I doubt your ship is accessible this eve."

"I'm very resourceful."

She glanced back at the Musketeer. "Another time for the lemonade, sir?"

"As you wish, my goddess." He bowed grandly.

The pirate took her hand and led her to the dance floor. He leaned in too closely. "You look beautiful." The alcohol on his breath burned her eyes.

She glanced in his direction, trying not to inhale too deeply, and inclined her head. "You're kind to say so."

A quadrille began, and Hannah relaxed; not only did she know this dance well, but partners changed so frequently that there would be little time for conversation. Still, the pirate studied her carefully. She barely glanced at him. If she gave him little notice, he'd see she had no interest in getting better acquainted.

As they left the dance floor, he leaned in. "Hannah?"

She turned her head slowly. "Who?"

"I know it's you, Hannah."

Tempted to shrink from him, she raised her chin. "I hope this Hannah person is either your sister or your wife, sir, or she may not forgive you for using her given name."

He took a firm hold of her elbow. "I know it's you. I told you that I would know you even in costume."

"Thank you for the dance." She wrenched her arm out of his grasp and walked away from him.

To her relief, other gentlemen less interested in her identity asked her to dance the next few sets, and she lost sight of the pirate. As the evening wore on, her confidence increased. She hadn't missed a step and conversed easily with everyone she met. Perhaps a mask was all she needed to find her poise. She smiled the whole time, blissfully moving to the music and with other dancers. Who would have believed a secret identity would be so liberating?

She often spotted the dashing Musketeer, and through the course of the cotillion, she changed partners to dance with him briefly. "We meet again, *Monsieur* Musketeer."

"Are you enjoying your visit among us mere mortals, Aphrodite?" His smile teased, warm and almost intimate without being threatening.

"Very much. I believe there are a few couples who may need my assistance falling in love, but others seem to be getting along famously without me."

He chuckled. "Have you chosen someone for me?"

"I am not a matchmaker, sir. I merely watch over and help lovers who have already found each other."

"Ah, unfortunate. Couldn't you make an exception for me?"

"Perhaps."

The sequence took them apart and returned them to their partners. At the end, they bowed and she lost sight of him. The pirate appeared across the room, but she moved out of his line of sight. After a lively country dance, Hannah took a moment to catch her breath, and the Musketeer found her again.

He smiled. "What must I do to win the favor of the goddess of love, that she might help me find a lady?"

"You pose an interesting problem. I have not yet decided what to do about you."

He stepped nearer, a bit more closely than strictly proper. "Am I a problem because you are tempted to match me with yourself?"

She smiled secretively. "Is that your wish?"

"At this moment, I wish that more than anything." The intensity of his eyes almost stripped away her carefully constructed ruse and touched the real woman inside.

In an attempt to put up her shields lest he cast some kind of spell over her, she tossed her head and laughed. "A lofty goal—to be loved by a goddess."

"To be loved by a good woman is a lofty goal, as well." He gently enfolded her hand in his. "What is your loftiest goal, Aphrodite?"

For a moment, she could hardly speak. His words touched a place deep in her heart. "I wish more than anything to be loved by a good man."

"Dance the supper dance with me; you can determine if I meet your definition of a good man." He smiled, his tone teasing as if still in the role of a swashbuckling Musketeer, but that intensity in his gaze suggested a deeper meaning. The warmth of his hand bathed her entire body.

The pirate appeared. He gave the Musketeer a brief once

over, pointedly looking at their hands. Holding hands was intimate, bordering on scandalous. She withdrew from the Musketeer's touch. Even Aphrodite knew boundaries.

In a clear dismissal of the Musketeer, the pirate turned to Hannah. "The supper dance is next. Stand up with me." He grabbed her hand.

The Musketeer stiffened but remained silent, waiting for her to speak. Which was nice, really, since so many men seemed to speak for her.

She pulled out of his grasp. "I'm afraid I cannot. This gentleman has already asked for the supper dance."

"So sorry, good sir." The Musketeer held out his arm and waited for Hannah to take it.

The pirate gripped her elbow. "Why are you toying with me?"

More annoyed than alarmed, Hannah turned her head slowly to make eye contact with him and drew from a cool reserve inside her. "Release me."

The pirate looked down as if only now realizing he'd seized her.

"The lady asked you to release her." The Musketeer took a step closer to the pirate. "Do so this instant, or I shall be obliged to intervene."

The pirate let go of Hannah. With a sullen glance at the Musketeer, the pirate affected a bow and left, listing off to one side as he walked.

"Cur," the Musketeer muttered. "Has he been bothering you all night?"

"He keeps insisting he knows me. He's harmless." But her elbow burned where his fingers had dug into her skin.

"Shall I warn him away?"

"No, don't bother. I'm sure he won't try that again." Still, Mr. Hill had never been so rough before; he'd always treated her like glass. He might be emboldened by his costume, or by drink.

The Musketeer's gaze followed the pirate's back. "He bears watching."

His protectiveness should have been endearing, but all her life, people had tried to manage her. It grew tiresome. Still, the Musketeer was right; Mr. Hill's behavior suggested he might not be as innocuous as she had believed.

The beginning notes of the supper dance began, and the Musketeer's mouth curved. "A waltz. Fortunately there are no patronesses who must be begged for permission."

Hannah returned his smile. "A goddess needs no mortal permission."

He grinned. "Of course not." He bowed with a flourish and held out his hand, waiting for her to extend hers.

The pirate had simply grabbed her, but this man waited for her to give her hand to him. She placed her hand into his and stepped into dance position with him. He led her with ease borne from practice and inherent skill. Instinctively she matched his subtle clues, and they moved together as if they'd been partners for years.

His voice wrapped around her with all the warmth of his touch. "There is something very different about you, Aphrodite. You are extremely self-possessed, and you stand apart from the others. It isn't arrogance or coyness; I can't pinpoint what it is about you that captures me."

How could she resist such beautiful words? It had to be the flattery of a *roué*, but it sounded sincere. Still, they were in costume. He clearly played a role just as she did. "I'm sure every mortal feels this way about a goddess."

"I'm beginning to believe you *are* a goddess. It's refreshing to have found a woman who doesn't want anything from me."

"Do women often want things from you?"

"Usually." His mouth pulled to the side in a mixture of bitterness and resignation.

"Does your Musketeer costume come with a name? I feel rather strange that I don't know what to call you."

"You may call me Bennett."

He smiled, and her insides took on the consistency of pudding. If she weren't careful, she would be in danger of losing her heart to this charming stranger.

Four

The goddess in Suttenberg's arms tilted her head to one side. "Bennett?"

An uncomfortable heat crawled up to his collar. Why in the world he'd told her to call him by his Christian name, he couldn't imagine. Not even his mother called him Bennett. Was this a sign of his ancestors' blood coming to haunt him?

"Is that your given name or your last name?"

He gave one of his signature mysterious smiles. "It is a name by which you may call me."

"Then I shall assume it is a last name, and not a Christian name, or people would be scandalized."

"You're a goddess; mortals' opinions shouldn't matter."

The smile she gave him in return suggested a host of secrets.

"Besides," he continued, "for all they know, we might be married."

"We might be married to other people." She turned a

searching gaze on him, her golden-brown eyes leaving him mildly exposed. "You aren't, though, are you? Married?"

"No."

"Truly?" For the first time all evening, vulnerability crept into her tone.

So, the goddess of love wasn't quite as impenetrable as she'd led him to believe. That crack in her cool, regal perfection warmed him, gave him hope. Strange, but he'd never wondered if a woman desired him; it had always been a safe assumption that women wanted him for something— his money or his title or the status of being seen with him. A few less virtuous women wanted him for more pleasurable, but less honorable reasons. All seemed to have their own agendas.

"I give you my word, I am not married." He'd never been so glad to utter those words.

Her expression took on an intensity he hadn't seen all evening. "I do not speak to *Monsieur* Bennett of the French Musketeers. I speak to *you,* the man behind the mask."

He gazed directly into her eyes. "I give you my word as a gentleman, I am not married." He paused, relishing the almost imperceptible relaxing of her shoulders that suggested she cared. "And you?"

She smiled and glanced away, suddenly demure. "No."

Demure. Odd, she hadn't exhibited that quality all evening, not even as she'd danced with other partners. Yes, he'd been watching her. Closely. To the point of almost ignoring his other partners. He hoped the casual observer would remain ignorant of his interest in the goddess.

Unlike other balls, when practically every eligible female and her mother stalked him in attempts to capture a duke, he hadn't caught her looking at him at all. He should have found a way to hide his identity years ago. Tonight none of his partners stalked him, a refreshing change, but none of them intrigued him like this Aphrodite. He'd danced with many ladies in mask, but she alone occupied his thoughts.

He led her through the steps, holding her closely. For the first time he agreed that waltzing was, indeed, an extremely intimate dance. Who was the woman behind the mask? What were her secrets?

He peered at her. "If I cannot ask you any personal questions while you are in the persona of Aphrodite, how can I possibly get to know you—the real you?"

"You seem resourceful."

He huffed his amusement at the polite thwarting that bordered on encouragement. "Very well. Tell me something about yourself that doesn't reveal your identity, but discloses an aspect of your true self."

She tilted her head elegantly to look into his eyes. "Today is my birthday."

"Is it?" Too bad he couldn't give her an appropriate gift. Or a birthday kiss.

"My favorite color used to be lavender, but after years of mourning, I now detest it. My new favorite color is pink."

Before he could express his condolences that she'd been in mourning, she pursed her lips into a tiny pout, so irresistible that he could hardly prevent himself from leaning in and kissing her. Right there. On the dance floor. In front of the entire assembly.

Her voice refocused his thoughts. "I hate blood pudding. I love the smell of lilacs. I put cream and sugar in my chocolate. I adore strawberries. I have never been outside of England, but I want very much to see all of the British Isles. And France. And maybe Germany someday—I've been studying German. And I like Shakespeare's comedies. I've read them all." She smiled. "Does that satisfy your curiosity?"

"It's a start."

Her mouth curved deeply, surpassing amusement and traveling into genuine, unrehearsed pleasure. How refreshing not to find a practiced smile. "And you?"

He thought back, trying to bring forward similar personal details that wouldn't give away his identity. "I don't believe I have a favorite color, but I'm partial to both green and blue. I hate bread pudding. I love the smell of books. I put cream and sugar in my coffee. Eating strawberries makes my neck develop red marks and itch. I like Shakespeare's comedies, too, but I haven't read them all. I have a desire to see Italy, but I don't speak Italian. My mother's mother was German; she insisted I speak German when I conversed with her. I called her *Oma*. But after she died, I forgot most of the language."

Strange, but everyone of his acquaintance, including his family, probably had little to no knowledge of the trivial facts—except the strawberry reaction—that he'd revealed to this mystery woman.

She grew more fluid in his arms. "It's a pity you don't remember the German language. While it sounds harsh to our ears, it is imagery-rich and poetic." Her smile faded, and her golden-brown gaze fixed on him. "Do you think it improper for women to read and learn?"

"No, I applaud it. I enjoy reading and learning, and encourage others to do so."

Her smile was both relieved and delighted. How charming to find a woman who revealed her emotions instead of playing coy.

His gaze focused on her lips again, and the desire to kiss her struck with more force than before. He'd certainly seen his share of attractive women, and he'd lost count of the number of them who had offered themselves to him—with various implied stipulations and prices, of course—but he couldn't remember the last time he'd suffered such acute desire. Artlessly elegant, mysteriously genuine, her contradictory traits fed his fascination.

The waltz ended, and his arms practically refused to release her. Still, he took himself in hand and stepped away before he carried her off to a dark corner to thoroughly kiss her. He couldn't do that. He refused to abandon his gentlemanly duty to treat a lady with respect just to satisfy a primal instinct that was quickly getting harder to control, probably thanks to his tainted bloodline.

As she stepped away, she smiled a genuine display of dazzling joy that nearly knocked him off his feet. "Thank you for the lovely dance. My dance master was not nearly so skilled."

He studied her more closely, searching for clues to her identity, her age. Though she followed his lead with more grace and skill than most, her comment made him wonder. Her mouth and the lower half of her face suggested youth, but with the upper part of her face and her eye area covered, he could only place her somewhere between sixteen and forty. "That was your first waltz since you came out, wasn't it?"

Again that mysterious smile. "My, you are getting personal. I don't mind telling you that I write with my left hand and that my hair color comes from my mother, but I won't give you any clues to my age. Besides, a goddess does not come out. If you must know, my dance master was the most skilled dancer who partnered me in the waltz, so I naturally compare all others to him."

A pertness touched the angle of her head, and she brushed lovely, long fingers over her gold necklace. The gesture drew attention to that hollow between her collarbone that his mouth ached to kiss.

She couldn't be more than thirty. Could she? She said she wasn't married, but she could be a widow. That would explain her mourning comment. But it might be a parent or a sibling she mourned. Not knowing was about to drive him mad. Yet not knowing filled him with exhilaration.

He could be patient. He'd enjoy this guessing game until he took off her mask. And kissed her thoroughly. Not necessarily in that order.

He bowed low and offered his arm. "Supper, I believe, my goddess."

She wound her arm around his, an innocent gesture he'd experienced hundreds of times, but tonight it became a sensual experience that sped the current of his blood into something more closely resembling a raging river after a storm. How could he eat in this condition?

With the intriguing lady at his side, he puffed out his chest as he led her to dinner. As liveried footmen brought dozens of dishes for the first course, he smirked and gestured to a nearby bowl. "I believe it's blood pudding. Shall I pass it to you?"

She grimaced. "I'll be sure to give you an extra helping of strawberries, sir."

He shivered exaggeratedly. "Greek mythology should have taught me never to anger a god, or in this case, a goddess."

"Anger, no, but tease gently? Perhaps. I suppose men cannot help themselves. My brother certainly took great delight in teasing me."

"Older or younger brother?"

Her smile dimmed. "Older."

Very gently, he asked, "The reason you wore mourning and then half mourning long enough to dislike lavender?"

She nodded and sipped her wine, not meeting his gaze.

"I'm very sorry."

She stirred her soup, staring into it as if her appetite had fled. "Thank you."

So, she wasn't a widow. The knowledge shouldn't please him so much. He changed the subject to bring back her smile. "You said you like the smell of lilacs; do you prefer them over roses?"

Her mouth curved upward a little. "For smell? Yes. For pure beauty? Hmm. Roses look and smell lovely, as do camellias, but lilacs have more character. And roses are given so often they've become cliché."

"Noted."

She smiled as if he'd passed some kind of test. "Do you believe ladies are too fragile to do anything more than lift a teacup?"

He blinked, trying to find a direction she might be headed. He finally settled with honesty. "No, I believe ladies, at least some ladies, have strength most men underappreciate. But if a gentleman is taking proper care of her, she shouldn't have to do anything strenuous. However, according to my mother, childbirth was assigned to women because the Almighty knew men weren't strong enough to handle it. She says men have no tolerance for pain and turn into great babies."

She laughed softly. "An interesting point of view."

"It's true. I cry real tears when I get a hangnail," he jested.

A full-bodied, husky laugh burst out of her. He stared, amazed at the rich, sultry sound. A few men nearby turned their heads. She pressed her lips together, shaking her head, and took another bite of soup.

"I like to go for long walks," she said. "Some people of my acquaintance feel I'm too delicate to walk."

"Because you are so petite?"

"I was frequently ill as a child. But seldom now. Still, everyone watches me as if I'll break. Sometimes I go for long walks when they think I'm napping. I feel alive when I walk."

"I like to walk, too. I also love to ride."

Her expression clouded over. "I don't like to ride."

"No?"

"Horses frighten me—perhaps another reason I'm treated as if I'm made of glass."

Her confessions evoked a protective instinct inside. He pictured himself accompanying her on her rambles, listening to the husky sweetness of her voice, watching the sunlight glisten in her hair. Was she wearing a wig or was all that hers? She had said her hair color came from her mother, but was what he saw real? He studied the top of her golden head but could not be certain if it were genuine or an expertly crafted wig.

"I promise not to treat you as if you are made of glass." He looked into her soft brown eyes.

Hmm. Brown eyes and blond hair was an unusual combination. Still, his steward was colored thusly, so the possibility existed that she was a true blond. Had he met any blond, brown-eyed ladies recently?

The corners of her mouth lifted. "I would very much appreciate you treating me like a person and not a glass ornament."

They fell silent as the servants took away the first course and brought the second. He sifted through everything she'd told him, looking for clues as to her name. Clearly he hadn't learned enough about her.

"You mentioned not liking horses; did you never learn to ride, then?"

She shook her head slightly. "I haven't tried in years. I'm so nervous that the horses always get jittery."

"They can sense it."

"I doubt anything frightens you."

He paused. "Dark water. I dislike swimming in water so murky that I can't see the bottom. I have an irrational fear that a monster will swim up from the depths, grab me, and drag me under. Childish, isn't it?"

"No, not childish; it suggests a good imagination." She lowered her voice. "I can swim. My mother said it was an unladylike activity. When we went to the seashore, we used bathing machines, but sometimes my friends and I snuck out and swam freely. It was glorious."

He chuckled at the rebellious gleam in her eye. Would she trust him with such information if they were unmasked? Probably not. He'd certainly never told others much of what he had revealed to her. Was it their masks or something about her that encouraged him to disclose personal details? Perhaps it was that sense of home that enfolded him in its embrace in her presence.

He steered the conversation to other topics. He tossed out casual comments about national events, and her views on social reform, the poor, the roles of landowners, and other subjects he didn't normally discuss with ladies. She met him head on with thoughtful, intelligent replies. When she didn't have an answer, she simply stated she'd have to do some more reading on the matter before she could comment.

He quirked a brow. "Do you like the smell of books?"

"Love it. A library is always my favorite room in a house."

Convinced she was quite possibly the most perfect woman he'd ever met, he probed further, discovering a thoughtful, insightful lady who surprised him on every level. He was tempted to fall down on his knees and beg her that moment to marry him.

How quickly could he obtain a special license?

No, he couldn't spring such a life-changing question on her. She deserved to know him better. But surely she'd be pleased to marry the Duke of Suttenberg. Wouldn't she? He'd never worried if a lady would accept his proposal as a duke, but now that he'd met one who didn't know of his title, he had to win her on his own merit. Was it enough? An uncharacteristic uncertainty edged into his confidence. This was his chance to learn if he, Bennett, the man, deserved the love of a woman like his Aphrodite.

"You're thinking very hard, Bennett."

His Christian name spoken in her voice sent a ripple of awareness over him. "I am."

"About?"

"I'm not ready to tell you just yet."

After dessert was served and consumed, without the appearance of a single strawberry, the guests left the table.

He escorted her, sorely reluctant to release her. "I suppose it would be terribly improper of me to ask you to dance a third time."

With her lips deliciously curved, she nodded. "I am the goddess of love, not the goddess of scandal."

"Very well. I'll resist."

As they headed toward the ballroom, some wild compulsion seized him, scattering all reason. He ducked into a nearby room, pulling her with him. She looked up at him with that mysterious smile and went unresisting with him.

She glanced around, her eyes lighting up. "The library."

"We're not here to read." He closed the door. The stillness of the room, with the noise of the guests muted on the other side of the door, fueled his impulses. He turned to her and placed his hand over hers where it rested on his arm. "I'm about to ask you a very mad, very improper question."

"Oh?"

"What is your Christian name?"

Again came that mysterious smile. "No names. Not until it's time to take off our masks."

He let out an exaggerated sigh. "Very well. Then I'll continue to call you Aphrodite. And I must apologize because I'm about to do something very rash with a lady whose name I don't know."

She went still.

He slid his hands up her arms to her shoulders and drew her toward him. He tried to move slowly, to give her time to protest or resist, but he honestly didn't know if he could stop himself even if she asked him to. With one hand moving from her shoulder to her back, and the other touching that sweet curve of her cheek, he leaned in and kissed her. Her intake of breath broke the silence. For a heartbeat, he feared she'd deny him, reject him, until her mouth softened, grew pliant. Her lips' silky texture astonished him, and the contact sent a concussion through his body like a cannon blast. Clearly, it had been far too long since he'd properly kissed a woman. While most of his body heated to a level of incineration, something deep in his heart sighed as if finally reaching a long-sought refuge. A choked groan escaped him.

He kissed her over and over, each time adding to an inner well he didn't know had dried. Though she kissed sweetly and with some natural skill, following his lead the way she had on the dance floor, she clearly had little experience kissing. Her innocence could not be ignored. This was a lady whose pristine virtue he had trod upon, and she'd be ruined if they were caught.

Reason cut through his primal hunger, and he forced himself to end the kiss. He held her soft body against him, trying to rein in his galloping heart. After pressing his lips to her brow, he pulled back and looked at her face.

Her mouth, moist and overly full from their kiss, curved at the corners, and her eyes remained closed. Then, like the strike of flint against steel that sparks flame, everything about her changed. She opened her eyes and stared at him as if he'd just insulted her.

And he had. He'd dishonored her, taken unfair advantage. And he wasn't truly sorry. Except for her expression.

He touched her cheeks softly, briefly, before holding his hands out to his sides in supplication. "Please. Please don't look at me like that. I swear to you, my intentions are honorable." He swept off his hat and mask.

She blinked, her brows drawing together as if she couldn't believe her eyes. Her gaze drifted up to that blond patch of hair that marked generations of dukes in his family. "You . . . you told me your name was Bennett. But you're . . ." She seemed to have trouble breathing. "You're the Duke of Suttenberg."

"I am. And I meant no disrespect. Please, will you—"

Before he got out another word, her hand blurred and a sharp pain exploded on his cheek. Stunned, he stared.

Her mouth spread into a scornful frown. "I am not a trollop, and I will not dally with you. Your Grace!" She threw his title at him like a curse, turned, and fled the room.

That was the first time in his life that anyone had ever dared slap the Duke of Suttenberg. And it hurt more than he ever imagined, in more places than his cheek.

Five

Hannah fled the library, still grappling with the horrible truth. Her charming Bennett was the arrogant Duke of Suttenberg. How could she have liked him? Trusted him? Usually, she was a better judge of character. Keeping silent and observing those around her normally revealed much about them. But no, she'd played the flirt, and now she must face the consequences.

At least no one had happened upon them when they'd been alone. Kissing. What had come over her? She'd behaved foolishly. With complete lack of sense. She might have been ruined.

With the back of her hand, she wiped her mouth. No matter how hard she tried, she couldn't fully erase the sweet, exciting bliss that had consumed her when Bennett kissed her.

Clearly, her reaction only stemmed from having fallen prey to a philanderer. Odd, the Duke of Suttenberg didn't have that reputation. But a man who went about luring girls he'd just met into isolated rooms and kissing them had no concern for the reputations or hearts of his victims.

She marched so quickly that she had to hold up her skirts to keep them out of her way, heading to the main staircase, intent upon locking herself in her room. A voice caught her attention.

"Wait!"

She glanced back. With his Musketeer hat and mask in place once again, Bennett—the Duke of Suttenberg—strode toward her.

Going anywhere alone while he pursued her would invite another unwelcome encounter. She changed directions and practically ran to the ballroom, slipping in between guests and worming her way toward the center of the room. The candles burned low in the wall sconces and chandeliers, casting a flitting light over the room.

Voices slurred with too much drink mingled with husky whispers and laughter. Couples stood close, ladies gossiped, girls who were newly out giggled, men rocked back on their heels and eyed ladies. Footmen carrying trays of glasses wound through the guests. With so many eyes upon him, the oh-so-falsely-proper duke wouldn't accost her and create a public spectacle.

As she stood shielded by the crowd, she took several breaths, each time regaining another scrap of her composure. Soon the night would be over. She could do this. She was Aphrodite, the confident goddess who cared not for mortals.

After squaring her shoulders, she lifted her head and impassively eyed the crowd. Nearby, Mrs. Potter, dressed as a swan, fanned herself, flirting with a slender man wearing a domino, whom Hannah was pretty sure was a Buchanan twin. There. She'd make a game of discovering the identities of the guests. Of course, she didn't know all the guests, having only come to stay with her sister a few times before she moved in with them this past summer. Still, she recognized several members of the local gentry. Each gave themselves away in little ways—body shape, posture, gestures, particular ticks or habits.

The final dance was announced. Another waltz. She let out a strangled groan, shutting down memories of the way Bennett had led her—firm, yet gentle—in a dance that seemed invented for those few glorious moments she'd spent in his arms when she'd believed he was perfect, before he'd revealed his true character.

Mr. Hill, the pirate, turned his head in her direction. He straightened, clearly spotting her. With a growl of annoyance, she moved away from him. She didn't have the patience to deal with him right now. But he pushed through to her.

"Wait," he said as he caught up to her. "Dance with me." He stepped closer, too close. His breath reeked of liquor, and he swayed on his feet.

"No, thank you. I'm finished dancing for the evening."

He frowned but rallied. "It's too warm in here. Shall we catch our breath outside on the terrace?"

Why did men always think women wanted to be alone with them? If he thought she'd go with a man who was three sheets to the wind, he didn't know her very well.

"No, thank you."

"Then let's find a place to sit. The sitting room off from that door?"

"No, that would be unwise."

"Then—"

She held up her hand. "Sir, I have no desire to wound your feelings, but I do not wish to go anywhere with you. Not ever."

He swayed first toward then away from her, as if he stood on the deck of a ship. "But I adore you. I desire you. I—"

"Please, don't. It's best that we do not continue our association."

His mouth fell open.

"Good evening, sir." She bobbed a faint curtsy and started to leave, but he grabbed her upper arm.

His mouth twisted. "Because I'm not the brother of an earl? Is that it? I'm too common?"

Her face heated as anger simmered her blood. "Are you calling me a snob?"

"You think you're too good for me, you with your lovely dowry and noble connections, now that your sister has nabbed herself an earl. But you're nothing but an upstart little social climber."

A third voice cut in. "Apologize to the lady this instant, cur."

Bennett stood next to her, his hand on the hilt of his rapier. But he wasn't her Bennett; he was the rude Duke of Suttenberg. Annoyance that he'd once again intruded into her life, with the growing realization that no man believed her capable of lifting a finger for herself, turned the simmer in her blood to a boil. He was just as bad as Mr. Hill. She wanted to throw something at the both of them.

Before she could speak, Mr. Hill snarled, "This conversation does not concern you, boy."

"It does concern me, so leave her be." The duke's voice, unclouded by drink, and his form, so tall and straight, formed a sharp contrast to the drunk man. Not that she wanted his interference.

Mr. Hill's gaze darted from the duke to Hannah, and he sneered. He turned as if to leave. Over his shoulder he cast one last barb, "That proud little doxy isn't worth it."

With a quick backward step and a metallic scrape, the duke stood in the *en garde* position with his rapier gleaming in his hand, the point touching the base of Mr. Hill's neck.

A few nearby guests let out gasps of horror and delight at the sensational development. Hannah stared in open-mouthed shock. He'd actually drawn a weapon at a ball. Unbelievable.

"Apologize to the lady this instant, or I will not hesitate to draw your blood." The duke's voice, barely audible, cut through the din in the room.

Mr. Hill seemed to snap. Perhaps the abundance of alcohol, or his stung pride, drove him to recklessness, but he pulled out his cutlass, albeit more slowly than his sober opponent, and crossed his curved sword against the narrow blade of the rapier. "I'll teach you to interfere with me, boy!"

Stunned, Hannah gasped, "No."

Mr. Hill lunged forward and swung his sword. The Duke of Suttenberg's blade bent under the weight of the blow. With a quick flick of his wrist, he disarmed Mr. Hill. The cutlass clattered as it hit the floor. Mr. Hill staggered back, swaying drunkenly, and nearly fell.

Cole appeared and hauled Mr. Hill to his feet. Then, turning to the staring crowd, Cole smiled brightly. "Well done! Very entertaining! That's the best end to a ball I've ever seen!" He applauded as if the brief fight had been planned to amuse the guests.

Next to him, Alicia also clapped. "Bravo!"

Hannah joined in, admiring her brother-in-law's quick thinking. Apparently, the guests closest to the fight believed Cole's ruse. Their faces relaxed, and they took up the applause. Mr. Hill looked around as if he were in a daze.

While the assembly applauded the "show," Cole shook Suttenberg's hand. "That was a very realistic performance. Thank you."

The duke put away his rapier, then made a low, flourishing bow to the assembly. Cole patted Mr. Hill's back and led him away, still congratulating him on his acting skills.

Suttenberg turned to Hannah and opened his mouth, but she held up a hand to stop him. "Don't."

Nothing he could say would excuse his behavior. First the kiss, then the spectacle he created. The duke had fooled society into believing he was the perfect Englishman, but he was a discreet womanizer with no sense of propriety.

Turning away, Hannah touched her mask to assure herself it remained securely in place and pushed through the dispersing crowd. She'd had enough of tonight's ball. How could he have humiliated her that way? True, Mr. Hill's words had been nothing short of unforgivable, but they were only words. Suttenberg had actually drawn a weapon. If anyone knew what had really transpired, Hannah would be the source of gossip for months. Alicia's grand plans to launch Hannah into London society next Season would be tainted by tonight's altercation. With luck, the guests would remain ignorance of the truth.

Hannah ducked into the servants' stairway. Taking the main staircase would reveal to Suttenberg that she was a guest of Cole and Alicia's. If she had her way, he'd never know who he'd shamed, first by kissing her, then by drawing a weapon over her.

She seemed to be doing a lot of hoping that nothing about tonight would be linked to her. Fate was seldom that kind.

Lifting her skirts, she practically ran up the stairs to the family wing, dashing past a startled maid, who flattened herself against the wall and stared at the intruder in the servants' domain.

Unmasking the Duke

Safe in her room, Hannah rang for her maid and stood in front of the mirror, stripping off her costume jewelry. In the mirror, her flushed face stared back, surrounded by a halo of disheveled, limp curls. Outside her window, the clattering of carriages and hoofbeats kept up a steady rhythm as the guests departed. Not that it mattered. Even if the ball weren't over, Hannah wouldn't have gone back out there for all the tea in China.

Alicia burst in. "What happened?"

Hannah bit her lip as hot tears blurred her vision. "It was so humiliating. I can't believe it."

"Who were they? I thought the Musketeer resembled the Duke of Suttenberg."

Hannah nodded. Though tempted to keep it all secret, she'd never hidden anything from her sister. "The pirate was Mr. Hill. He'd had too much to drink and became a bit aggressive. He—" She swallowed and turned away, too embarrassed by what had occurred.

"What did he do? Did he touch you?" Alicia's voice rose in alarm.

"No. But he called me a social climber and a . . . a doxy."

Alicia gasped. "That scoundrel. He will never be welcome in this house again. I vow I will publicly snub him."

"Please don't. I don't want anyone to know or even suspect their fight was real, nor that I was the center of it."

Calming, Alicia shook her head. "No, of course you don't. What happened then?"

"The duke pulled out his rapier and demanded Mr. Hill apologize. And you know the rest." She sank down onto the chair by her dressing table.

"His Grace is the absolute model of gentlemanly behavior. That he defended you comes as no surprise. But I cannot account as to why he'd draw a weapon at a social gathering. It's so unlike him."

"Yes, well, he isn't the model gentleman you think he is."

Alicia let out a long breath and actually smiled. "It was noble of him to rise to your defense. Still, if it weren't for Cole's quick thinking, the whole thing could have gotten out of hand."

"I hope everyone believed it was staged." Hannah hugged herself, still smarting over the duke's forward behavior. Did he truly think because he was a duke that every girl would abandon her virtue?

Alicia pulled off her white wig and smoothed her hair. "The guests were still bubbling over about the realistic display as they said good-bye, and even congratulating me on having such entertaining floor show. No one seemed to think the lady in the goddess costume had any part of the show."

"Good." Too bad the sword fight wasn't the only thing to have gone amiss.

How could she have been so foolish as to have allowed a man she'd met only that evening to kiss her? He probably thought her fast. Maybe she was. That kiss had been the most supremely perfect moment of her entire life. She'd never experienced such lovely pleasure, nor such astonishing sense of belonging.

At least she'd had the presence of mind to slap him. That should dispel any presumption that she could be coaxed into behaving like a hoyden again.

"You're still overset, dearest." Alicia knelt in front of her and drew her into an embrace.

Her sister's touch and the strong emotions she'd experienced all evening collided. A sob wrenched its way out of her.

Alicia pulled away and looked at her. "Hannah, dear, what is it? Did something else happen?" She smoothed a stray strand back from Hannah's face, her touch affectionate, motherly.

The entire story came pouring out of Hannah—all her bliss, her joy, her heartbreak that the kiss meant so little to him, his attempt to use his rank to justify his taking advantage.

Alicia listened without judgment. When Hannah finished talking, Alicia hugged her again. "Going with him alone into a room wasn't the wisest course of action, but after what transpired between you two, I can't say I blame you. And you're right, a man like His Grace should have known better. Frankly, I'm shocked he'd treat a lady in such a way. Don't worry any more about it, dearest. If you never want to see him again, I'll make sure of it."

"I don't." For the moment, she was content to let her sister take care of her.

"Then you shan't. He's probably figured out who you are by now, but duke or no duke, he cannot make you see him. If he calls upon you, we'll turn him away. It's as simple as that."

Hannah let out an exhale, releasing her tension, and leaned against her sister, basking in her affection and the sense of order she exuded. All would be well. Hannah had survived her ball without tripping or getting tongue-tied, thanks to her false confidence due to her costume, and hadn't brought public embarrassment to Alicia and Cole. How she'd ever survive London, she couldn't say. But the Season was months away. Maybe by then she would develop some poise and grace without the aid of a mask. And she'd certainly avoid going into a room alone with a man ever again.

As she went to bed, the memory of Bennett's arms around her, his mouth kissing her so tenderly, crept over her. If only it had been real. Having tasted such sweet pleasure made her long for more. The next time she kissed a man, she'd be sure his intentions were more honorable than the duke's.

Six

Still wearing his Musketeer costume, Suttenberg stood in the study of Tarrington Castle, awaiting the arrival of Cole Amesbury, the Earl of Tarrington. No doubt, after the earl finished seeing his guests out, he'd return and demand an explanation. Suttenberg paced to the windows.

If Tarrington called him out, what would he do? He respected, even liked, the earl. He couldn't fight him. Would an apology suffice? Drawing a weapon at a party was a serious offense. But then, so was kissing a lady he'd only just met. He couldn't believe he'd done either. Had he completely gone mad? Perhaps his maternal grandfather's Italian blood had finally taken over as he'd always feared it would.

He ran his hand over his face, remembering the well-deserved slap, and paced back toward the other side of the room. He'd always prided himself on doing everything exceptionally well, on exceeding societal expectations. He served faithfully in Parliament, did his best to care for his properties and tenants, achieved a fearsome reputation for fencing and fisticuffs, avoided gambling and excessive drinking, and never trifled with ladies' hearts or their virtue. But tonight he'd broken every social and personal rule. Worse, he'd lost his Aphrodite.

Tarrington entered, eyeing Suttenberg as if he'd never seen him. "What were you drinking tonight?"

Suttenberg let out his breath. "I don't even have that as an excuse."

Tarrington sat and laced his fingers together. "Well, at least now I know you're human. For years I wasn't so sure." His lips quirked.

"I apologize for my conduct."

The earl waved him off. "The guests think it was an act."

"Thanks to your quick thinking."

Tarrington inclined his head. "My wife considers the evening a success. Everyone will talk about it for weeks."

"Still, I cannot excuse my temper."

"What happened? Did he insult you?"

"He insulted a lady."

Tarrington nodded sagely. "I have risen to the defense of many a lady, once to the point of dueling." Frowning, he stared down at his hands.

Suttenberg didn't pry. "It would have been better form to challenge him rather than draw a weapon."

"No need to flog yourself—no harm done."

"You truly aren't angry?"

The earl grinned. "Angry? Are you kidding? Even if no one else knows it, I had the singular experience of witnessing the mighty Duke of Suttenberg in a rare moment of weakness. It may never happen again, so I'm relishing in it." Chuckling, Tarrington got up and clapped a hand on Suttenberg's back. "No one got hurt. No one became truly alarmed. The matter is closed."

The muscles in Suttenberg's shoulders loosened. At least he hadn't offended Tarrington, and he didn't have to face the prospect of a duel. Yet the earl's words offered little comfort. He'd behaved badly toward his goddess. He had to find her and beg her forgiveness. And convince her to give him another chance.

Tarrington interrupted his thoughts. "Is there something you want to talk about?"

Suttenberg looked up. The earl watched him carefully.

Perhaps he'd gotten into a habit this eve of speaking frankly. "You wouldn't happen to know the identity of a young woman dressed as a Greek goddess, would you? She had long, blond curls. That might have been a wig, I suppose, but it looked genuine."

Tarrington cocked his head. "Shy?"

"No, she was very poised and a little flirtatious."

"Hmm. I saw more than one goddess. My wife's sister is blond, and she was dressed as a goddess, I believe. But she is painfully shy, especially at large gatherings. I can't imagine her flirting."

"Your wife's sister? Miss Palmer, isn't it?"

"That's her. You've met her a few times, I believe."

A few times? This morning, Miss Palmer did say something about strawberries. He nodded as if he remembered. "I met her this morning, didn't I? Pretty little thing. Very young. I don't believe she could be my Aphrodite." He let out a long breath. "Would you ask the countess? I must find her."

"Oh? A lady caught your eye, huh?" A brow raised, and the earl's mouth quirked to one side. "I don't recall you showing preference for a lady before."

"No, 'tis true. But this one was different."

"And she gave you no clue as to her name?"

"None. And then I made a fool of myself and kissed her."

Tarrington choked. "You kissed her?"

Suttenberg put his head into his hands, surprised that he'd confided in Tarrington, and reliving the shame all over again. "Truly there must be something wrong with me. I don't blame her for slapping me. By the time I caught up to her, the pirate was talking to her. Apparently she spurned him, and then he grew insulting. And I snapped." He raised his head, expecting a condemning stare.

Tarrington's expression was a mixture of disbelief and amusement. "I'd like to meet the girl brave enough to slap the Duke of Suttenberg. Of course, you were in costume, so . . ."

"Ah, no. I removed my mask after I kissed her. She knew my face and called me by name before she slapped me."

"You do have a problem."

"I have several, in fact. I must come to terms with my own behavior. I must find a girl whose name and face I do not know, and I must convince her to give me another chance."

Tarrington nodded. "I'd only known my wife a few moments before I became equally obsessed."

Footsteps neared, and the door flew open. The Countess of Tarrington burst in, eyes snapping and chest heaving. The men leaped to their feet as the countess marched up to Suttenberg, wearing an expression of outrage.

"You kissed her?" she demanded.

Taken aback, Suttenberg could only nod.

"You scoundrel!" She raised her hand, and for the second time in his life—both in the same night—a lady slapped the Duke of Suttenberg.

Seven

Sitting in Alicia's sun-drenched parlor, Hannah glanced at the clock and sipped her tea while Alicia played hostess to her neighbor, Mrs. Potter. They rhapsodized about the triumphant ball two nights past, and all the delights of the evening, sprinkled liberally with speculations on who had worn what costume and who had been seen in whose arms.

At this, Mrs. Potter stopped and glanced at Hannah as if remembering her presence, before she returned her attention to Alicia. "Well, you know what I mean, of course, Countess."

Hannah nearly rolled her eyes. Just because she was newly out didn't mean she knew nothing about the foibles and passions of men and women. And after the ball, she had a better understanding.

Mrs. Potter smiled at Hannah. "And how are you, my dear? You didn't overtax yourself?"

"No, ma'am. I am quite well."

"I do worry about you. When you had to leave my dinner party a fortnight ago with a sick headache, I really was concerned. Young ladies with delicate constitutions cannot be too careful."

Hannah's hackles rose at the insinuation that she was so sickly neighbors must worry for her. She tried to sound gracious. "I'm quite well. Thank you for your concern."

"You know, my great aunt suffered from the sick headache, and she found it helpful to use leeches once a month. You might try that."

Nearly choking on her tea, Hannah gasped. "Oh, er, thank you. I'll keep that in mind."

"And don't exercise too much. My aunt simply couldn't tolerate going for walks." Mrs. Potter tutted. "She never had children, poor dear."

Hannah's stomach dropped at yet more proof that she'd never know the joys of motherhood.

Alicia broke in. "I keep a careful eye on her, as well, to be sure she doesn't overdo it."

Mrs. Potter said hurriedly, as if she feared she'd somehow offended her hostess, "Oh, yes, I'm sure you do, Countess. I'm sure you do. Well, I must be off."

After they bade farewell, Hannah let out a sigh of relief. Just to be contrary, she turned to her sister. "I'm going for a walk. A long one."

Before Alicia could reply, Hannah went to her room and changed into a sturdy pair of walking boots and took up a wide-brimmed hat. She carefully wove a hatpin into her hair to keep it in place. After donning a spencer against autumn's chill, she went outside. Meandering through the gardens didn't satisfy today; a good ramble through the country called to her. Forgoing the driveway, she took a circuitous route past the gardens out toward the river leading to the lake. The river, slow-moving and sluggish, gurgled in the autumn stillness. A songbird trilled overhead. She strolled along the river, following it toward the lake, passing the bridge over which the main drive crossed.

After a bend in the river, she came upon the lake. It spread out before her in golden shimmers. Swans floated on the surface, leaving V-shaped wakes. Wild geese crossed the sky against the azure backdrop. She walked along the edge, as waves lapped against the shore. The solitude filled her with peace. But she couldn't stay much longer or she'd be late for dinner. Reluctantly, she turned back and followed the river toward the castle.

As she stepped over the path strewn with rocks and blanketed with a damp carpet of leaves, her foot slipped. She sat down hard. Pain splintered up her leg.

"Oh bother!" Her clumsiness usually originated from nervousness in the presence of others, but she certainly had her share of ungraceful moments in private, as well.

Sitting awkwardly on the damp ground, she carefully righted her legs. She tried to climb to her feet, but pain in her ankle stopped her. She paused, resting, and tried again to put weight on that foot. This time the pain lessened. Perhaps she could walk out the soreness. At least she hadn't fallen in the water, which would be more her usual style.

Her ankle throbbed worse with each step. She found a boulder and sat, careful to keep her ankle straight. The song of the river filled her ears, and she watched it ripple toward the lake, momentarily forgetting her discomfort and her desire to return home. Gold and red leaves fluttered from above to land on the surface and ride the current like tiny boats. The shadows grew long, and the temperature cooled. Alicia would worry if Hannah didn't return home soon.

Hannah stood and continued. Each step sent waves of pain up her leg. At least she could walk, if a bit slowly. If she followed the driveway, she'd have the smoothest path and the shortest distance back to Tarrington Castle.

A horse's hoofbeats approached from behind. A lone rider astride an enormous stallion cantered around the bend in the narrow driveway. He rode beautifully, like one born for the saddle. Hannah moved to the side of the road to allow the rider plenty of room to pass without bringing the frightening animal too close.

The rider slowed to walk next to her. "Are you in need of assistance, miss?"

The Duke of Suttenberg's smooth voice drew her gaze. He sat astride, looking at her like she was some kind of waif. Her cheeks heated. Not him. Not the duke who'd kissed her like she was some kind of tart.

With any luck, he'd go away and take his big, scary horse with him. "No, thank you."

He leaned in as if to peer at her around her hat. "You look familiar. Have we met?"

What a question! She lowered her head to use the brim as a shield. However, he never seemed to remember her the other times they had been introduced, so the odds of him knowing her face or name now seemed unlikely. At least he didn't mistake her for a servant today.

"I don't think so." She flushed at the lie. But telling him any different would be pointless. As often as they'd been introduced, how he never seemed to remember her was a mystery. Either he had the worst memory of any person alive, or she was truly forgettable—to all but the Buchanan twins and Mr. Hill.

Go away, go away, go away, she silently chanted. She couldn't bear it if he discovered her to be the hussy who had dressed and acted like Aphrodite and brazenly kissed strangers. And liked it. But hated herself for liking it.

"You're limping. Have you injured your foot?"

"I'm fine. No need to worry. Continue on." She made a point of walking on her fiery, throbbing foot as evenly as possible.

He stopped his horse. Just as she began to believe he would leave, the creaking of leather drew her attention again. With practiced grace, he dismounted and walked next to her, leading his horse by the reins. Good heavens, the beast was huge! But at least the tall man next to her walked between her and the animal. He appeared to have control over the creature.

"I cannot leave you here to limp along this road, miss. Are you going to Tarrington Castle?"

She wanted to deny it, but since she walked along the private drive leading to the castle, the truth seemed obvious. And she couldn't concoct a believable story as to why she would be here otherwise. "I am."

"Then please allow me to assist you. You shouldn't be walking on an injury."

She shivered at the thought of putting herself at the mercy of a horse again. Or the duke. "I can't ride your horse."

He rubbed his chin. "You could sit across the saddle, even if it isn't a sidesaddle."

"I can't. I will walk. It isn't far now."

He stopped. She moved more quickly to put some distance between herself and the duke and bit her lip against the pain. Seconds later, the creaking of leather and metal reached her ears. She looked back. He unbuckled the saddle, carried it to the side of the road, and set it down. She turned around to watch. What on earth was he doing?

He went back to the horse, took up the reins, and trotted toward her, leading the horse. As he reached her, he gestured to the horse where only a blanket remained on his back. "You can sit in sidesaddle position on the blanket. He's very steady. He likes ladies; he won't throw you."

To ward him off, she held up her hands. "I'm not riding that horse, not now, not ever." She made no comment on his claim that his horse liked ladies. She didn't want to know how many ladies had ridden his horse nor under what circumstances.

Narrowing his gaze, he bent down a little and peered at her face under her hat. "Aphrodite?"

The blood left her head so quickly that she nearly lost her balance. Her mind emptied of all intelligent thought. "W-what?"

The corners of his mouth lifted. "It is you! Aphrodite. But I suppose it's Miss Palmer." His smile spreading, he removed his hat, and that shock of blond hair nestled among his ebony waves mocked her.

She let out a frustrated sigh. She should never trust fate to keep her secrets.

"I've been trying to talk to you ever since I found out who you are, but the countess won't let me near you." He rubbed his cheek, and his smile turned rueful. "The Countess of Tarrington is a formidable woman."

Hannah folded her arms and glared. "I can't imagine why my sister wouldn't want you near me."

His smile faded. "You're still angry with me."

"Your powers of observation are truly astounding, Your Grace." She practically snarled his title.

"You have every right to be angry, but please give me another chance. I'm not normally so rash."

"Really," she said dryly.

"Miss Palmer, please, if you knew me at all, you'd know I normally have excellent control over my impulses."

"How kind of you to lose control at my expense." She shifted her weight onto her good leg.

"I was completely undone. You were so elegant and mysterious and witty." Glancing down, he smiled and brought up his hand filled with a small bouquet. "I brought these for you."

Lilacs. He'd remembered. She squelched her delight at the gesture and made no move to accept them.

His gaze darted over her face. "You are even more beautiful without the mask than I imagined. Younger than I suspected, though." A tiny crease formed in his brow.

She let out an exasperated huff. "Do you recall meeting me before the masque?"

He paused. "Yes, I believe we were introduced a few days ago."

"We have, in fact, met on five separate occasions prior to the ball."

"Five?"

"Yes. The first time was at a dinner party a year ago. You barely glanced my way, so I'd be surprised if you remembered me. The second time was at your brother's house early this summer. My sister and I came for tea. It was a short visit, and again you barely looked at me. You seemed preoccupied. Or perhaps simply disinterested."

His eyes searched the air as if reading an invisible book, trying to find the memories that matched her words.

"The third time was last month. A group of us had a picnic and picked blackberries. I dropped my basket, and you helped me pick up my spilled berries."

He let out a long exhale and fingered the stems of the lilacs.

She pushed on. "That same afternoon, you bit into a tart and realized it was strawberry. But since you only ate one bite, you suffered a very mild reaction. The fifth was the morning of the ball when you came to visit my brother-in-law. You mistook me for a servant!"

He winced.

"Do you remember any of that? No? Of course not. You only remember the brazen flirt wearing a mask."

"Miss Palmer, in my defense, I seldom pay attention to ladies as young as you. You're what? Fifteen? Sixteen?"

"Eighteen!"

"Nearly half my age. And if those very young ladies I meet are clearly without Town polish, I make a point not to look at them a second time—especially if they are beautiful; I don't want to tempt myself. I never wish to raise a lady's expectations, and I have a great many duties, so I cannot let myself become distracted by someone I cannot court."

"You were very distracted at the ball, it appears."

He paused, his expression softening. "I certainly was. If I had known who you were, I would not have danced with you a second time, probably not even a first. Nor would I have . . ." He made a circular wave. "You know."

She wouldn't let him off that easily. "Kissed me?"

He winced again. "I'm sorry if I made you feel unnoticed the previous times we met. I do believe I remember you at the picnic. You were wearing pink, weren't you? I don't think you spoke the entire time."

"No, I'm not normally one for conversation, especially in large groups."

"You certainly spoke at the ball."

"That was easy. I wore a mask, and we were playing a guessing game." Her leg ached in earnest, and dark shadows reached across the road. "I'm going home. My sister will be worried about me." She took another step, but her ankle had stiffened and the pain doubled.

"Please ride my horse." A light of understanding brightened his face. "You're afraid of horses. I remember."

She gritted her teeth and kept limping.

He kept pace with her. "We'll go slowly, and I'll be right here to steady you. You won't fall."

"No," she ground out. She bit her lip to keep from crying out with the pain.

He raised his voice to a stern tone. "Hannah Palmer, I am giving you two choices: either my horse carries you, or I carry you."

At his threat, she pulled out her hatpin, brandishing it like a weapon. "Touch me and I swear I'll . . . I'll put out your eye!"

He paused, sizing her up. With a single, swift motion, he stepped in, grabbed her by the wrist of the hand that wielded the hatpin, and pulled her against his chest. For a few terrifying heartbeats, he held her trapped against him. Every nerve ending blazed with awareness.

He parted his lips, those tempting lips that had taught her a pleasure she'd never dreamed would be so sublime. Instead of kissing her, he said, "Just so you have no delusions that your 'defense' would protect you if I meant you harm."

She stared into his eyes, unable to look away.

He dropped his voice to a whisper and loosened his grip. "But I have no intention of hurting you. And I'm sorry I spoke to you in such a heavy-handed manner." He released her and stepped back, leaving her off-balance and aching for his touch again.

Clearly only a practiced *roué* had such effect on sensible young ladies like herself. Or maybe she was so hopelessly green that she was prime to fall victim to any smooth charmer—which didn't paint a delightful picture of her future in London.

He moistened his lips and continued speaking softly. "I cannot leave you to walk injured in the dark. I know I broke your trust when I kissed you, but I give you my word as a gentleman, I won't take advantage, and I won't let you fall off my horse nor be harmed in any way. Please, *please* allow me to take you home."

Between the burning in her foot and ankle, and the desperate sincerity in his expression, not to mention his achingly handsome face, she relented—probably another lapse in judgment. She and the duke clearly brought out those qualities in each other.

Resigned, she nodded. "Very well."

Mingled relief and satisfaction overcame his features. "Here."

He handed her the lilacs. As he lifted her into his arms, she held her breath. Their bodies pressed together intimately. Though slim, he possessed strength aplenty to hold her without visible effort. That patch of blond hair caught her attention. Was it as soft as it looked? He smelled divine, all male and desirable. His lips caught her fascination. Only inches from hers, they reminded her of how sweetly they'd kissed her.

Her confusing exhilaration from the singular experience of being in the duke's arms changed to fear as they approached the horse. The beast loomed large, an unpredictable creature with big teeth and uncertain temper, likely to spook at anything. Her breath came in ragged gasps. She closed her eyes. The duke carefully sat her upon the blanket on the horse's back with her legs on the horse's left side. She made the mistake of opening her eyes. The ground fell away at a dizzying distance. The horse shifted his weight underneath Hannah and turned her cold. With the duke's arms around her, and his head level with her waist, Hannah tried to control her labored breathing. The horse shifted again.

"You're safe," the duke murmured. "Relax."

With one arm still around her, he used his free hand to pet the horse's neck and murmured, "Easy, boy. Be a gentleman."

The horse's ears swiveled back to listen, and he snorted, still prancing a little.

"She needs your help," continued the duke. "Let's go slowly and take the lady home."

As the horse settled, the duke eyed Hannah. "Good, you're sitting more comfortably now. Let's go. I'll stay right next to you."

He urged the horse to a sedate walk, but Hannah's fear compounded with every step. The horse took several small sideways steps, probably feeling the tension in her body. The duke murmured soothingly, to her or to the horse, she wasn't sure which, but neither of them calmed. She squeezed the lilacs so hard that she crushed several blooms.

With a quick glance at her face, the duke said, "This isn't going to work. I'll have to ride with you."

He led the horse to a stile next to the road. Using the stile as a mounting block in the absence of stirrups, he swung up and settled her in front of him, then reached around her to take the reins. She blushed so hotly she could have caught fire. She was practically sitting across his lap and letting him embrace her. There were just so many things wrong with that. The heat from his chest warmed her left side, and his arms around her created a sensation of safety and danger all at once.

"I won't let you fall," he said. "Trust me."

"I'd probably trust you better if I didn't know you," she said between clenched teeth.

"If you truly knew me, you'd have complete faith in me," he said tightly.

She glanced up at his face. Only inches separated their mouths. "To do what? Compromise me completely?"

Anger rolled over his features, but then he let out a long exhale and composed his face. With his arms around her, he urged the horse forward again. Under the duke's confident command, the horse obediently pranced along the road.

Finally he said, "I'm sorry. It was ungentlemanly of me. I should have never behaved that way. But I was pretty sure I'd found the perfect lady, and I couldn't think straight."

Pleasure seeped into her. But his "perfect lady" was a role she'd played at a masque, a lady who didn't exist.

"And I'm sorry I drew my blade," he continued. "When that man insulted you, I lost my head. You seem to bring out a side of me I didn't know existed."

Her conscience pricked her, and she softened toward him. "Perhaps it was the mask. I did and said things I don't normally, either."

"Can we start anew?"

She stiffened. "What do you mean?"

He looked wounded. "Nothing nefarious, I promise. Simply begin our acquaintance in a more . . . traditional way."

"We did. I hardly said two words to you, and you instantly forgot my existence."

He flinched. A few seconds passed. He spoke in the same thoughtful tones he'd used as the Musketeer, as Bennett. "The difference was the way you carried yourself. You were confident at the masquerade ball—poised, mature, witty—so I deemed you approachable. Meeting you as the very young and inexperienced sister of the Countess of Tarrington, not to mention how shy you seemed, well, it made you unavailable. So I avoided looking at temptation. It's hard to remember what one doesn't allow oneself to see."

His explanation made sense in a way. After her parents died and she wore black crepe for mourning, she avoided looking at gowns and hats in cheery colors because she couldn't have them. Later, she didn't look at them because her family was too poor to afford such finery.

Tarrington Castle came into view, its silvery white spires beckoning in the dimming light like a lighthouse to weary sailors. But it no longer held the appeal she'd expected. Inside the castle, she was alone. Oh, she had Alicia and Cole and their sweet baby, but no family of her own. Bennett's strong arms around her enfolded her in comfort and reassurance. It might be counterfeit to love, but the sensation was hard to ignore. In his arms, her fears about riding the horse had taken a step back—not quite leaving, but at least not leaving her quaking.

Did Bennett often hold ladies in such a way? She looked down at the lilacs, a thoughtful gesture, to be sure. But was that only the gesture of a libertine? She might merely have been one in a long line of ladies he'd tried to seduce.

Bennett met her gaze, his features soft and imploring. "Will you forgive me?"

She moistened her lips. "If I ask you a blunt question, will you give me an honest answer?"

He paused. "Very well. You have my word. I owe you complete honesty."

"Do you often kiss ladies?"

His body stiffened. After a moment, he lowered his mouth to her ear and said softly, "No. I don't often kiss ladies, or women of any kind. Despite my behavior toward you, I am not such a scoundrel."

He hadn't been seeking a dishonorable liaison with her. Yet that relief was tempered by the sad truth that he'd kissed Aphrodite, not Hannah Palmer, which meant he'd never kiss her again. Would another man's kiss be so moving? Surely if she found a man she loved, his kiss would eclipse Bennett's. Of course, she still had the London season to survive. And that ugly little fear that she couldn't have children whispered at the futility of dreaming of a family.

The horse snorted and strained against the reins, ratcheting up Hannah's fear, but Bennett held his mount under control. But can one really control a horse—even a man as commanding as the Duke of Suttenberg?

His chest rumbled against her. "You said you loved Shakespeare's comedies. Which is your favorite?"

As she considered his question, her nervousness eased enough for her to sit more comfortably. "Either *Much Ado about Nothing* or *Twelfth Night*."

"What do you like about them?"

"Strong women. In fact, many of his plays have strong women—*The Taming of the Shrew*, for example. Katherine's strength was misplaced at first, but at least she refused to be a doormat."

As they discussed Shakespeare's plays, the trip flew by. Enfolded in his arms, she relaxed against Bennett, soaking in the sensation of being held.

As the sun sank behind the horizon, they arrived at the front door of Tarrington Castle. Then it hit her; she no longer trembled in fear. She'd been so occupied with her conversation with Bennett that her fear had vanished. Amazed, she glanced at him. He'd probably brought up the subject of Shakespeare to keep her mind off her fears. Whether he'd done that out of kindness or necessity, she could not say.

He dismounted and lifted her down. "Can you walk or shall I carry you?"

"I'll walk." She took a cautious step but hissed in her breath.

He swung her into his arms and carried her up the stairs to the front door. Resigned, she put her arms around his neck. She really shouldn't enjoy the safety and well-being that overcame her when he carried her. In fact, she should still be angry with him. But after these past few minutes in his company, she had quite forgiven him. He'd transformed into the Bennett who captured her attention at the masque—considerate, attentive, gentle—not at all the duke who owned the world and viewed everyone as objects to serve him.

Inside, Cole, wearing his overcoat, stood, giving orders to several men who held lanterns. Alicia stood nearby, pale and silent. She turned at Hannah's arrival.

"Hannah!" Alicia rushed forward but stopped short. "You're touching my sister again, Suttenberg."

The men fell silent.

Hannah put up a hand. "It's not what you think. His Grace was kind enough to help me when I twisted my ankle." She smiled in an attempt to lighten the mood. "You know me, my usual clumsy self."

Alicia folded her arms and glared at the duke, obviously unconvinced. Cole dismissed the others and strode toward them, his gaze thunderous.

As Bennett set her down on a nearby chair, he whispered, "You're stronger than you know, just like Katherine. Or Aphrodite." Without waiting for her reply, he stood, facing the others. "I found her limping near the bridge and I could not, in good conscience, allow her to walk so far on an injured foot."

Alicia and Cole wore equally concerned expressions bordering on anger.

She couldn't allow her sister and brother-in-law to believe the worst of Bennett's actions this afternoon. "That's true. I don't know how I would have made it home without his aid."

Alicia glared at the duke but spoke to Hannah. "What did he do, carry you all the way home?"

"No, we rode his horse."

Her sister's amber eyes opened wide. "You rode a horse?"

Hannah nodded. "I didn't think I could do it, but His Grace walked the horse and kept my mind off of it." At Alicia's look of alarm, Hannah rushed on. "We discussed Shakespeare, and I wasn't nearly so afraid."

"Suttenberg?" Cole looked at the duke for verification.

He donned his ducal mien, all traces of her Bennett vanishing. "I give you my word, I did not touch her in an improper way. I admit to a lapse in judgment at the ball, but I hope you know I'd never take advantage of an innocent girl."

Cole let out his breath and dragged a hand through his hair. "Of course. My apologies for doubting your honor. When Hannah didn't come home, we grew anxious. Then you come in carrying her . . ."

"It looked bad," the duke finished. "Understandable." He bowed to Hannah. "Good evening, Miss Palmer. I hope your ankle heals quickly."

"Thank you for your assistance." She blocked out the memories of his arms around her while they rode and while he carried her to the house. And she most especially blocked out the softness of his kiss at the ball and the stirrings inside her heart.

Alicia crouched in front of Hannah. "Which ankle?"

Hannah lifted her injured foot and held still while Alicia unfastened the boot to examine the damage.

"This changes nothing, I trust?" the duke said. "You're still coming to my hunting lodge in Netherfield in two weeks' time?"

Cole and Alicia exchanged weighted glances. Alicia nodded briefly. Cole's expression relaxed, and he said, "Yes, we're still coming."

The duke smiled. "Excellent. Until then." His gaze rested on Hannah briefly, and her Bennett peeked through his ducal posture. He bowed and strode away, his lean body filling out his suit beautifully. Blushing, Hannah forced her attention back onto her foot.

Alicia stared at her, and her voice took on an incredulous tone. "You like him."

"No!" Hannah put a hand over her eyes. "Oh, I don't know. He was so charming at the ball. And just now, when he brought me home, he was so kind. He took off his saddle so I could ride, and he didn't make me feel foolish for being so afraid. But it's pointless. I'm beneath him."

Alicia sat next to her. "Why do you say that?"

"He's looking for someone who'll be the perfect duchess, not someone young and shy like I am. I'm not mature enough, nor do I have enough Town polish." Not to mention he needed someone to bear children and protect the ducal line. Fate had made her a failure in the most basic feminine duty. She curled her hand into a fist in helpless anger.

"Being a duchess brings on a great deal of responsibility, not to mention public scrutiny," Alicia agreed. "Everyone looks to a duchess for comportment, dress, everything. She is usually held as some kind of example to follow, but if she slips up, people are delighted to find evidence she's no better than they. People can be pathetic sycophants to a duchess's face but ruthless behind her back."

Cole broke in. "She's right. Suttenberg is always doing everything he should and excelling at it. Naturally, I found it vastly startling, not to mention amusing, to learn he'd lost his head at our ball. It reassured me the rest of us mere mortals aren't as far behind him as it appears."

"You're an earl," Hannah said. "You aren't far behind him in rank."

"Not just rank, but in everything. He seems so perfect. Like my brother Christian." He smiled ruefully.

Hannah nodded at the mention of Cole's handsome younger brother. But Christian fell short in comparison to her Bennett, the Duke of Suttenberg. Intelligent, witty, accepting—even encouraging—of her ideas and dreams, and thoughtful, Bennett truly was as amazing as people thought. He wasn't perfect, but that added to his appeal. Oh heavens, was she losing her heart to him?

Foolish girl! Her feelings were irrelevant. She wasn't meant to be a duchess: she disliked attention, she lacked poise, and most of all loomed that horrifying possibility that she couldn't bear children so crucial to the continuation of the line.

She stared at the lilacs in her hand. "I understand what you're saying; liking him would be pointless."

Alicia touched her arm. "No, not pointless at all, dearest. Your dowry is respectable and being Cole's sister-in-law raises you from the level of a country squire's daughter, and you're so beautiful and kind that everyone admires you. You have no reason to believe yourself beneath consideration. But a duchess is not an easy role to bear."

"I wouldn't want people to watch me and talk about me, nor have false friends." Hannah shook her head. "I won't give him another thought. When we go to his hunting lodge, I will content myself with his library and gardens. The visit will be a pleasant diversion, nothing more."

Alicia hugged her, and they turned their attention to her ankle. Cole carried her up the stairs to her room. Though he was broader and more muscular than the duke, being in his arms invoked none of the pleasure of being in Bennett's. She sighed. She'd have to put thoughts of Bennett out of her head.

But that night before she retired, she carefully pressed Bennett's lilacs between the pages of her favorite book.

Eight

The Duke of Suttenberg stood in the small drawing room of his hunting lodge and tried not to look too often or too longingly at Hannah Palmer. He must resist temptation. Though he'd discovered in her an uncommon delight, someone as young and inexperienced as she would crumple under the pressures required of a duchess. He wouldn't do that to her. Besides, he was nearly twice her age.

But she drew his focus. She stood serenely, almost aloof, watching the others with an aura of quiet dignity. While the earl and countess conversed with everyone, Miss Palmer seemed content to observe.

Since the houseguests were all assembled, he began the formal greetings. He led his mother to the Tarringtons. "You remember Lord and Lady Tarrington, of course, Duchess?"

Voices in the room hushed as they often did when he spoke, and the guests turned to watch him.

"Certainly." Mother spoke confidently, unconcerned with the attention.

Lord Tarrington bowed low. "You're looking well, Duchess."

Lady Tarrington curtsied gracefully. "Lovely to see you again, Your Grace."

"Congratulations on the birth of your son," Mother said.

She received equal looks of pride. "Thank you, Your Grace," the earl said. He gestured to Miss Palmer. "Please allow me to introduce Lady Tarrington's sister, Miss Palmer."

With flushed cheeks that only added to her beauty, Miss Palmer curtsied without lifting her gaze.

"My, you are even more beautiful up close," Mother said.

Blushing, Miss Palmer stammered, "Th-thank you. Your Grace."

Suttenberg smiled, hoping to steady her nervousness. "I trust your ankle has healed?"

She took her lip between her teeth briefly, those lush, sweet lips he'd kissed once. "Yes, Your Grace. It's . . . well." Her blush turned crimson, and her eyes narrowed as if she were in pain.

Apparently the question had the opposite effect. Mother looked at her in—was that sympathy or pity?—and moved on to meet the others. Pity was never a good sign. The duchess pitied the unfortunate, not ladies who won her approval. Miss Palmer took a step back and bumped into a small table. It teetered, setting a vase to wobbling. She turned and tried to catch the vase but knocked over a small picture in a frame.

Some of the younger guests giggled. Miss Blackwood,

the daughter of a marquis that his mother hoped he'd consider, stared at Miss Palmer as if she were a street urchin.

After throwing a withering glare at the uncharitable girls, Suttenberg went to Miss Palmer. He steadied the vase and righted the picture frame. "No harm done," he said.

After darting him a glance, she closed her eyes and swallowed as if trying to prevent tears.

Poor girl. She'd never survive the spotlight always shining on a duchess. Odd, but when she'd pretended to be Aphrodite, she'd been so poised, so confident, not the bashful, clumsy girl he saw now. Even when she'd been limping and frightened of his horse, she hadn't been so awkward.

Miss Palmer's sister, the Countess of Tarrington, went to her and squeezed her hand, giving the girl a sympathetic smile, then straightened her posture as if giving unspoken guidance. Miss Palmer followed suit, but kept her gaze downcast, her cheeks still reddened.

To keep attention off the distraught girl, Suttenberg continued guiding his mother to each guest as if nothing had happened. He greeted Miss Blackwood and her parents without undue warmth, lest they be too encouraged by his attentions, and he welcomed Mr. Gregory, a longtime friend of the family, who managed to show both deference and friendly affection for them both.

Suttenberg clapped Gregory on the shoulder. "Always glad to see you, Gregory."

"You as well, Your Grace." Mr. Gregory smiled and glanced at the duchess, his smile turning affectionate. "You're radiant, as usual, Duchess."

As Mr. Gregory and Mother exchanged pleasantries, Miss Palmer practically disappeared into the background. After the butler announced dinner, they filed into the dining room and sat to a sumptuous meal, but Bennett hardly tasted it as his focus returned often to Hannah Palmer. She seldom spoke to her dinner companions. Trying to keep to his vow to avoid temptation, and to spare her the guests' focus, he hardly looked at her all evening. But she occupied his thoughts all night, even as he tried to sleep.

The following day, after he took all interested guests out to enjoy a morning hunt, he returned home while many of the guests went on an extended ride. Inside the stables, he brushed his hunter, enjoying the uncomplicated pleasure of bonding time with his horse. After he'd finished, he headed for the hunting lodge, absently glancing at the pasture behind the stables where some of the horses grazed. Miss Palmer stood with her arms crossed on top of the fence, her chin resting on them, her attention wholly focused on a pair of colts prancing as if performing a dance for her. Despite his best intentions, he went to her.

He leaned against the fence and watched her, admiring the soft curve of her cheek. His fingers itched to touch it. Puzzled by her rapt attention on something that clearly terrified her, he asked, "What is it about horses that frightens you?"

With a little start, she turned to him and smiled ruefully, "I have always been afraid of them; I feel small and helpless next to such big creatures. But when my brother Armand got a new horse, he wanted so badly for me to ride with him. So he brought out one of the smaller mares and convinced me to ride. I had no sooner found my seat when something spooked the horse, and she started running. I was terrified. I was sure I would fall off and die."

"But you didn't."

"No. I stayed on somehow. My brother caught up to us and pulled the horse to a stop. He pulled me off and held me, telling me over and over he was so sorry. I shook all over. I realized how very little I could control such a big, strong animal. And I don't really understand them. They seem so volatile. They are beautiful, and I love watching them—from a safe distance."

He nodded. "If you understand them, they may not seem so frightening. For example, look." He pointed to a colt with his ears pricked forward. "He's curious. But look at those two at the top of the hill. See the position of their heads? They're aggressive. When they put their heads down and flatten their ears, they're angry. And that one is pawing. He's about to charge. But those four are relaxed—you can tell by their heads and their postures. That one over there, the little mare, she's listening to us. See how her ears are turned our way?"

Her face brightened. "I see." Her smile turned rueful. "You know, I'm surprised I haven't noticed that before. I'm normally fairly observant about people. I'm surprised I didn't see that about horses."

"You have to spend time in their company to discern little clues like that."

"Yes, I suppose you're right." She returned her chin to her resting position with her arms atop the fence. "But they're easily spooked. Can that be predicted?"

"Sometimes. Sudden movements or loud noises will often do it. Some horses are more high-strung than others." He turned to study her. "What do you observe about people?"

She began an astonishingly accurate and detailed discourse about each of his guests—their names, habits, and relationships—ending with, "Dr. Power doesn't mind everyone asking him for free medical advice. He's such a gentle, fatherly sort of man. Oh, and Miss Blackwood has set her cap for you, in case you didn't notice."

He nodded. "I did notice. My mother wants me to notice her in return. She fits all my mother's requirements. From the exterior, she seems ideal, but she's too calculating. I'm not entirely sure she has a heart."

Miss Blackwood would not stoop to help a lady who couldn't remember the steps during a dance the way Miss Palmer had. And he could never allow a woman like Miss Blackwood to see the weakness deep inside him, a weakness he feared would reveal itself if he let down his guard.

She smiled as if they were comrades. "I didn't want to say that about her; it would have been impolite. She probably rides beautifully." Her tone turned wistful.

"She does."

Miss Palmer slumped a little. "I'd never make a good wife for a duke or a lord. I'd be better suited for a country squire—someone who won't seek London society."

He ached to tell her that it didn't matter. With a lady like her at his side, he wouldn't feel so alone, wouldn't feel the need to keep up pretenses every moment of the day. But she was right; she'd be happier living the country life with a man who wouldn't subject her to moments when her shyness would cause her to become flustered and knock over vases, to the delight of gossips.

Her voice drew him from his thoughts. "Mr. Gregory and your mother have a particular fondness for one another."

He chuckled softly. "Oh, no, Mr. Gregory is a longtime friend."

"He doesn't want simple friendship, and I don't believe she does, either."

"Why do you say that?"

"They converse like old friends, but every once in a while, they cast longing glances at one another. And once he looked at her with such admiration that I almost teared up. He seems a fine man."

Odd, but Mother had never mentioned Mr. Gregory in that particular way. He'd have to ask her about it later. His mother remarrying? He turned that over in his mind. Honestly he was surprised she hadn't yet. He'd been five when his father died, and the duchess had been alone ever since. She was still an attractive woman, only in her early fifties, and had a great deal to offer a husband—wit, intelligence, kindness. Certainly she ought to remarry if she had that desire. Suttenberg agreed with Hannah Palmer; Gregory was a fine man.

Miss Palmer's voice broke in to his thoughts. "Your mother is a gracious lady."

He studied her face. "Do you think so?"

"I do. She wasn't condescending at my awkwardness when you presented me to her or when I acted like a clumsy fool. And she's inordinately fond of you."

He smiled. "She is, fortunately. And I hope to stay in her good graces."

"Surely you're not worried. Why, with such a paragon of a son, she must be very proud." She smiled as if enjoying a private joke.

He shook his head. "I'm no paragon, as you well know."

A small chestnut horse trotted to him, nodding her head and nickering a greeting. He smiled affectionately at the old mare. She stretched her neck out over the fence. Miss Palmer stiffened but didn't step away.

"Good morning, Daydream." He rubbed the mare's nose and ran his hands along her neck.

"Are your mother's expectations so high?" Her nonjudgmental compassion as she gazed at him had an odd effect on his tongue, loosening it in a way that it normally would not.

"I became the Duke of Suttenberg at the age of five."

She nodded and recited, "Bennett Arthur Partridge, the Fifteenth Duke of Suttenberg." She smiled. "The current book of Peerage is expected reading for any young lady who will have a Season in London." She sobered and touched his sleeve. "What happened then?"

"My mother explained that my rank carried a great deal of responsibility. I not only must learn to manage my lands, but be an example of a peer of the realm to everyone who would watch me. My father had a reputation for excellence, and she wanted me to follow his legacy."

"A heavy load for a five-year-old." She regarded him somberly.

He rested one arm on top of the fence while the other continued rubbing Daydream, who nuzzled him and wuffled in his ear. "She told me the time for catching frogs and learning my letters in the nursery was over. I went to school the next day and spent the rest of my life trying to live up to family ideals."

She covered his hand with hers. Warmth soaked in from the contact all the way to his heart. For a mad instant, he almost tore off their gloves and touched her hand-to-hand, cheek-to-cheek, lip-to-lip.

Softly, she asked, "What would happen, do you think, if you failed to live up to that ideal?"

"I'd disappoint her. That alone would be unbearable. And I'd disappoint everyone who relies on me to do it right—my younger brother and sister, their children. I'd be a failure."

"Don't you think that's only a natural part of being human—having weaknesses?"

"I'm a duke. I'm not allowed to have weaknesses."

"Everyone has weaknesses." The softness in her eyes became almost too difficult to bear.

He let out a long, slow breath. "I do have a terrible weakness. My grandfather on my mother's side was Italian—hot-blooded and passionate. He dueled a dozen men, killing over half of them, and had a dozen lovers, leaving illegitimate children scattered over four countries. In the end, his temper proved his undoing. He started a fight, and his opponent killed him. If I let go of my self-control, I'll be just like him."

She said nothing for a moment, just sat there squeezing his hand. "You aren't like that. And you won't become that, not even if you let go once in a while."

"I might. Look how I behaved at the ball. I kissed you, someone I'd only just met, and I drew a sword."

"Well, then, clearly the answer is to avoid masques. And pirates." A teasing light entered her soft brown eyes.

He shook his head, uncomfortably aware of how much he'd confided in this sweet girl. "Most of my friends don't know anything I told you."

"Do you have the wrong friends, or do you have an aversion to allowing them to see the real man inside?"

He hesitated. "I'm not certain."

"I'll keep your confidence," she said gravely.

He gazed at the lovely lady next to him. How could he could have been so foolish as to have overlooked her before? At first he'd been blinded by his quick assessment that she was too young and shy and awkward. He'd almost missed the joy of knowing her, of knowing what it was like to reveal his true self to someone. Hannah Palmer was artless, with no hidden agenda, no practiced flirtatiousness, no carefully cultivated games.

And she allowed him to be his true self in her presence. He hadn't spoken to anyone with such candor in longer than he could remember. The idea of spending all his days with such an enchanting, genuine lady left him almost desperate with longing.

Daydream bumped Hannah with her nose. The girl leaped back.

"She won't hurt you," Suttenberg said soothingly. "This is Daydream. She's very gentle." He held out a hand to her. "Come meet her. She's the first horse I learned to ride."

Hannah placed her hand in his and let him lead her back to the fence. He put her hand under Daydream's nose to get her scent. After the chestnut snuffled, Suttenberg put Hannah's small hand on the horse's neck and guided her to stroke it.

"Look at her ears," he murmured. "And see how she holds so still? She likes you."

Hannah's mouth curved in a tentative smile. "I want to touch her." She removed her glove and put her bare hand on the horse's neck.

"She's softest right between the nostrils." He petted the area to demonstrate.

Hannah eyed him before she followed his lead, her lips curving upward in delight. "She's just like velvet."

They stood side by side, petting a horse as if it were the most natural thing in the world. He'd never felt so comfortable with a lady before—comfortable except for a growing longing to draw her into his arms.

If only he could keep her at his side and hold on to the relaxed, easy joy of having her near. A few loose curls slipped from her hat and framed her face. She glanced up at him with an almost teasing smile. The image of Aphrodite superimposed itself over her. Aching, burning to touch her, he traced a finger down her cheek.

"You're unlike anyone I've ever met," he murmured.

Warmth and affection shone in her eyes. No moment in his entire life had ever been as perfect as this. No lady had ever been so perfectly suited for him, the real him, Bennett.

He cupped her face with his hands, leaned in, and kissed her. She kissed him back, with more heat than before, and he slipped into a sweet bliss he only experienced with her.

"Marry me," he whispered as he broke the kiss. "I need you. I want you."

She stared, her mouth working silently, then said, "I thought we agreed I'm not suited for the role of duchess."

He pulled her in against his chest, savoring the softness of her body and the way it molded against his. "I don't care. I don't care if you can't ride and don't like large gatherings and get flustered when everyone watches you. I need you for quiet moments like this, when I can be who I really am and tell you my thoughts. When I'm with you, I forget I'm the Duke of Suttenberg, and I become just Bennett Partridge."

She put a hand on his cheek, the same cheek she'd slapped after their last kiss. "You'd soon regret marrying me—your mother would disapprove, I'd embarrass you in public, I'd fail you in some crucial way. Something will happen, or fail to happen, and you'll wish you'd married someone more like Miss Blackwood—with a heart, of course." She raised up and kissed him softly. "Thank you for the offer, but I must decline."

He tightened his hold on her. "Don't. Please don't."

"Perhaps we oughtn't spend time together alone." Regret dimmed the light in her brown eyes. She stepped out of his arms and walked away.

Pain pierced his heart. His hot blood screamed at him to run after her, to do whatever he must to secure her in his life. Control. Maintain control. He fisted his hands and turned away. He must accept her logic, however cruel. She wasn't suited for London life and all that would be required of her as a duchess. His duty came above his own need, the need for a wife he could love, a wife who would love him for who he was.

He hung his head and almost gave in to the urge to weep.

Nine

Hannah sat in her bedroom with her fingers to her lips, reliving the glorious kiss of Bennett Arthur Partridge, the Fifteenth Duke of Suttenberg, and made no attempt to suppress the tears streaming down her face.

Bennett. He wanted her to love him for the man, not the duke. And heaven help her, she did love him. His proposal seemed so sincere, as had his kiss. She'd almost accepted. The idea of sharing her life with a man of such strength and gentleness, of sophisticated polish and the type of kindness that he removed a saddle to let her ride his horse, who confided his most private fears, who kissed her like she was the most important and loved woman in his life, left her breathless with wonder. Oh, she yearned to accept.

His proposal had probably been another momentary lapse, like those that had driven his actions at the ball. If she'd accepted, he, as a man of honor, would have followed through and married her. But he'd grow to regret it. And he'd resent her when she failed him at every turn. Not only would she be the duchess everyone would ridicule, which would shame him and his family, but she'd fail him as a wife in her most basic role, that of bearing a future duke. He needed an heir; to deny him that would be unthinkable. The sorrowing suspicion that had plagued her for years sharpened into true pain. Now that it was Bennett's children she wanted...

The harsh truth glared at her. She lay down on the window seat and gave in to her grief. After a time, her tears dried. She stared at the trees swaying in the autumn wind, casting off their gold and crimson leaves, as if casting off hope for life.

Alicia came in, carrying the train of her riding habit over her left arm. "How was your morning? Did you enjoy your walk?"

Hannah pushed herself up to a seated position and hoped her sister wouldn't detect her sorrow. "It was . . . pleasant."

Alicia sat next to her, her cheeks wind-kissed pink. "I'm so glad to hear it." She let out a happy sigh. "It was a lovely day to ride. The men caught several pheasants for dinner, so we'll eat well tonight."

Hannah tried to muster some enthusiasm. "Good. I haven't have pheasant in ages."

Her performance didn't convince her sister. "Do you have another headache? You know, you should consult Dr. Power. He's a sought-after physician in London."

"No, I'm well." She drew in her knees and hugged them.

"What then?"

"I don't think I should go to London."

"Because you bumped into a table last night under the duchess's scrutiny?"

"Not only that. I just . . . I don't think the kind of man who'd want to marry me will be there."

"Where do you think he'll be?"

"Living in a small estate in the country."

Alicia put an arm around her. "Oh, my dear, you have much to offer any man. Don't make assumptions about them; you'll be wrong most of the time." She smiled wryly, probably remembering all the assumptions she'd made about Cole. "Give it a month. If you hate London, we'll go home and see about finding you a poor country squire."

Of course, Hannah's failure to produce heirs might disappoint even a poor country squire, but at least the fate of a duchy wouldn't be at stake. And she couldn't bear such disappointment in Bennett's eyes. She almost let out a moan. She must not think of him as Bennett; he must be His Grace or the duke forevermore.

"As you wish." She glanced at Alicia, too weary to continue this conversation with her emotions so raw. "I think I feel a headache coming on. Perhaps I shall take a nap."

Alicia stood. "I'll let you rest." She closed the door quietly behind her. But a few minutes later, Alicia returned. "I hope you don't mind, but I asked Dr. Power to look in on you."

Oh dear, caught in her lie. But if he was a sought-after London doctor . . .

"Very well. Send him in." Hannah stood.

The silver-haired Dr. Power entered. "Miss Palmer? I understand you are suffering from a headache?"

"I'm better now. But . . ."

He passed an assessing glance over her. "Can I do anything for you?"

"Doctor, may I ask you a question?"

"Of course." The kindly gentleman took a few steps nearer.

She let out her breath, shaking all over. If a renowned doctor confirmed her fears, it would cement them forever. And if she knew ahead of time that she couldn't have children, she should not, in good conscience, marry anyone, unless perhaps to a widower who already had them. Maybe the doctor knew of a treatment or a way she could still bear a child.

The idea of sharing her life or having children with anyone but Bennett left her empty.

The doctor adjusted his spectacles. "Anything you tell me will be kept in strictest confidentiality."

She nodded, clasping and unclasping her hands, and drew a shaking breath. "I wondered if you have much experience with women who get headaches so strong that light and noise becomes intolerable and often last all day, sometimes longer."

"Yes, I have a few patients who suffer from that malady."

She hesitated, afraid to ask the question; afraid of its answer. "I was sickly as a child, and while I'm healthier now, I still have those kinds of headaches. And I wondered, are they symptoms of something worse? Something that make it difficult for a woman to bear a child?"

He gestured for her to sit and took a seat next to her. He gave her a fatherly smile. "No, miss. I know of no correlation between those kind of headaches and the ability to procreate."

She held her breath. "Truly?"

"Yes, absolutely."

She pressed a hand to her chest, hardly daring to believe it. The dark fear she'd borne for years dissipated, but didn't entirely vanish. It seemed too perfect to be real.

As if sensing she needed further proof, he added, "My patients who suffer from the sick headache, also known as migraines, have many sons and daughters. There is no reason to believe you won't, when the time comes."

She searched his face. A respected London doctor surely knew what he was about. And she'd observed his confidence and sincerity over the course of their visit. As the reality of his assurance sank in, she almost sobbed in relief. She might still be a green, unpolished girl who suffered from shyness and awkwardness, but at least she might know the joys of motherhood. If she ever married.

"I can't tell you how glad I am to hear that."

"Have you carried that fear all your life?"

She nodded.

"There are many reasons why women cannot conceive or deliver healthy babies—some for reasons we may never understand except that it is God's will—but your headaches should not preclude you from bearing children."

"Thank you. I'm so relieved." Tears welled up in her eyes as the last of her fears vanished.

"I'm happy to have provided some comfort to you." He patted her hand and left.

Hugging herself, Hannah leaned her head against the window. She might be a mother someday. A weight lifted from her soul.

But her ability to produce heirs didn't make her capable of fulfilling the role of a duchess with all its responsibilities and pressures—not to mention being married to a paragon, whom everyone would think had settled for someone without his charm and elegance.

Perhaps someday she'd find another man who would kiss her the way Bennett had and who would help her stop dreaming about the man she could never have. She didn't know whether to laugh or cry at the absurd thought.

Ten

Trying to forget the sweet girl who'd stolen his heart, Suttenberg threw himself into his duties, meeting with his steward, hosting his guests, hunting, fencing, and providing entertainment. His efforts mocked him as meaningless.

On the last night of the house party, Suttenberg sat next to his mother. With a little luck, his guests would view his mood as stylishly aloof instead of wounded. How would he ever find a lady who would take Hannah Palmer's place in his heart? He'd never believed love would happen so quickly, nor take such hold of him.

Against his will, he glanced at her—so lovely and untouchable that it almost hurt to look at her. She sat amid a small group of guests, watching them with that assessing way of hers, giving almost no input unless questioned. Sometimes her answers brought laughter, some brought pensiveness, but mostly she remained quiet, content to observe. Miss

Blackwood eyed her with cold disdain, but Hannah appeared to give no notice except for glances akin to amusement.

The duchess leaned over and spoke in his ear. "You're right, Suttenberg. Miss Blackwood would be a perfect duchess, except the primary emotion she possesses is contempt." She paused. "Pity Miss Palmer is so shy. Not only is she uncommonly lovely, she's intriguing and has a depth I've only just noticed."

He nodded, not trusting himself to speak. Remembering his vow to pay more attention to the gentleman that Hannah Palmer suggested had captured his mother's affection, he looked about the room for Mr. Gregory. Their longtime friend, a gentleman with a modest estate, glanced at Mother, a soft smile flitting over his features. Mother smiled back and let out an almost imperceptible sigh.

Suttenberg eyed his mother. "Why is it that you never remarried?"

"Oh, well, you know . . ." She waved a hand.

"No, I don't know. Tell me."

She studied her fingers, looking almost wistful. "I am the Duchess of Suttenberg. I cannot marry just anyone."

"Why? You've been alone a long time. I have the estate well in hand. You have a generous jointure. Why couldn't you follow your heart?"

"It wouldn't be right if I were to marry too far below my station."

"I can't imagine why not. Who would dare gainsay you?"

"Well, no one, of course, but any good man would know not to reach too high."

"Any good man would follow his heart." As the words left his mouth, he gave a start. If he hadn't heard himself utter it, he would never have believed he'd made such a statement. As he turned it over in his mind, it rang true. Whether it was a secret belief he'd only now acknowledged or a profound change in his principles, he couldn't say.

His mother stared at him in wonder. "You are the last person I would have expected to hear speak those words."

He let out an uneasy laugh and tried to shrug. "If he's respectable and will treat you well, then he's surely not beneath you."

She said nothing for a while. Finally she turned tortured eyes upon him. "I have found someone. But you wouldn't approve. And I can't disappoint you."

Aghast, he stared. He lowered his voice. "You are in love with someone, but you haven't married him because I wouldn't think he's good enough?"

She flicked an imaginary speck off her gown. "I know all too well how important image is to this family. To you."

"Hang the family image. Do you love him?"

She let out a sigh. "Yes."

"Does he love you?"

She glanced at Mr. Gregory, who caught her gaze. His features turned to alarm as if he suspected they discussed something that distressed her. "Yes, I believe he does."

Suttenberg stood and offered a hand to her. "Come with me, please." They crossed the room to Mr. Gregory. "Sir, please join me in the conservatory."

Mr. Gregory paled and glanced anxiously at the duchess. "Of course, Your Grace."

Unbelievable that a man who had known Suttenberg since he was an infant addressed him with such deference. Was he so pompous and untouchable that he drove everyone away, including suitors of his sister and mother?

He led them to the conservatory. "Close the door, Gregory, if you please."

The gentleman did so, looking as if he were about to be tied to a post and lashed.

Suttenberg eyed him. "Your estate is small but fairly prosperous, is it not?"

Gregory blinked. "Yes, Your Grace. You yourself have helped me with crop techniques, my tenants are hardworking, and we turn a modest profit every year."

"So, you aren't destitute?"

"No, Your Grace."

"Has anyone ever accused you of being a fortune hunter?"

Mr. Gregory stepped back in surprise. "No, Your Grace."

"And you aren't a rake? You don't gamble or drink excessively or trifle with women?"

"Oh, no, Your Grace." He looked more horrified with every question.

Suttenberg paced across the floor amid a plethora of tropical plants, enjoying himself but trying to look grim and thoughtful. "So, you have much to offer a wife?"

"I . . ." Gregory trailed off. "I think so, but that depends on the lady."

Suttenberg nodded. "I understand that you have formed an attachment for the duchess."

After another glance at Mother, Mr. Gregory drew himself up and spoke to them both. "Yes, Your Grace. I have loved the duchess for years."

"Did you declare yourself?"

He hung his head. "As much as I want to, no. I know when I'd be reaching too far above me."

Suttenberg turned to his mother. "Do you love him?"

"Yes," Mother almost sobbed.

"Do you care about his rank or his wealth?"

"No."

"Would you marry him if he asked you—if I gave my blessing?"

She looked like a child about to reach for a longed-for gift. "Yes."

"Then for heaven's sakes, Gregory, you have my blessing. Will you two just get married and stop mooning over each other?"

Mr. Gregory and the duchess ran into each other's arms. Suttenberg turned away to give them privacy.

The duchess's voice stopped him. "Bennett."

He froze. She hadn't called him by his Christian name in years.

She gave him a dazzling smile. "Perhaps you ought to take your own advice, son. If love is good enough for me, it's good enough for you, as well."

He paused with his brows raised.

"I believe there is a lovely girl in the other room, perhaps without all the qualities one would expect from a duchess, but with many qualities desirable in a wife—a girl you can't seem to keep your eyes off of." She smiled as she rested her head on Gregory's shoulder.

Suttenberg made no comment as he left the conservatory. He shouldn't be surprised Mother had noticed his preference for Hannah Palmer, despite his attempts to keep his feelings hidden. She was right; Hannah might not be as cool and poised as some believed a duchess must be, but she was in possession of every character trait he most admired. And he loved her. He should take his own advice.

He sought out Lord and Lady Tarrington, inviting them to join him in the library. They eyed him curiously as he paced. "I have a problem. I have fallen in love with Hannah. I asked her to marry me yesterday—I hope you will forgive me for not seeking your permission first—but she refused. She said she's not the kind of person who would make a good duchess. But I cannot let her go. And I believe she has feelings for me, as well."

Tarrington grinned. "Permission granted. But she must willingly agree to marry you; I won't coerce her."

"Nor would I want you to, of course. Lady Tarrington?"

She narrowed her gaze. "You kissed her again, didn't you?"

He gulped. "I did. I can't seem to control myself around her. She is the most wonderful, remarkable, genuine lady I have ever met, and I am quite hopelessly in love with her."

The Countess of Tarrington stepped forward and raised her hand.

He tensed.

She patted his cheek and smiled. "Then go and woo her—gently."

He almost shouted his happiness. After giving instructions to the nearest servants, he practically raced to the drawing room where the other guests gathered. "Ladies and gentlemen, I suggest we dance. Miss Blackwood, since you are such an accomplished pianist, will you play for us? Begin with a waltz, if you please."

Without any expression, even surprise at the request for a waltz at the beginning of the evening, the cold beauty stood and went immediately to the piano. The gentlemen helped servants push furniture to the edges of the room and roll up the carpets to transform the drawing room into a small ballroom.

Suttenberg went to Hannah and held out a hand. "Dance with me, my Aphrodite, I beg you."

She blinked, and a slow smile curved her delicious lips. Her chin lifted, and her posture straightened. "I'm not certain I ought to dance with a mere mortal such as you at two different balls."

"Then I thank you from the bottom of my heart that you have deemed me worthy of your divine presence once again."

As he took her in dance position, his body sighed as if finding its missing parts. She slipped completely into the goddess role and moved with him with all of his Aphrodite's grace and poise.

While he spun her around the room, contentment and joy wrapped around him. "You know, a goddess could easily play the role of duchess."

Her façade slipped for a second. "A goddess does whatever she wants. A duchess has to obey society laws and have large parties and ride horses."

"A duchess doesn't have to do anything. Most view her as almost a goddess."

"But she's expected to follow certain conventions. And a duke needs a duchess who will."

"Not this duke."

Her eyes widened, but he said nothing further. Instead, he kept conversation on lighter matters, flirting with her as he had at the masque and enjoying her flirting in return.

As the dance ended and they bowed and curtsied, he took her hand. "Take a turn about the gardens with me?"

She went still, considering.

He held his breath. If she refused, he'd try again and again. He would not lose her.

Eleven

Hannah paused. Did she dare go outside alone with Bennett? He had a habit of kissing her when they were alone, unless she was limping.

She glanced at her sister, who smiled so broadly at her that a light seemed to come from her. "You appear to have won over my sister," Hannah said.

"At least she didn't slap me this time. I'll have to tread more lightly around your family—very strong women. Katherine would be proud."

She smiled at the reference to the Shakespearean characters they'd discussed. She could apologize for her sister's conduct, but apologizing for the actions of a countess seemed presumptuous. Besides, at the time he'd deserved it. She settled for giving him a saucy grin that would have pleased Aphrodite.

As Bennett led her outside, Hannah inhaled the chill, earthy air. A bright moon bathed the gardens in a soft glow.

Their feet crunched in a carpet of fallen leaves. The pale patch in his hair seemed to glow in the semidarkness.

Chill bumps peppered her arms. "Perhaps I should have gotten a shawl."

He took off his coat and draped it around her shoulders. "Don't go in just yet, please."

She cocked her head, as daring as she'd been on the night of the masque. "Are you going to kiss me again?"

"Most certainly. But first I must tell you something. I love you."

Her breath stilled. He loved her? Despite all her shortcomings?

He took both of her hands in his. "I want you at my side wherever I go. I want to share with you my estates and introduce you to my tenants. I want to show you what London has to offer and take you to the seashore where we'll swim together. I want to tell you what I'm thinking and feeling, knowing I can trust you to accept me as I am, a human with fears and weaknesses. I want to hold you in my arms at night and wake up with you in the morning. I want you to always be honest with me and tell me what you think." He drew her closer, gently, as if giving her a chance to step away if she wanted. But into his arms is where she longed to go.

She opened her mouth to speak, but he put a finger over her lips. "I want to get old with you. I don't care for parties and balls; those aren't required to serve in Parliament. And on the occasions we do attend a gathering, if you remain quiet, everyone will think you're mysterious."

She latched on to the sentiment her sister had expressed once. Perhaps they were both right.

Bennett continued, "If you only choose to surround yourself with your closest friends, people will think you are discerning. If you only have small parties, society will view them as exclusive. When you find yourself obligated to enter society, bow to the queen, and so forth, all you need to do is pretend to put on your Aphrodite mask and you'll be perfect. The rest of the time, be your genuine self. I love you as you are."

He loved her. He truly loved her! And he had given such carefully worded, wise counsel that she actually dared believe him. The moment he called her Aphrodite, she automatically fell into the poise she'd adopted at the ball while in costume. So she could do it at will. Now that an expert had assured her that she had no reason to fear that she'd fail to produce an heir, her greatest fear of all, her other concerns faded away as too meaningless to consider.

"Please, Hannah, please marry me. I promise I'll live every day trying to make you happy."

A little ripple of pleasure ran over her skin at the sound of her given name uttered in his voice. She kissed his finger still over her lips.

He removed the finger and offered a sheepish smile, but intensity, almost desperation, darkened his eyes.

Stepping nearer, she placed a hand on his chest. His heart thumped against her palm. "Before I give you my answer, I want you to promise me something."

"Anything." He ripped off his gloves and touched her face, running his fingers up and down her cheeks, a pleasantly distracting motion.

She touched that blond patch of hair that contrasted so sharply with his dark waves. It was, indeed soft, but no softer than the rest of his hair. "Promise me you will only wear your mask of the paragon in public, and when you're alone with me, you will be yourself."

He awarded her the most glorious smile she'd ever seen.

"You are the only one with whom I trust to be myself, and if you call me Bennett, I will have no trouble remembering."

"Then I shall, Bennett. And if you can be the real you in my presence, I can be Aphrodite in public as your wife."

"As my duchess."

She smiled, no longer terrified at the thought. "As your duchess."

He wrapped his arms around her and kissed her. The explosion of warmth and pleasure nearly took her breath away.

The love, the sheer passion, pouring into her through his kiss transported her to a realm of joy and beauty she'd never dared dream. Every inch of her body sighed as the missing piece to the puzzle of her life fitted into place. All her life had led to this single, glorious, perfect moment. And she belonged there. With him.

Twelve

Hannah smiled at her husband as he escorted her into the ballroom at Tarrington Castle. Though this year the Countess of Tarrington's ball was not a masque, as last year's had been, Hannah firmly wore her Aphrodite persona as if she were in costume. When she entered a room on the arm of the Duke of Suttenberg, such a feat came easy.

He glanced at her, the corners of his lips curving and his eyes shining with adoration. "You look beautiful, my goddess."

"You are handsome as ever, my delicious mortal," she purred.

Abandoning his usual reserve, he broke into a broad grin.

All eyes fixed on them, and murmurs of what a handsome couple they were, and how mysterious the duchess was, rippled around the room. Hannah only smiled. They were, indeed, a handsome couple, and she'd grown comfortable smiling mysteriously when she could think of nothing to say. As the Duchess of Suttenberg, she'd managed not to embarrass herself or her husband during the London Season, and she'd even bowed to the queen and backed away wearing a hoopskirt and train without tripping. And, if her suspicions were correct, she now carried Bennett's child. How different she was from the girl she'd been a year ago.

Alicia and Cole greeted them. Hannah hugged her sister, whom she now outranked—a thought that always made her shake her head at the ironies of fate. As she caught the glances of familiar faces, she nodded. Fortunately, she'd built a reputation for having little to say.

As the duke paused to speak with someone, Mr. Hill approached. "Good evening, Duchess."

She turned her head slowly and said with cool reserve, "Mr. Hill."

"I—" He glanced at the duke. "I just wanted to congratulate you. I wish you all the best." He smiled tentatively.

"Thank you, Mr. Hill."

After casting another furtive glance at the duke, Mr. Hill bowed and backed away. Nearby, the Buchanan twins flirted with young girls barely out of the schoolroom.

The musicians struck up the dance introduction, and Cole and Alicia headed up the line. The duke led Hannah to stand next to them. Others lined up behind them. As the dance began, Hannah smiled at her husband, admiring the grace with which he moved, the beauty of his face, the signature blond shock of hair surrounded by dark waves. Sometimes she still could hardly believe he was hers.

As the set ended, he grinned mischievously at her. She knew that grin. Trying to keep a silly smile off her face, she went with him into the library. Bennett tugged her into his arms and kissed her so thoroughly she wasn't sure she could continue standing.

After he ended the kiss, he chuckled. "I couldn't help myself. You looked so tempting, I just couldn't resist."

"How very fortunate for me." She put a hand on either side of his face and caressed his cheeks. "And now, allow me not to resist."

She kissed him until he groaned. "Aphrodite, you must leave off or I won't be able to go back into that room full of people. I am only a mortal, after all. There is a limit to my endurance."

"I'm counting on that," she said huskily.

They cast off their masks of the duke and the goddess and spent a few minutes together as just Bennett and Hannah, the happiest people at the Autumn Ball.

ABOUT DONNA HATCH

Donna Hatch is the award-winning author of the best-selling "Rogue Hearts Series." She discovered her writing passion at the tender age of 8 and has been listening to those voices ever since. A sought-after workshop presenter, she juggles her day job, freelance editing, multiple volunteer positions, not to mention her six children (seven, counting her husband), and still manages to make time to write. Yes, writing IS an obsession. A native of Arizona, she and her husband of over twenty years are living proof that there really is a happily ever after.

Visit Donna's website: DonnaHatch.com
Twitter: @DonnaHatch

What's in a Name?

Nancy Campbell Allen

OTHER WORKS BY NANCY CAMPBELL ALLEN

My Fair Gentleman
Beauty and the Clockwork Beast
A Timeless Romance Anthology: European Collection

Isabelle Webb Series
The Pharaoh's Daughter
Legend of the Jewel
The Grecian Princess

Faith of Our Fathers Series
A House Divided
To Make Men Free
Through the Perilous Fight
One Nation Under God

One

Penelope Timely used two hands to steady the piece of paper she read for a second, and then a third, time. The words swam in a jumbled mass the longer she stared at the paper, and she eventually lowered it to her lap, meeting a gaze identical to her own. Her twin sister stared at her, mouth agape, green eyes wide, dark golden curls hung in suspended animation before Persephone finally blinked and closed her mouth.

"Well, you'll have to go in my place, Penny." Persephone nodded as if the matter were good and settled. She glanced over her shoulder and lowered her voice. "That way I shall have plenty of time to spend with Gilroy, and Aunt Millicent will be none the wiser."

Penelope gaped in outrage, searching for words that were, for once in her life, absent. She blinked and looked at the paper again. "The duke wants to meet you, Persephone; he thinks he's been corresponding with *you*."

"Well, but he hasn't been, now has he?" Persephone

pulled a chair close to Penelope's and flounced into it. She took the letter from Penelope's nerveless fingers and smacked it on the kitchen table with an impressive *thwack*. "He's been corresponding with you, so therefore it's you he must meet."

"I only did this for your sake," Penelope snapped and, at Persephone's wild-eyed censure at her vocal volume, lowered her voice to a furious whisper. "I wrote to him because you begged me to and said that, as we would never, *ever* meet the man, it hardly signified which of us was the author!"

Persephone pouted prettily in a way that Penelope, despite bearing her sister's identical features, could never quite manage. Her efforts always resulted in more of a grimace. And therein lay the difference between the two. Everything about Persephone's personality and inner glow, well, glowed. Her interests represented those every gently-bred and reared young lady's should. She *enjoyed* embroidery. She *enjoyed* flower arranging. She *enjoyed* painting landscapes with water colors. The only thing Penelope ever wanted to paint were trilobites.

"Penny." Persephone grasped Penelope's hands and gave them a hearty squeeze. "The letter says he'll be here for the Ellshire Village Autumn Masquerade Ball and Festival, and even then only for the second day. All you will need to do is sit near him and chat during the supper picnic and bonfire. Simply engage in your customarily inappropriate conversation, and he will be instantly repelled." Persephone's eyes twinkled, and she clapped her hands. "Problem solved! He returns to London, I am free to pursue my *tendre* for Gilroy, and all will be perfect!"

"All will *not* be perfect, Persephone!" That her sister was a true nitwit never came as a surprise to Penelope. What did come as a surprise, time and again, was the fact that

What's in a Name?

Persephone always managed to pull Penelope into her ridiculous schemes, and when the jig was up, she somehow emerged smelling like the proverbial rose, while Penelope smelled like something that had crawled out of the stables.

"*She* is going to know. Somehow," Penelope stabbed a finger toward the parlor where their aunt sat, entertaining the vicar's wife, "she always finds out. She loathes me, and this is going to be one more reason she'll feel justified!"

The pretty pout appeared again, and Penelope refrained from rolling her eyes, but only just. "Penny, what makes you think she loathes you? I'm certain you're exaggerating."

Penelope leveled her sister with a flat stare. "The fact that she says, 'Penelope, you are loathsome. Go change into a day dress that doesn't have dirt smudges along the hem.'"

"Oh, now see? Telling a person she's loathsome because her dress is dirty is not nearly the same as *loathing* someone."

Penelope closed her eyes. "Persephone, this will never work. This is a disaster in the making, I can feel it."

"Nonsense." Persephone patted Penelope's hands and stood, smoothing her dress. "Now I must Plan." She tapped a finger against her lip, and Penelope stifled a groan. Things never went well when her sister Planned. "We shall say that you have developed a ferocious megrim by the afternoon of the second day of the festival. That way, when you are pretending to be me in the duke's esteemed company, I can be elsewhere with Gilroy. Aunt Millicent will be expecting to see only one of us in attendance that evening, so my presence won't be missed. Or rather your presence. Oh, stuff it, you know what I mean." Persephone waved a hand in the air. "Now, you shall wear one of my dresses, of course. Do not eat any sweets between now and the festival."

Penelope stood and snatched the duke's letter from the table. "I am going for a walk in the meadow," she said through clenched teeth. "Your debt to me is herculean, Persephone Timely, and I shall one day collect!" Penelope stomped to the kitchen door that led to the small garden just outside. "And furthermore, I'm not the one who sneaks extra strawberry tarts into her room each evening! Perhaps your dress will have to be taken *in* to fit me!"

Persephone gasped in outrage and spun on her heel, while Penelope narrowed her eyes and left the kitchen, feeling at least a small moment of victory.

"Don't eat any sweets between now and the festival . . ." she muttered as she left the yard, closing the white wooden gate behind her and setting off for the expanse of land behind the home, which in the spring was filled with wildflowers and butterflies, but now in autumn had begun to mellow and turn colors. There was a bite to the air, but rather than return to the house and retrieve her wrap, Penny wrapped her arms around her middle and walked briskly away from the modest home—her aunt and uncle's home, not hers or Persephone's.

Mama had loved her girls, had babied Persephone, and indulged Penelope's quaint interests in science and paleontology, often remarking fondly that Penny was so very much like her papa, who had been gone those many years. It was those very interests and traits that now stood to Penelope's detriment in Aunt Millicent Fanbecker's eyes. She had never liked the girls' papa and had been most irritated when her sister married such a strange, unconventional man, even though he was a baron. When Mama died two years ago, Millicent had taken the girls into her home because, of course, it was the right thing to do, and perhaps some of that audacious behavior could be eventually shamed out of that strange Penelope. Persephone was the darling, of course, and without Mama's gentle presence in her life to love her unconditionally, Penny felt very much alone indeed.

A gust of wind blew against her face, and Penny sucked in a breath. She rubbed her arms and quickly made her way across the long expanse of the meadow and into the trees that bordered the property. She picked her way through the underbrush, her feet crunching on leaves that had begun to fall. The path was familiar, and she was surprised she'd not worn a trench through it by now. A dry creek bed lay within the wooded area, and it was there she'd discovered a treasure trove. Fossils, one after the other, had revealed themselves to her patient hands in the past two years—her precious trilobites and sea creatures that had lived eons ago in the ocean that had since receded and now lay less than a mile away.

Her fingers itched for a small trowel and brush to search even further, but it was cold, and almost evening, and there was the matter of That Letter still clutched in her fingers. She looked at it again, trying to slow the thudding of her heart. The problems with actually meeting His Grace, the Duke of Wilmington, were so massive she hardly knew where to begin. She placed her cold fingertips against her forehead where she felt the beginnings of a real headache forming.

Aunt Millicent's husband, Uncle Horace, had a cousin who lived in London and was often invited to tea with the Countess of Everley, whose husband's sister had married the tenth Duke of Wilmington. His Grace had died two years earlier, leaving his one and only son as heir to the dukedom. The duchess was most diligent in her search for a wife for her son, who at his eventual death was in danger of passing the title to an odious distant relation, and such a thing would never do. And yet the new duke showed no interest in any one particular young lady, and in the last two Seasons had refused to step one immaculately polished boot into Almack's to peruse the latest flock. He had been introduced to, and summarily dismissed, each and every young debutante his mother paraded before him, telling her that he was looking for a Woman of Substance.

Uncle Horace's cousin mentioned to the Countess of Everley that there was, in fact, a very polished and beautiful young lady who lived near the country estate and whose father had been a baron. It was a station significantly removed from a dukedom; however, desperate times called for desperate measures, and if the young lady in question were indeed polished and beautiful, the chasm could be bridged—at least overlooked.

And so the duchess had written to Aunt Millicent, through the Countess of Everley and Uncle Horace's cousin, that her son, His Grace, the Duke of Wilmington, would be most interested in an introduction to Millicent's polished and perfect niece. She was sending along a note from His Grace—whose handwriting had looked suspiciously feminine to Penny—introducing himself and requesting a response, if the young lady would be so kind.

Penny wandered to her favorite tree stump next to her fossil sanctuary and sat, elbow on knee and chin in hand, the latest letter from His Grace dangling between her fingertips. It was a disaster of epic proportion; she could find no less dramatic phrasing to describe the predicament. Of course, the duchess meant her son wanted to correspond with *Persephone*. The perfect one. And after Millicent approached the girls with those initial letters in hand, all aflutter and beside herself at Persephone's good fortune, Persephone had cornered Penny and begged her twin to write the letter for her. Persephone couldn't be bothered with it, and as Doctor Gilroy Fitzroy, new to the village and most sought after indeed, had shown an interest in her, she couldn't possibly dream of betraying that interest by corresponding with another.

Penny had eyed her sister rather flatly, telling her that as her aim was to marry and establish a family of her own, what better place to do so than at the side of one of the country's noblest? His status, not to mention fortune, far eclipsed that of a lowly village doctor, a tradesman. Persephone would hear none of it, however. Her heart was taken, it was a matter of True Love, and that was that. It was actually one of the few times Penny had to admit a certain grudging respect for her sister, whose usual flights of fancy and demonstrations of vapidity were enough to have Penny's head pounding within an hour. Persephone was choosing her heart over a potential fortune, and Penny could hardly fault her for it.

So, to appease her sister, Penny had written the duke a charming note, signed Persephone's name to it, and it had been dispatched posthaste to London. Penny never expected to hear another word from His Grace, but she must have written something that caught his eye, for he responded himself—his handwriting notably more masculine this time—and Penny, in spite of herself, had been charmed by the dry wit evidenced in the bold scratches of the quill. She drafted a return note, again signing her sister's name, and had begun a correspondence of once, and then twice weekly letters. She had a stack of them at the bottom of her vanity drawer, tied with a blue ribbon and hidden beneath a box of fossils.

Six months' worth of letters, each more detailed, charming, and compelling than the last. His Grace was in his young thirties, passed through Eton and Oxford, took a personal interest in his estates, and enjoyed picnics and walks along the river in the rain. But most of all, he had an avid interest in, nay, *obsession* with paleontology. Penny closed her eyes, remembering the letter she'd received from His Grace admitting such an odd, and as he termed it "boring", interest. She had nearly swooned. And so now, six months later, His Grace, the Duke of Wilmington, believed Persephone Timely to be an avid hunter of fossils and disdainer of all water-colored landscapes and pointless embroidery.

Penny shivered again at a gust of wind and opened her eyes to look out over the autumn landscape. She had somehow assumed that she and the duke would never cross paths. He would never try to meet "Persephone" in person. That the beautiful world she lost herself in between his letters and hers would somehow suffice. That she would never be forced to admit her subterfuge, would never have to bear the scrutiny of a duchess who would find her significantly lacking as wifely material for her son, and would never have to face the wrath of Mean Aunt Millicent when her duplicity was discovered. She didn't think she would ever have to tell Persephone, "If by chance he comes to visit, you must pretend to be interested in ancient animal bones. Oh, and you also despise the color pink, much preferring blue." That would be well-received indeed. Persephone's dresses were always of the pink variation. Penelope's were, of course, blue.

And now he was actually going to arrive. She was going to have to pretend to be Persephone, which might be plausible if they were alone and she could merely speak for herself. But they wouldn't be alone, and others around them would be expecting Persephone to be, well, Persephone. The thought of not only trying to balance such a scene, but also to actually act like her sister, had her feeling slightly nauseated. She had been foolish in the extreme to imagine such a scenario would never occur. She had been so caught

What's in a Name?

up in the joy of actually having made a friend, a true friend, whose interests so perfectly mirrored her own. She realized the depth of her affection for her faceless friend when they were four months into their correspondence and he asked her to please, if she would, address him by his Christian name, Henry. And she had given him leave to call her by her Christian name, as well.

Penny frowned, feeling a sting in her eyes that she most certainly did not want there. She hadn't given him leave to use her name, but her sister's name, and she had shrugged off the sense of unease even then, wanting to hold her fantasy world close to her heart where it would safely stay.

"Fool, fool, fool," she muttered aloud and looked again at his most recent letter. He was coming to the village festival. Estate business would keep him away for the first day, but he was most looking forward to making her acquaintance for the second day's activities. She stood, restless, and wrapped her arms tightly around her middle. She didn't want to meet him as Persephone. She wanted to meet him as Penny. She would prefer him to be plain in appearance, although she supposed she could stomach it if he were thin and elegant, blond, most likely, and poetic. Not too terribly tall as to be intimidating. Or even if he were a bit portly, she wouldn't mind. It would make her feel less conscious about herself, for in spite of her identical likeness to Persephone, she never quite felt beautiful. She always felt awkward and out of place, because no matter how much she tried to be everything she should, she just . . . wasn't. Time and again, young men who assumed they would find the same package in her as in her sister had turned away disappointed.

Persephone could have her handsome doctor, and they would have handsome children who could paint watercolored bowls of fruit or embroider or set broken bones. Penny had no illusions about making a good match herself, because she couldn't hold the charade for so long. And rather than marry because it was expected, and be miserable in it, she'd rather be the spinster aunt who was content to sit in the dirt and dig for bones with a little shovel. She was just fine with that image in her head, until she imagined a life where she would never be irritated by little children underfoot or sit in companionable silence next to her sweetheart before the fire in the evenings with a good book.

And as for Henry . . . her heart ached a little, and she placed her hand to her chest. The Henry of her heart was gentle, not handsome enough to turn heads, and wasn't really a duke. Because Penelope Timely would never be a duchess.

Two

Henry Phillip Johnathan Arthur, eleventh Duke of Wilmington, flipped through the papers in his lap as the carriage continued on its way to his ancestral seat, Wilmington, which bordered the village of Ellshire. He was glad to leave the bad air and noise of London behind, welcoming the air that wafted through the carriage window he'd opened as soon as the big city was far enough behind him.

"Honestly, Henry, it grows colder by the minute," his mother, the Duchess of Wilmington said and pulled her fur-lined wrap closer to her thin, elegant frame.

"Apologies, Mother." The corner of his mouth lifted in a smile. "Might I assume the heating brick has outlived its purpose?" Henry slid the window closed, wishing he'd decided to ride alongside the carriage on his horse rather than reviewing estate business en route as a means of efficiency. His heart thrummed in anticipation, however, at the reason he'd decided to do so in the first place. The more work he could accomplish before reaching the estate, the more time he would have to pursue the primary reason for his visit. And Persephone Timely was well worth the inconvenience of riding in the carriage with his mother, who was never warm and despised the brisk, country air.

"No matter. We'll arrive in less than an hour." His mother smiled at him. "I must admit I was rather surprised you expressed an interest in the Ellshire Autumn Festival this year. Especially since you've not given it two thoughts since you were ten years old."

Henry shrugged, busying himself with his documents again, trying for a nonchalance he wasn't sure she'd believe. "I really should be more involved in the estate business, wouldn't you say? I've visited all the others this year. Wilmington is the ancestral seat, after all."

The duchess snorted. If duchesses were to do such a thing. "You only visited the other estates all year to avoid being in London for the Season."

He finished reading a page and scrawled a quick signature at the bottom. "I would never do such a thing, Mother."

She sniffed. "You would. You would, and you did. Rather makes me wonder if you've decided to remain a bachelor your whole life."

Henry glanced up at her, again with the half smile. "When I find a woman worthy of my time, I'll express an interest."

"How can you find such a paragon when you refuse to even look?"

He sighed. "It's distasteful, Mother. Like walking through a market and choosing the best piece of fruit. But how do I know it's not bruised or rotted on the inside?"

"You know very well the patronesses at Almack's are

discerning and extraordinarily exacting in their approval of each Season's debutantes. You'll not find a rotten piece of fruit in that esteemed assembly."

At that, he laughed and couldn't help himself. "Exacting in their examination of a young lady's breeding and decorum. They're all the same, those young women. Not a personality expressed among the lot. And those that manage to speak comment only on the weather."

"A duchess needn't have a personality. She must know how to host a ball and look elegant."

"Mother." He gave her his full regard as her eyes widened in innocence. "You have more of a personality than anyone I know, duchess or not. Male or female. What if Father had followed your brand of advice when looking for his bride?"

"We found each other."

"Exactly! And it didn't happen at Almack's. It was a horse race, as I recall?"

She turned her nose up and looked out the window. "I do not recall."

"Is it so much to ask that I want something more, something like you two had?" He felt the customary pang at the loss of his father. The tenth Duke of Wilmington had been a good man. An honorable man.

"When affections become engaged, the parting is all the more painful." Her confession was little more than a murmur, and he wasn't certain he'd heard her. He experienced a swift surge of love for his mother and leaned forward to clasp her fingers.

"I miss him too. Every day. And I want something more than a cold, polite marriage."

She smiled at him, her eyes suspiciously bright, and Henry sat back in his seat to allow her to collect herself. She wouldn't appreciate an acknowledgment of her near-tears. But if all went well with Miss Persephone Timely, he knew his mother would be very pleased indeed.

Penny entered the parlor the following afternoon slightly windblown, with her bonnet looped over her arm, sketchbook in hand, shawl falling from her shoulders, and very much unaware that they had visitors. She took in the scene with a modicum of confusion. Persephone sat ramrod straight on the settee, an elegant woman of indeterminate years sat across from her, and the largest man the home had likely ever seen stood at the hearth, his hands behind his back and feet set apart as though standing at ease before a military commander. His hair was as black as night, and his eyes were a startling sea foam green. He regarded her with a fair amount of what she could only assume was surprise as Aunt Millicent, also seated and adjacent to the other woman, motioned toward Penelope with a subtle flare of her nostrils.

"And this is my dear sister's other daughter, Persephone's twin."

Penny raised a brow at her aunt. Persephone's twin, was it? She now had no name of her own?

Persephone delicately cleared her throat, and Penny thought she might have detected a sympathetic wince. "Your Grace," she said to the man and then looked at the older woman, "and Your Grace, my sister, Miss Penelope Timely. Penny, may I introduce His Grace, the Duke of Wilmington, and his mother, the Duchess." She turned back to the guests. "We are, as you can indeed see, twins." She smiled at Penny with wide eyes and patted the seat next to her on the settee.

Penny's feet adhered themselves to the floor, and her

astonished gaze fitted itself to the large man, her brain scrambling for a sense of cohesion, of rational thought. He wasn't supposed to be in the vicinity yet—and certainly not in the front parlor! He also wasn't at all how she imagined him to be. The reality was much, much worse than she'd supposed. He was well over six feet, looked as though he could easily till the earth with the best of his tenants, and he was so handsome her breath stuck in her throat. Her carefully constructed fantasy world crumbled around her as she began to see spots before her eyes and reminded herself to take in a much needed gasp of air.

"Penelope!" Aunt Millicent snapped her out of the fog and gave a curt nod.

"Oh!" Penny bobbed a slightly unsteady curtsy and managed, "A pleasure to make your acquaintance, Your Graces," before she made her way to the settee on legs that felt near collapse. She sank next to Persephone, painfully aware, as she breathed deeply in and out, that her hair was in disarray from being outside in a fairly impressive breeze and her bonnet still hung limply over her arm. She knew without looking that Aunt Millicent was glaring daggers at her; she'd told Penny more than once to keep the bonnet on to protect the coiffure.

Penny subtly attempted to tuck the errant strands of hair behind her ears and refused to make eye contact with her aunt. Her brain still spun in confusion as to the presence of Their Graces and why on earth Real Henry looked nothing like Letter-Correspondence Henry. Life was cruel. They might have at least enjoyed some pleasant conversation at the autumn festival had he not looked so very . . . overwhelming. Now she would be fortunate to be able to string two sentences together. She focused on Persephone's voice, which seemed as though it was reaching her at the end of a very long tunnel.

"... made arrangements to be here in time for both days of the autumn festival, isn't that lovely?" Persephone grasped Penny's fingers and clasped them tightly.

Penny managed to mumble something in the affirmative and look up, very much up, at the man standing at the hearth. His attention was focused solely on her face, a light smile playing on his lips. He blinked, then cleared his throat. "I must admit, the resemblance is remarkable. I wonder if even your relations have difficulty distinguishing between the two of you."

Aunt Millicent laughed, and Penny looked at her, making a concerted effort to abstain from narrowing her eyes. "Oh mercy no, Your Grace. They are as different as night and day, these two. Well, you can surely see just in demeanor alone."

Heat suffused Penny's cheeks, and she straightened her shoulders, mortified that her aunt would be so dismissive in front of company.

Aunt Millicent waved a hand in their direction. "Persephone is beautifully accomplished in all domestic arts. Penelope feels more at home running around in the woods." The woman's smile was wide, but didn't quite reach her eyes.

Penny wished more than ever that the house were situated over a sinkhole—not a large one, perhaps, maybe just one directly under her side of the settee. She happened to glance at the duchess, who regarded Penny with an assessing eye. Penny braced herself for a blast similar to the one lobbed by her aunt. Even the most veiled barb had the propensity for bloodletting.

"Miss Timely," the duchess said. "I must admit you remind me of myself at your age. I much preferred fresh outdoor air to the confines of the parlor." She smiled a bit, and the expression placed a stamp of beauty on features that hadn't dimmed with age.

What's in a Name?

Penelope nodded, at a loss for words, finding her throat suddenly tight. It had been a very long time since anyone had attempted to alleviate her sense of embarrassment. Her mother had been the last. Penny glanced at the duke, who was looking at his mother with one brow raised. The duchess returned his regard with one brow of her own cocked.

"Penny is an amazing artist," Persephone said, and Penny wanted very much to kick her. Persephone would have no way of knowing that Penny had told the duke on more than one occasion about her preferences in sketching and watercolor.

The duke tilted his head, his expression one of polite interest. "Oh, may we see your sketchbook, Miss Timely?"

Penny's heart stuttered to a stop and then resumed with a ferocious *thump*. Her sketchbook was full of fossils and rock formations. "Oh, I couldn't," she stammered. "I . . . that is, rather my efforts are quite . . ."

"Show them your sketchbook, Penelope," Aunt Millicent ordered.

Aunt Millicent clearly had no idea what Penny had been sketching for the last two years.

Penny glanced desperately at Persephone, whose eyes suddenly widened in awareness. "Oh, Aunt, you know how modest Penny is concerning her artwork. I never should have mentioned it; she is most humble about it."

Penny clutched the sketchbook in her lap and wished for a sinkhole big enough to sink the whole settee this time.

Persephone, mercifully, changed the subject. "We are most thrilled you will be in attendance at the entire festival, Your Grace," she directed to the duke. "And you will take part in the masquerade ball, of course?"

He inclined his head and gifted Persephone with a smile that made Penelope's heart race. "I have it on good authority, in fact, that the ball will be held at Wilmington this year. I suppose it might be rather awkward for me to decline."

Persephone laughed her perfect, delicate, duchess-appropriate laugh, and Penny died a bit. The entire affair was rapidly progressing from bad to worse. Not only would the man be at the masquerade ball, it was to be held in his home. His extremely large home. Where she would feel gauche and very much an impostor. Why was the ball not to be held in the village square, as always?

As though anticipating the question, the duchess said, "The local farmers are quite convinced we shall have inclement weather tomorrow night, and we cannot very well cancel such a grand event."

"Of course not, Your Grace," Aunt Millicent gushed. "And how wonderful and kind of you to open your home to the villagers."

Penny rolled her eyes. As though Millicent wasn't a villager herself. She felt the duke's gaze on her and glanced at him, chagrined beyond words to have been caught. His lips twitched, but he remained quiet.

Persephone's grip on Penny's hand had tightened to an uncomfortable degree. "I do hope the bonfire and supper in the park will go ahead as planned the following night," Persephone said. "It would be such a shame for rain to spoil the whole of it."

"I suppose it remains to be seen." The duke smiled again, and Penny felt a surge of fury at her sister, who had sucked her into a mess that was sure to leave Penny humiliated and brokenhearted. Perhaps the worst part of it all was the fear that she would no longer exchange letters with Henry—that either something she said or did in the next two days would ruin all prospects for future correspondence. And the crowning indignity of it all was that she was going to pretend to be Persephone. There was no way out of it now. She didn't imagine in a million years that His Grace would look kindly upon being duped.

Three

enry looked at the two young women seated side by side on the small settee and wondered how Miss Persephone Timely had convinced her twin to correspond with him in her stead. He had known there was something rather off about Persephone's demeanor after the first ten minutes he and his mother had visited with her and the superficial aunt. Persephone wasn't at all what Henry had imagined, not that he was disappointed in her appearance, quite the opposite, but she just wasn't the *same* as the woman with whom he'd exchanged letters and bits and pieces of his soul. He decided she must simply be nervous, or putting on a show for her aunt, her behavior something the relative perhaps expected of her.

But then.

The front door had opened, and the breeze blew in a version of Persephone that quite took his breath away. For those few moments before she realized she wasn't alone, she had a light in her eyes—almost like laughter—and a freshness about her that brightened the entire room. The smile on her lips had died, faded in the face of her confusion, and he realized as he saw the shock in her eyes at Persephone's introductions that he was looking at the woman he'd actually been writing to. It was all there in her slightly mussed attire, the fact that she'd been enjoying herself outside, the fact that her bonnet was looped over her arm rather than on her head. *This* was the one who had quite captured his heart with her intellect and dry wit, with her unusual interest in paleontology—and she had quite set his blood pumping with that delectable admission.

Twins. Of course. For a reason clearly unbeknownst to the aunt, Penelope had stepped in for Persephone when the duchess had written that blasted embarrassing letter requesting an introduction between her son and the paragon, Miss Timely. He had been beyond irritated with his mother when she'd handed him "Persephone's" first letter and admitted her hand in the introduction, and he'd had every intention of tossing the thing into the fireplace. There was something, though, in the wit behind the letter writer that captured his interest. She couched her own amusement at the entire tableau with all the right words and phrases. The sarcasm, though veiled, registered with him immediately. He couldn't help but respond.

The letters had increased in length and substance, and he'd desperately wanted to meet her in the flesh. More than once he'd forced himself to stay away from Ellshire, completely enthralled with the woman's letters and not wanting to put a premature end to a correspondence that was not only enjoyable and funny, but heartfelt and real. Because they'd never met, she had no preconceived notions about him. She didn't know what he looked like, nor he her, and he had made a point to not describe himself. Those very physical traits that had served him well with ladies of all sorts in his years at Eton and Oxford had become tiresome of late. The money, the title, his appearance. He was gushed at by debutantes and winked at by the ladies of the *ton* who were bored in their own marriages to wealth and titles. Persephone knew only that he was a duke, and had a rough idea of his age. And those things never came up in the course of their written conversations. Except he now knew, as surely as he was the Duke of Wilmington, that the woman he'd been sharing his heart with was Penelope, not Persephone.

Penny.

He tried the name in his mind and quite liked it, again taking in her windblown appearance and wanting very much to grasp her hand and yank her from the room, away from her mean-spirited aunt and well-meaning but superficial twin sister. He was grateful beyond words to his quick-thinking mother, who had rescued the young woman from the aunt's cruel comments. Anyone who knew the duchess, however, would have known the act for what it was. He held back a snort. His mother? Enjoying the fresh air? He could no more see the duchess running through a meadow with a sketchbook in hand than he could see her on the moon. She *had* met his father at a horse race, however. Hmm. It merited some thought.

He took his eyes from Penelope with some effort and regarded Persephone, who was laughing merrily at something the duchess had said and carrying the conversation well. Her sister seemed too mortified to say more than a handful of words. His hands itched to grab Penny's sketchbook and examine her drawings. He would bet his entire ancestral seat it was full of trilobites and seashells. His lips twitched, and he found his gaze straying to her face again. One of her dark blond curls escaped from behind her ear where she'd tucked it and framed her face, coming to rest just beneath her jaw line against her neck.

She looked at him—probably against her better judgment—and his heart quite stopped for a moment. He found her absolutely stunning. Persephone sat with her skirts perfectly draped, likely her feet and ankles placed together just so in proper formation on the floor. Penny's knee bounced a bit, and her fingers clutched the sketchbook so firmly her knuckles were white. She placed her sketching pencil behind her ear, probably without even realizing she did so, and chewed on her bottom lip as her gaze skittered away from his and landed instead on her aunt, whose glacial stare was enough to make *his* insides shrivel a bit. It was with a surge of protective anger that he watched Penelope's shoulders slump just the slightest bit, and she quickly removed the pencil from her ear.

When she was his duchess, he would stand behind her, with his hand on her shoulder, and he would lean down and whisper in her ear that she was twice the woman her aunt was and that she ought never to give the woman the satisfaction of seeing her wilt. He frowned. *When she was his duchess?* Where had that come from? He examined the thought from all angles and realized it didn't matter. He had known in the back of his mind that he wanted this one woman when they were only three months into their correspondence, and he decided he would meet her at the Ellshire Village Autumn Festival. What he hadn't expected, though, was that the woman of his affections was playing a bit of a game that had him rabidly curious.

He really should get her alone for a moment and tell her he knew what she and Persephone were doing. But then, he found himself more than a little intrigued—and not a little aroused—at the thought that she may well have determined to see the thing through to the end. That she was uncomfortable was clear to him. That she had the courage to pull the deception off, however, he knew beyond a shadow of a doubt. And as he looked again at Millicent Fanbecker, he was inordinately proud of his future wife. He barely resisted the impulse to rub his hands together.

Let the games begin.

Four

Penny walked along the bustling village street with Persephone, and regrettably, Aunt Millicent, the following day. She wore Persephone's signature pink clothes, and tried very hard not to roll her eyes every time she caught her own reflection. The effort to be Persephone for the duration of their visit to town was weighing on her most ardently, and she threw a scowl at her sister from beneath her annoyingly pink bonnet.

Persephone was convinced she could feign a sore throat and slip into the small apothecary where Dr. Fitzroy kept his practice. She'd begun priming that particular pump earlier in the morning, telling Aunt Millicent—as Penelope—that she was feeling scratchy in the throat. Millicent had dismissed her with barely a glance and a suggestion to gargle some salt water when they returned from the village. She also expressed, through pursed lips, a concern for Persephone's health, stating that if Penelope should make her sister ill, all prospects with His Grace might well be squashed. Penny didn't understand why His Grace would lose interest in someone merely because said someone had a scratchy throat, but she kept this to herself.

The village bustled with significantly more excitement than usual. The autumn festival was upon the town, and anticipation hung heavy in the air. Vendors with carts full of gourds and pumpkins stood next to storefronts boasting sales of all sorts, ranging from ribbons, to gloves, to the most recent fabric from London. The village's two small cafés were filled to capacity with townsfolk and visitors, and three stands next to the cafés sold roasted chestnuts and cups of chocolate, warm and lovely. The air smelled crisp and fresh, and Penny closed her eyes for a moment, enjoying the cool breeze that carried delicious scents up and down the streets.

"Perhaps a cup of chocolate might soothe your throat, Penelope." Penny gestured to the stands and nudged her sister. Hot chocolate would be just the thing to soothe her own irritation at having to wear pink.

"No sweets," Millicent interjected from behind the two girls. "I do not want to pay the seamstress to take your seams out. Besides, Persephone, I'm surprised you would even suggest it, knowing that the next few days with His Grace are crucial! You mustn't put on an ounce!"

Penny's nostrils flared, and she clenched her teeth together to keep from saying something she'd regret. She glanced at Persephone, who regarded her with a scowl.

"No, I shall be fine without any chocolate." Persephone slowed her steps and cast her eye across the street. "But I do wish to stop by the apothecary and see about some soothing drops. I should hate to share a sickness with you, dear sister. Aunt Millicent has the right of it. You really cannot afford to become ill."

Penny glared at Persephone, but slowed her steps. She

wanted to tell Persephone that she was going to ruin their charade before it had even begun; Penny never gave credit to anything Aunt Millicent said, and their aunt would likely notice the comment.

"Well!" Aunt Millicent slowed her steps, as well. "That is very astute of you, Penelope. You see, dear, even your sister realizes you must remain in good health."

"I suppose we should cross the street, then, and visit the apothecary," Penny said through tight lips.

Persephone looped her arm through Penny's. "An excellent idea."

The threesome crossed the street, and Penny wondered how Persephone planned to have any sort of meaningful conversation with Dr. Fitzroy when not only was she pretending to be someone other than herself, but with her draconian aunt standing watch.

Her answer came soon enough as they neared the shop and Aunt Millicent pulled back on Penny's arm. "You needn't accompany her in there, Persephone. In fact, we probably ought to limit your close association with Penelope for the time being. We don't want her illness spreading. It's bad enough that you must ride in the same coach together." Millicent frowned and motioned at Persephone with her chin. "Go in, then. We shall wait here."

Persephone scampered into the shop with more energy than someone ill probably ought. Penny looked at her aunt for a long moment, surprised that she was surprised. "But she's alone, Aunt, and unchaperoned. It's not at all proper. What of her reputation?"

Millicent waved a hand in the air. "Honestly, Persephone, do you truly believe your sister's reputation is at stake? We needn't worry she would speak overlong or intimately with anyone; the girl is entirely too much like your dead father." She wrinkled her nose in distaste. "He never did carry on a normal conversation, either."

Penny felt heat rising from her chest. It spread across her neck and into her cheeks, and she wondered if her head might explode into a bright ball of red flame. "Our papa was a good man, Aunt Millicent. And our mother loved him very much."

Millicent eyed her askance and sniffed. "I warned her. She acted the fool over that man from the moment they first met. But she wouldn't be dissuaded once her mind was set."

Penny drew in deep, even breaths and turned her head away slightly in hopes of catching another cool breeze. "He was landed gentry, Aunt. Surely he might have found favor in your eyes for that alone, no?"

Millicent let out a puff of air. "Title or no, he was odd. He never mixed well with society. It wasn't as though that match led to any advantageous connections for your mother."

"Perhaps she wasn't interested in advantageous connections," Penny said softly. "Perhaps she only wanted the love of a kind man, and children."

"Persephone." Millicent placed a finger under Penny's chin and pulled her attention back. "You know very well that love is not currency, nor does it help one's station in life. You are not sounding like yourself today."

Penny's eyes misted. "Perhaps I am merely missing Mama today."

"I expect maudlin sentiment from your sister, not from you." Millicent's taut features softened slightly. "Ensnare the interest of His Grace, my girl. All such thoughts will fly away most handily when you are a duchess."

"Yes, Aunt." Penny placed her finger under the bonnet ribbons, wishing she could just take the thing off.

What's in a Name?

Persephone always tied her bow snugly under her ear. Penelope preferred her bonnet bows to hang loose somewhere around the middle of her neck, which probably explained the reason it was forever flying off.

"Mrs. Fanbecker!" The shrill voice of the vicar's wife sounded down the street, and Millicent turned with pleasure toward the woman. "Just the woman I was hoping to find!"

Millicent smiled. "Mrs. Jonas, what a pleasant surprise!"

Mrs. Jonas was the large to Aunt Millicent's slim. Together they resembled Jack Sprat and his wife. "I have the recipe I mentioned to you the other day when Mr. Jonas and I took tea with you. It's here somewhere in my reticule." The portly woman opened her reticule drawstrings and plunged her hand into the recesses, fumbling about and muttering some.

Penny took advantage of her aunt's momentary distraction to turn her attention elsewhere—anywhere. The insults to her father's memory hung heavy in the air, and she missed her parents fiercely. She looked into the street, and something sparkled, catching her eye. It was a rock, and a beautiful one at that.

Penny slipped quietly away from the two women, moving into the street, her eyes solidly fixed on the object, and imagined wistfully that it was an embrace from her father. She bent down, her gloved hand reaching for it just as a shout rang out from someone close by. As her fingers closed around the rock, she looked up at the commotion, only to be shoved to one side amidst a flurry of pounding hooves and the flash of a very large horse.

Penny lay sprawled in the middle of the street, with a very heavy body atop hers. The wind had been knocked from her lungs in a painful *whoosh*, and she struggled to catch a decent breath. The figure atop her rolled to one side, and she felt a hand on her shoulder.

"Miss Timely, are you hurt?"

She knew the voice—had been entranced by it the night before in her aunt's parlor. The pink bonnet had slipped down over Penny's face, and she lifted an unsteady hand to shove it away from her eyes. A handsome face and a pair of sea foam green eyes came into focus as the offending bonnet moved out of the way.

"Your Grace," she managed, drawing a shaky breath. "I . . . there was a rock . . ." Penny looked at her hand to find her fingers locked in a death grip around the object that had sent her into the street in the first place. "I don't know what happened . . ."

His face was pale, his brows drawn. "A horse—must not have been thoroughly broken in—very nearly ran you down." He put his hand behind her shoulders and helped her into a sitting position. She registered a gasp from an onlooker and swallowed as His Grace tugged the hem of her dress down over her shoes.

Penny closed her eyes at her own stupidity. "I apologize, Your Grace. You put yourself in harm's way. I ought to have paid closer attention."

"Persephone!" Aunt Millicent's screech carried through the street and likely into the next village. "Whatever has happened?"

"My aunt doesn't know I like rocks," she mumbled, hoping for all she was worth that the duke would keep her secret. He would be expecting Persephone to be enamored of geology, but Aunt Millicent knew very well that Persephone was not.

"Your secret is safe with me," he whispered.

She looked at him, then, his face still quite close to hers. It was as though time stood deliciously still for just a moment. The color seemed to be returning to his face, and the corner of his mouth quirked in a smile. Her breath hitched, and she noted the clean smell of his clothing, the sharp, smooth line of his jaw. She closed her eyes for the briefest of moments and wished the world would melt away.

The world did not, in fact, melt away, and the noise around her returned with a rush as Millicent reached her side and clawed at her arm, pulling her more fully upright. "Your Grace!" Millicent seemed to foam at the mouth as she searched for words that, apparently, eluded her. "You have saved Persephone's life!"

Penny winced as Millicent hauled her upright, and she fought back a scowl. Shouldn't injuries be assessed before forcing an accident victim to stand? She rotated her head on her shoulders, stretched her limbs just a bit. Nothing seemed broken, just most likely bruised.

"Nothing any other gentleman wouldn't have done, I'm certain," His Grace said as he rose and dusted his pants and the elegant, if slightly dirty, line of his impeccably tailored jacket. "I merely happened to be the closest at hand." He smiled. "Fortunately."

Penny bit her lip. Why, oh, *why* did he have to be so handsome? She searched his face for a flaw, desperately hoping to find one. Alas, he was perfection itself. Adonis. A thing from which marble statues were designed. There was no hope for it. Henry was beautiful, and Penny was lost.

"What is that filthy thing?" Millicent reached for Penny's wrist with a talon-like grip and pulled it closer for inspection. "A rock?"

Penny blinked. "I don't know how . . . I'm not sure why . . ."

Millicent shook her wrist with a strength that, frankly, surprised Penny. "Drop it, Persephone. Your gloves will be filthy."

Penny refrained from telling Millicent that her entire dress was likely filthy after taking a tumble into the street. The rock, though, remained firmly clutched in her hand. She couldn't drop it. It was a hug from her papa.

"I'll take it for you, Miss Timely." Henry placed his large hand around hers, and Millicent released Penny's abused wrist. His long fingers brushed gently across her knuckles, and she slowly relaxed her grip. "There we go," he whispered. "I shall keep it safe."

"Your Grace, how can we ever repay you?" Aunt Millicent was beside herself, basking in ducal glory as the rest of the village looked on amidst murmurs, clucks of approval, and sighs from young girls at the clear gallantry of His Grace, the Duke of Wilmington.

"Nonsense, the privilege is mine. I'm happy to assist." Henry smiled at her and subtly slipped the rock into his coat pocket.

Penny swallowed and met his eyes, feeling her own mist over just a bit. "Thank you, Your Grace," she managed, and curtseyed, feeling slightly sore and yet wonderful all at once.

"I ask only that you save me a waltz at the masquerade ball."

"Of course she will, Your Grace," Millicent gushed and curtseyed, as well. "And she will be wearing pink, as always."

Penny glanced at the duke in some dismay. She'd told him she hated pink. If he remembered, though, he didn't comment on it. He smiled at her, one brow raised. She swallowed again.

"Pink. Of course. Her favorite color."

Penny looked at him sharply. Was he toying with her? She couldn't be certain, and she hadn't flirted enough in her life to recognize it definitively. Perhaps he'd just forgotten. After all, it wasn't as though the subject of her favorite color came up with every letter exchanged.

What's in a Name?

Millicent pulled Penny toward the sidewalk just as Persephone emerged from the apothecary on the heels of Dr. Fitzroy.

"My goodness, Miss Timely, are you hurt? May I be of some assistance?" The doctor looked at Penny with clear concern and kind, intelligent eyes, and Penny was struck by the thought that her sister seemed to have fallen in love with a man of some actual substance.

"She is just fine," Millicent snapped. "*His Grace* has already seen to her welfare."

Penelope wanted to tell the good doctor that her arm had been nearly ripped from its socket by her overzealous aunt.

Persephone locked eyes with Penny, shock clearly written on her face. She rushed forward and grabbed her in an embrace. "Pen, are you well?" she whispered.

Penny nodded. Persephone pulled back and looked at her face for a long moment as though assuring herself of the truth. She looked over Penny's shoulder at the duke and pursed her lips ever so slightly, the way she always did when she was Thinking, just before she began Planning.

"Thank you, Your Grace, for coming to my sister's aid." Persephone smiled at him and then wiped a smudge of dirt from Penny's face.

"Don't touch her, Penelope," Millicent hissed, even as she smiled at curious onlookers and urged Penny forward. "You'll make her sick! I hope you managed to get a remedy for whatever it is you seem to have contracted." Millicent flicked a glance at Dr. Fitzroy and dismissed him just as quickly.

"I believe I did indeed, Aunt Millicent. Dr. Fitzroy has prescribed exactly what I need to be well." Persephone blushed and cast a backward glance at the doctor, who lifted a finger in farewell.

Penny raised a brow but said nothing to her sister, who seemed entirely pleased with her visit to the apothecary.

Millicent yanked on Penny's arm, threading her own through it. "That was an absolutely brilliant maneuver, Persephone!" She leaned in close, excitement rolling off of her in waves. "A bit risky, perhaps, but brilliant nonetheless! However did you think so quickly? I didn't even see His Grace until the whole of it was over!"

Penny gaped at her aunt. She thought the whole incident had been orchestrated? "I . . ."

"You're stunned, dear. I shouldn't be surprised if you haven't knocked your head about somewhat. That was quite a daring plan, but when a clear objective is within reach, one should sacrifice to achieve it."

"Quite," Penny muttered. They neared the carriage, and Penny absently registered Persephone patting down the side of her dress that had taken the most abuse when hitting the road, while Millicent continued clucking nonsense. Penny's thoughts trailed back to the moment when Henry had slipped her rock into his pocket. And her heart melted.

Five

Penny glanced at her sister, who sat beside her in Aunt Millicent and Uncle Horace's carriage on the way to the Wilmington estate for the Ellshire Autumn Masquerade Ball. Her hands were clammy inside the magenta elbow-length gloves and the mask she clutched in her fingers was itchy—she'd already tried it on. And she hated magenta. It was the most intense and offensive form of pink imaginable.

Persephone avoided her gaze, staring out the window rather than face the scowl Penny had permanently etched on her own features. Persephone wore Penny's masquerade gown, which was a beautiful combination of sapphire and the palest ice blue. Penny had actually been looking forward to wearing the ensemble. It was extravagant in the extreme, and Penny sincerely doubted she'd ever have a chance to wear it anywhere ever again. Aunt Millicent had insisted Uncle Horace loosen the purse strings on the girls' trust for the occasion, and the modiste had spared no expense. Truth be told, Penny knew Millicent couldn't have cared less whether Penny wore something new or an old day dress for the occasion, but she could hardly be so blatant in her preference for Persephone and deny Penny a suitable gown. The neighbors would surely take notice.

Persephone had insisted that Penny must wear her pink ball gown and dance with His Grace in her place. Persephone had no idea what Penny had written in all those letters, of course, and she still couldn't bear to betray her heart's true love, Doctor Gilroy Fitzroy. Even though His Grace was stunningly handsome.

Penny batted her way through the jealous green haze that clouded her vision at her sister's statement and refrained from scratching Persephone's eyes out. But only just. Because yes, His Grace was indeed stunningly handsome, so much so that it hurt the eyes and quite ruined Penny's hopes for a gentle association with a pleasant but homely man, but also because the thought of him holding Persephone close while pondering on all the things Penny had written from her heart made her inexplicably furious. Plus, there was the fact that the duke had been quite dashing earlier in his rescue. She felt connected with him in a way that she absolutely wasn't willing to share with her sister—with anyone, for that matter.

So there she sat as the carriage rumbled along, trying to keep her posture and expression perfect for Millicent, who sat opposite them in the carriage next to Uncle Horace, who looked for all the world as though he'd rather be watching cattle graze. If Millicent suspected for even one moment that the girls had switched places, Penny's life would be miserable because, of course, it would be somehow Penny's fault. Their earlier escapades in the village had been but a test, really. Tonight would be the true measure of their success. Millicent would be watching them like a hawk.

What's in a Name?

"Penelope, I do hope you'll refrain from any inappropriate chatter this evening, especially if you actually find yourself dancing with someone. And for the love of heaven, if your throat is still bothering you, don't breathe on anyone, or sneeze." Millicent was watching Persephone with narrowed eyes, and Penny observed from the outside as her aunt's vitriol spilled onto her sister instead of her.

Persephone tore her gaze from the passing countryside that was fading in the face of the encroaching evening and gaped for a moment at Aunt Millicent. She then slouched a bit in her seat with a sniff. "Of course," she said in a petulant voice, and Penny wanted to slap her. She was surprised Persephone hadn't belched loudly and wiped drool from her chin in an effort to play at being Penny.

Aunt Millicent rolled her eyes heavenward with a little huff. "Don't know why I even bother," she muttered, and Penny tilted her head at the woman, never disliking her more than in that moment.

"Penny knows perfectly well how to behave in public, do you not?" Penny said, looking at Persephone.

Persephone gaped at her for a moment before nodding. "Of course."

Persephone had rarely, if ever, defended Penny to their aunt, and the fact that Penny had now subtly called her attention to it seemed to have the perfect twin flustered.

Millicent snorted something unintelligible but let the matter rest for a moment. She eventually recovered herself and looked at Penny, eyes shining. "Now, Persephone dear. You must use every charm you possess to engage His Grace's affection. You already have him quite intrigued, as we clearly saw today in the village. Why, I could tell just from the way he looked at you last night in the parlor that his interest was piqued."

Penny gritted her teeth but managed a smile she hoped was bright and sunny. "Oh, Aunt, surely he wasn't paying me any special regard," she said with a dismissive wave of her hand.

Persephone uttered a little sound that sounded suspiciously like denial. "But Persephone, I'm certain you must be mistaken! Whyever would he not have paid you special regard? You are all that is charming and beautiful."

"Exactly right, Penelope," Aunt Millicent said, barely sparing the blue-clad sister a glance. "You see, even your sister realizes it."

"But, Penny, I saw him also stealing a glance or two at you!" Penny fluttered her lashes at Persephone.

"Bah. Only because she looked an absolute fright." Millicent flicked a hand at Persephone, who now bristled noticeably and sat up a bit straighter in the seat.

Well, good! Let Persephone see firsthand what it felt like to be on that side of their aunt's painful derision. Persephone wasn't used to being dismissed, to being the lesser of the two girls, and even though Penny knew Persephone realized it was all a farce, she also now would know exactly how Penny felt every time Millicent knocked her down yet again.

Just because Penny was feeling perverse and entirely put out with her sister, she tapped her finger against her chin and struck a contemplative pose. "I do wonder if Doctor Fitzroy will be in attendance this evening," she mused aloud.

Aunt Millicent scowled. "Whyever should you concern yourself with him, Persephone? I told you when he first moved to the village that he is far beneath your potential."

Persephone sat up even straighter in the carriage seat. "But he is quite wonderful!"

Aunt Millicent shot a glance at Persephone. "It would stand to reason you would think so, Penelope." And then the woman actually brightened a bit. "Although, it may well be just what we need once Persephone is wed to the duke! Penelope, you might manage to catch the doctor's attention with your odd interests and love of the outdoors. You did spend time with him today at the apothecary, and your temperament far better suits you to be married to one of the working class. You would have a smaller household to manage, and your husband would never have to concern himself with his wife's inability to entertain people of polish. Then you will make a match, and I shall have done my duty to my dear sister." She looked entirely pleased with herself, and Penny felt Persephone bristle.

Penny reached for Persephone's fingers and winced slightly as her sister clamped on like a vise. Whether Persephone was angry at the insinuation that the doctor was less than perfect or she worried that Penny would actually pursue the man herself, Penny wasn't certain. She only knew as the mansion loomed in the distance that she looked forward to the upcoming evening with equal parts excitement and dread.

Six

His Grace looked over the crowded assembly with a watchful eye from behind his black mask, refraining from checking his timepiece. Again. The Timely twins were late, and he tapped his thumb against his thigh in irritation. He hadn't slept well at all the night before, thinking continually about the young woman who would dance with him tonight. And then after seeing her nearly mowed down in the street earlier by a stampeding horse, he found himself anxious for her arrival.

He knew she would be passing herself off as Persephone, again, but surely she wouldn't try to act like her sister. She must know she'd revealed her true self in all those letters to him—that had been clear as day from observing the two in their parlor. To act like Persephone now would be to show him the face of a stranger.

His mother appeared at his elbow and took his arm. "Are you watching for someone in particular, Henry?"

What's in a Name?

"No." He glanced at her shrewd assessment of him and bit back a sigh. "Yes."

"Might it be Miss Timely?"

He nodded reluctantly, not sure why he wanted to keep his relationship with the woman to himself for just a bit longer. The duchess knew her introduction had given life to a correspondence with Miss Timely, but she didn't know to what extent. His mother believed their exchange equaled no more than a handful of letters. He had well over thirty, wrapped in twine and stacked in a lockbox he'd kept under his bed since boyhood; it contained fossils and some of the more unique rocks he'd found around the estate. He flushed when he thought of the fact that he still owned the lockbox full of childhood treasures and of the laughingstock he would become were his friends to learn of its existence. Perhaps equally mortifying was the presence of one small trilobite he'd picked up at the Natural Museum when Persephone—no, *Penelope*—had expressed her fondness for the things. He'd brought it with him and was carrying it in his coat pocket, nestled against his heart, at that very moment.

He rolled his eyes at himself and focused again on the ballroom entrance while his mother greeted the vicar and his wife. His heart stuttered when he finally noted the presence of two women, dressed in identical gowns and masks, except for the color of each ensemble. From the letters, he knew the woman he sought *should* have been in blue. So, it was with a wry smile that he crossed the floor with his eye on the woman in pink. He blinked a bit. Very bright pink. Her face in the village when her aunt had told him the color to expect on her had very nearly made him laugh aloud. She'd looked absolutely disgusted and then tried to disguise it. And failed.

He watched the ladies as he drew near, his stomach clenching in curious knots, anticipation humming through his body. He saw the moment Penelope registered his presence as she grabbed her sister's fingers as though clutching to a life raft. His lips twitched, and he came to a stop before the women and their relations, who stood just behind them. Executing a smart bow he'd learned before he could walk, he said, "Mr. and Mrs. Fanbecker, lovely to see you. And your charming nieces." They curtseyed. He took the blue-gloved hand in his, placed a kiss on the knuckles, and then glanced into the very green eyes behind the pink mask as he reached for the pink glove and kissed it, as well.

Miss Blue recovered herself first and placed a hand upon her nicely accentuated bosom. "Your Grace, however did you know it was us?" The perfect lips curved into a perfect bow, and he smiled at her.

"Well, Miss Penelope," he said in a stage whisper, "your aunt mentioned today that Miss Persephone would be in pink, and you would be in blue. And as you are the only two here who are mirror images of each other and the colors fit the description, I reached my assumption that you've now confirmed."

"Oh, Your Grace, so clever of you!" Millicent Fanbecker fluttered her purple fan that matched her purple mask. He considered giving the woman the cut direct, but that would do more harm than good to her niece.

"Mr. Fanbecker, the refreshments are delectable." Henry motioned to the corner of the room where the food was spread upon several large tables. "You must accompany your wife over and try one of everything."

The man's eyes brightened behind his simple mask, which did little more than give him the appearance of a portly raccoon. "I say, I believe I shall! Come, dear." He pulled on his wife's arm, and she, in turn, grasped Blue Timely's elbow as she nudged Pink Timely subtly forward.

What's in a Name?

"Penelope, come with us. I believe I see Doctor Fitzroy by the refreshments."

Blue's eyes widened, and a genuine smile spread across her face, a lovely blush highlighting her cheeks. "Persephone, I shall just be over there."

Pink took a deep breath, and Henry took one as well, noticing the equally well-accentuated bosom in magenta. The young woman managed a bright smile and a wave at her sister, who was now being unceremoniously dragged along behind her aunt.

Finally. They were alone. Well, he amended, as alone as a young woman was ever allowed to be with a single man who was not her relative. The entire village of Ellshire, and probably a few neighboring towns as well, had shown up for the esteemed event. The crowd around them milled, laughed, surged, but it all seemed to fade away as he studied Penelope Timely. She was truly lovely. And knowing that she would likely gasp in delight if she knew he carried a trilobite in his coat pocket made her all the lovelier.

"Miss Timely," he began, and she looked up at him with wide eyes. She bit her lip and then rubbed at it with her forefinger. He could almost hear the litany that must be coursing through her head. *Stand up straight, do not fidget, smile charmingly, definitely do not bite your lip.* She blinked and drew a shuddering breath.

"I do hope you're recovered from the incident earlier in town?"

"Yes, and truly, Your Grace, I am most grateful for your assistance."

"I also have something that I believe belongs to you." He smiled and pulled the rock from his outer coat pocket—the one she'd been clutching when he threw her out of the horse's path.

Her eyes lit up behind the mask, and she sighed. "Thank you, Your Grace! It looked so beautiful from a distance, and I wanted an opportunity to examine it up close." She flushed. "I ought to look before I step, I suppose."

"It is a rather interesting rock, Miss Timely. I believe it might be a geode. Have you ever broken one apart to see what lies inside?"

"No, but I've read about them! I'm most anxious to try it, then." She examined the rock carefully for a moment and then seemed to remember herself, because her gaze shot up and she looked for her aunt, he assumed. She hurriedly put the rock inside the reticule that hung from her wrist and cinched it shut.

"I must admit, from your correspondence, I am surprised to see you dressed in such lovely shades of pink rather than the blue you said you favor." He was a cad, well and truly, and he didn't bother to deny it as a flush stole across her cheeks. A very pretty flush, much like the one she'd worn when entering the parlor the night before.

She cleared her throat. "Pers—Penelope has taken a fondness for blue, lately, and as the dresses had already been commissioned, I thought to give her that ensemble." She winced, as though realizing the flimsiness of the excuse.

He smiled and offered her his arm as the orchestra struck up a waltz, the waltz he'd arranged to have played early on in the evening. "Would you do me the honor, I wonder?"

"Of course, Your Grace." She placed her gloved fingertips on his arm, and he was suffused in warmth that had him wanting to pull at his cravat.

They approached the middle of the ballroom, and he faced her, savoring the act of finally reaching for her, putting his right hand at her waist and pulling her close. He inhaled the soft scent that clung to her, something light and floral, as she placed one hand on his shoulder and the other in his hand. She trembled, and he slid his hand around to the small of her back, supporting her as they began to move.

"I thought we had moved beyond my title." He smiled down at her, shortening his stride to better accommodate hers. "You dispensed with the 'Your Gracing' some months ago. And I rather have the impression that I am making you nervous."

She locked her eyes onto his with a light shake of her head. And then as if she had finally decided to find her tongue, she spoke. "Henry." Her voice was soft and sent a jolt of awareness flooding through him. Had he not been adept at dancing, he might well have stumbled and taken her to the floor with him, which really may not have been all bad.

"I am not . . . that is, I am not nervous, truly. Well, perhaps a bit. It's only that you are not at all what I had expected." She blurted it out and then looked horrified.

He smiled down at her, that gentle scent again brushing over his senses as he spun her in a turn. "What were you expecting, Persephone?"

Something flickered in her eyes, and she shook her head. "Someone homely," she muttered, looking studiously at his cravat.

He choked on a laugh, not entirely certain he'd heard her correctly. "Home—*homely?*" He tilted his head, pulling her eyes up toward his face. "And you seem disappointed."

"No." She squinted at him. "Yes. You see," she chewed on her lip again, drawing his attention to her very pretty mouth. "My sister has always been the more gregarious of the two of us. I am typically far . . . less so. She finds herself much at ease in the company of people of all sorts. As my aunt mentioned last night, we are as different as night and day, despite the appearance."

"Interesting, that. In all the letters you wrote to me, you never once mentioned a sister."

She drew in a breath that served only to bring her body closer to his. He closed his eyes for a moment and bit back a groan. "I have lived in her shadow since the death of my mother," she continued. "And frankly, Your Grace, I have very much enjoyed our correspondence out from under that shadow."

"Henry."

"Henry." She relaxed in his arms the slightest bit and smiled. "When I think of you as Henry, I admit I find myself much more at ease."

His lips twitched. "Despite the fact that you do not find me homely?"

She blushed, but laughed. "Yes. Homely would have been of benefit to me, but I shall manage."

"My dear Persephone. You are the most interesting, humorous, and delightful woman I have the privilege to know. I wish you could see it in yourself."

Her gaze locked on his, and her movements slowed the tiniest bit, forcing him to adjust his own steps. A sheen formed over her intense green eyes, and she blinked, clearing her throat. "You could not have said anything kinder to me if you'd tried." Her voice was low, quiet. "I often feel very much like an oddity." She smiled, but it was tight.

He glanced at the refreshment tables, narrowing his eyes when he found her aunt, whose mouth was moving rapidly at her husband as he piled food onto a plate. "Mrs. Fanbecker, then. She is your mother's sister?"

Penelope nodded.

"And there is no love lost between the two of you." He would never have dreamed of embarking on such a personal conversation with any other woman than this one. He knew her, but not this part of her, and his anger at the relatives continued to grow.

"I am not what she wishes to see in a young woman. I remind her of my father, whom she quite despised. My sister is all that a well-bred woman should be. Aunt Millicent has grand hopes."

"Then she is a fool. For I am quite enthralled by the woman I've come to know over the past several months."

Her mouth dropped open, and it took everything in him to keep from stopping in the middle of the floor and capturing her lips with his. She cleared her throat and shook her head with a little laugh. "Then you are most singular, Your Grace. For most gentlemen find my sister's personality much more to their liking."

"As you said, I am singular. I am not most gentlemen." The strains of the waltz slowed and then came to an end, and he told his arms to release her. They steadfastly refused. "Would you take a stroll with me out on the terrace?" He winked at her. "It is well lit, I assure you, with plenty of chaperones scattered here and there."

Her lips twitched, and a smile lit her eyes behind the hideous magenta mask. "How thoughtful of you to provide chaperones for the event."

He reluctantly released his hold on her long enough to take her hand and pull it through his arm. He kept his hand atop hers, willing her to stay close to him, as though he could anchor himself to her side by securing that hand to his sleeve. "We do what we think best for the community, of course. It would never do for Ellshire's young women to move freely without a disapproving frown dogging their footsteps."

She laughed out loud, and it wasn't the polite twinkle of noise her sister displayed. It was a joyful sound, a genuine laugh that spread warmth through his extremities. He led her out onto the terrace that overlooked the estate's beautifully manicured gardens and flower beds that had been pruned back for the season in preparation for the coming winter. The air was cooler than he'd anticipated, and he frowned. "We should get your wrap," he said and turned to walk back inside with her.

"Oh, no, please? This is lovely. It was overly warm in there." She did indeed look flushed, and she wafted at her face with her hand before reaching up to scratch under the mask. "This thing..."

"Take it off."

She looked up at him, eyes wide. "I'm sorry?"

He shook his head. "The mask. Take it off."

"But it's a masquerade ball. Doesn't that quite defeat the purpose?"

"You forget I know who you are, Persephone Timely. There are no secrets between us."

Seven

Penny's heart dropped into her stomach at his softly spoken words. *There are no secrets between us.* No, except one huge secret, the fact that Persephone was supposed to have been the one writing to the duke, and now Penny had dug a hole so deep for herself she didn't know how to crawl out of it. She lifted her fingers to the mask, frustrated that she trembled. Her fingers fumbled with the tie at the back of her head, and she despaired of removing the mask without completely pulling her hair out of its elegant coiffure.

Henry twirled his finger in the air. "Turn around." He placed his hands on her shoulders and turned her away from him, and she felt his fingers at the ties of her mask. The cool air wafted over her eyes and nose, and she breathed deeply, rubbing at her face.

"That feels so much better," she sighed, and complied when he held her shoulders and turned her back to face him.

"Looks better, too." He grinned, and she thought she just might faint.

She shook her head, hating the fact that she had become a simpering female, prone to fits of vapors and sighing in delight at handsome gentlemen. But truly, as she studied the man before her, she asked herself one very simple question: *What do I have to lose?*

At that moment she determined to enjoy the festival with him to its fullest, to be nothing but herself, to enjoy spending time with the man she'd come to know through his written words. After all, she had the same face as Persephone, and she certainly found her sister pretty enough. And Henry found her fascinating. Perhaps it was time she pulled herself out of Persephone's shadow.

She smiled. "Now you must also remove your mask. It's only fair, you know."

"I believe I might require help, as well, then. It's only fair, you know." He grinned again, and her heart skipped a beat.

She twirled her finger, and when he turned around, she stood on tiptoe to untie the strings of his black masquerade mask. When he turned back, she stared for a moment before realizing she must either appear daft or quite rude. She tipped her head to one side and nodded. "Much better, also."

She still held Henry's mask in her gloved fingers, and he held hers. When she held his mask out to him, he shook his head.

"I believe I like yours better. I'm keeping it."

She choked on a horrified laugh. "You can't wear a pink mask! And besides, we'll have to go back inside eventually. You should know that at the Ellshire Autumn Masquerade Ball, all masks are to remain firmly in place until midnight."

"Well, then I'd say we've already broken the rules." He

studied her for a long moment, the teasing grin fading, the look in those light green eyes quite intense. "I made myself wait to meet you in person, Persephone. Did you know that? I wanted to come to you months ago."

Her mouth suddenly felt very dry. "Why didn't you?" she heard herself whisper.

"I didn't want to stop receiving your letters, and I knew that once I met you in person, I would want something more than a letter-writing friendship."

"Oh." Mercy. She barely stopped her hand from fanning her face. As she thought back over what he'd said, one word stood out to her more than the rest.

Persephone.

She closed her eyes for a moment and then turned to the railing, walking toward it slowly and gripping it with her fingers, her hand still holding his mask. Maybe it wasn't such a huge secret, the fact that she had written to him under false pretenses, under her sister's name. But that was the only part of that correspondence that had been a lie. Only that, the name she'd signed at the bottom of each letter. But he was a good man, an honorable gentleman. What would he think of her subterfuge? What would he think of a woman who would write to a duke and lie about her identity?

He joined her at the railing, and she felt the heat of his arm next to hers. "I've been too forward, it would seem," he murmured.

She shook her head, her throat aching. "Not at all, Your Grace. Truly, I . . ." She felt him watching her and turned to meet his gaze.

"Henry." He said it firmly, softly, his eyes locked onto hers and holding her there.

"Henry." She blinked against the sting of tears she would rather die than shed.

"You're shivering. It's cold out here. Come with me, Persephone." He grabbed her hand and pulled her along the terrace to the end, and she stumbled along beside him.

She noted belatedly that while the terrace was indeed well lit, there were no well-placed chaperones in evidence anywhere. There wasn't anybody out there at all, in fact. Henry paused at the top of the stairs at the end of the terrace and looked at her, one brow raised.

"Where are we going?" she whispered.

"Do you trust me?"

"Of course." And she did.

He led her down the stairs and around the side of the house, down a path to one of three glassed-in gazebos that each flickered with soft light from small stoves and candles within. "We won't stay away long," he told her as they climbed the steps of the farthest gazebo from the house. "You'll be ruined, and we can't have that."

"My aunt would be thrilled," she muttered as she moved closer to the wood-burning stove, extending her hands and reveling in the warmth.

"I can't imagine your aunt would want you ruined."

She heard the smile in his voice even as she shook her head. "My aunt would be so happy to have me off of her hands. She now has it in her head to marry me off to the village doctor."

He was silent for a moment. She looked at him and realized her mistake. Her aunt wanted *Penelope* to marry the village doctor, not Persephone.

She exhaled. "That is, well, she just . . ." Penelope rubbed her forehead and closed her eyes, hating that she'd ever agreed to write that stupid letter for Persephone in the first place. The charade was tumbling about her, and fast.

She turned at the feel of his hand on her elbow, and he

gestured to a bench seated close to the stove. She sank onto the soft cushion and sighed.

He sat next to her, one ankle propped atop the other knee, and regarded her carefully. "Let me understand this. Your aunt wants *Penelope* to marry the village doctor."

"Yes." She swallowed. "What did I say?"

Henry shook his head. "When did this come about? Has it been long in the planning?"

Penny shook her head and looked down at the black mask she still held in her hands. Her pink mask now rested atop one very well-muscled thigh, and she swallowed, feeling suddenly very warm. "Tonight, on the way here to the ball, in fact, she encouraged Penelope to set her cap for Doctor Fitzroy. She would then feel absolved of her responsibility to my mother if we both married. She despairs of Penelope ever making a match with anyone, regardless of trade or station, and she hit upon the idea just before we arrived here tonight."

"And how does Penelope view the matter? Does she fancy the good doctor?"

Penny thought of Persephone's love and affection for Gilroy, and the ghost of a smile played around her lips. "She does. Very much." Penny swallowed and turned her attention to the small fire in the stove. "My aunt is hopeful, of course, that Pers—"—she bit off a curse—"that I make a good match. A splendid match. Truly, Henry, we ought not to be out here long by ourselves. If she notices I'm gone, she will allow a certain amount of time to conveniently lapse and then launch a search for me in hopes of finding me in just such a situation. You would be forced to do the honorable thing, and I would rather face her wrath eternally than to see you coerced into a marriage you do not desire."

"And if I do desire it?"

His husky voice drew shivers down her spine, and she tore her gaze from the captivating flames to the light and shadows they cast on his handsome face. He wasn't grinning; there was no amusement anywhere, either on his features or in his demeanor. He placed his arm across the back of the bench and leaned toward her, his leg brushing against hers. "Perhaps you should let me decide for myself."

"Well, that's just the thing—you wouldn't be deciding. You'd be forced, and besides," she looked away again, cursing the burning sensation she felt in her eyes, "there are things you don't know about me, I haven't been completely—"

He placed his fingers on the back of her neck, his thumb rubbing slowly across her skin. "What's in a name?" he whispered, and she strained to hear it.

Confused, she wrinkled her brow and opened her mouth to respond when his lips found hers, effectively silencing anything she might have said and driving every sane thought from her head. He slid his other hand to her side and then around her back, gently pulling her closer until she was pressed tightly against him. With a sigh, she tentatively reached her hands to the hair at his collar and tangled her fingers in the thick, black strands. He groaned and deepened the kiss, tracing his tongue subtly across her lower lip before trailing his mouth along her jaw to a sensitive spot on the side of her neck, just below her ear.

She was on fire, every nerve ending, every cell. "Henry," she whispered, cradling his head in her hands. "I must tell you, I must..."

Henry found his way back to her mouth again and kissed her repeatedly, thoroughly, driving her to a pitch she had never known existed. He finally pulled his mouth slowly from hers and framed her head in his hands, his forehead resting on hers, breathless. Penny exhaled softly, caught on a tide of sensation and emotion that had her seeing stars.

Cold reality intruded when she heard laughter outside, and voices approaching from the direction of the house. She froze, and Henry pulled back, looking into her eyes. "I cannot pretend I'm not tempted," he said.

"To what?" She stared at him, confused.

"To get caught with you here, like this."

Her breath snagged in her throat, and she stared at him, horrified to realize that nothing would make her happier. "Henry, I—"

He shook his head. "I won't enter into this by ruining your good name." He looked at her intently, and something hovered at the back of her mind, something she was certain her muddled brain wasn't comprehending. "We will do this properly. I'll come to your house tomorrow and inform your uncle that I intend to court you."

He stood and pulled her up with him. He must have assumed, however, that she could walk. She felt absolutely boneless after his sensual assault, and she found herself slightly vexed that he seemed able to function perfectly well while she was two steps from falling on her face. He tugged her along behind him, slipping down the steps, out of the gazebo, and around behind the back. As the small group of people progressed past the first two gazebos, Henry pulled her quickly to his side and wrapped his arm around her waist. He ran with her from one gazebo to the next, shielding her and pausing to look around the corner before finally grasping her hand and running for the mansion.

Rather than heading straight for the steps, however, he veered off to the side and pulled her into the garden, where the trees, while having lost most of their leaves, still provided temporary shelter from prying eyes. He spun her around and fitted the mask to her face, tying it carefully and then patting rather ineffectually at the back of her head.

"I'm afraid I may have dislodged a couple of pins," he murmured, and she heard the amusement in his voice.

She laughed softly, torn somewhere between delight that he wanted to be with her, to make something more out of their friendship, and despair that it would all soon come crashing down when he realized she was a liar. She'd tried to tell him, more than once. And now, when she searched one last time for her voice, her words caught in her throat at the feel of his lips along the side of her neck. He pulled her shoulders toward him, her back against the solid plane of his chest, and she closed her eyes. He wrapped his arm around her waist when she sagged against him, and she shivered as his breath fanned against her skin.

"Go," he finally murmured. "Go back inside. I'll return in a few minutes. If we do not have another chance to talk before you leave, then know I will come for you tomorrow. Will you be there?"

She nodded, tears stinging in her eyes, and this time she was unable to keep them from falling. First one and then another escaped and trickled along her cheek beneath the mask. Before he might notice, she pulled from his embrace and ran for the shelter of the house, cursing herself for ten times a fool and wishing more than anything she could avoid seeing his face when she finally found the courage to tell him the truth.

Eight

Henry leaned a shoulder against the tree and watched Penny run for the house. He cursed himself up one side and down the other for not just letting her tell him what he knew she had to say. He hadn't wanted her worries or fears about what he might think to intrude on the moment. He'd wanted to show her that his affections for her were real, that it didn't matter if her name was Persephone or Penelope, that whatever reason she'd begun the correspondence as her sister must have warranted the subtle deception.

He cursed and exhaled, willing his ardor to cool enough that he might reenter the ballroom without looking like a teenage boy flushed from his first burlesque show. By the end of their conversation in the gazebo, he'd begun losing track of which sister they were actually discussing. When she mentioned that Penelope had tender feelings for the village doctor—Fitzgibbons? Fitzhugh? Fitzcad?—his heart had pounded in his ears, and he'd felt a mad surge of jealousy over a man he'd never met. But was she speaking of her own affections or Persephone's?

It was all confusing, and he'd allowed his emotions free rein, very nearly ruining her in the process. It would have been so much easier, of course, to do as he'd said and let them just be discovered together alone. Problem solved, special license obtained, married within a week.

But if Penny was in love with someone else, if her affections were truly engaged with another, he was going to have to find the integrity to let her go. He shook his head as he finally made his way back to the house. Integrity suddenly seemed very overrated. He reached the doors leading to the ballroom and stood there for a moment, searching for a magenta dress and dark golden curls that had been slightly mussed. He bit back a satisfied grin as he remembered her response to his less-than-subtle attack on her mouth. The grin faded and was replaced with a grim determination that when it came to Penelope Timely, he wasn't going to roll over without a fight. Her feelings for him, her genuine friendship with him that had risen from their letters and taken on a life of their own—they meant something. He could search all of England and well into the continent and never find another woman who was enamored of old fish remains and geologic formations.

His eyes continued a restless sweep of the crowded room, and he finally found her, standing with her twin and leaning forward to listen to a handsome young man who hovered close to the two women. A wave of jealousy washed over him as Penny laughed at something the man said, and he clenched his teeth together so tightly his jaw hurt. The vicar walked by Henry with a plate full of food, and Henry caught his attention.

What's in a Name?

"Who is that young man over there with the Timely twins?"

The vicar laughed as he popped a cheese ball into his mouth. "Masquerade ball, Wilmington. You're not supposed to know who anyone is until midnight."

Henry stared flatly at the man and refrained from snapping that it was almost a certainty everyone in that room knew everyone else, mask or no.

"That's the Ellshire village doctor, Gilroy Fitzroy. Handsome lad, fresh out of university. Lucky to have him here—he's already delivered three babies and cured a few fevers. Even rescued my grandson's puppy from the river last week."

Of course he had. The man delivered babies and rescued puppies. What kind of name was Gilroy Fitzroy, anyway? Parents must not have liked him much to have saddled him with that rhyming monstrosity. He took cold comfort in that thought as Penny smiled again at the doctor, and Henry felt it like a punch in his gut. His mind cast back on the conversation in the gazebo, uselessly trying to remember her exact phrasing. Either Penny or Persephone definitely had feelings for the paragon puppy savior, that much had been abundantly clear. He wondered if he could scare the physician away from Penelope by alerting him privately to her affection for dead sea creatures.

Disgusted with himself for being so petty, he leaned his shoulder against a pillar and observed the crowd as they counted down the minutes until midnight and then removed their masks with much cheering and laughter. His gaze found Penny's face once again, and he took immense satisfaction that her eyes were focused entirely on him, not on Fitzroy. Henry gave her a salute, his mouth quirking at her resulting blush. He hoped she was remembering every last moment of their episode in the gazebo.

There was one thing he knew for certain, the duke and the doctor were likely to come to blows.

Penny tore down the hallway after her sister and yanked the bedroom door open when Persephone slammed it in her face. "Have you completely lost your senses?" Penny hissed as she looked with growing horror at Persephone's resolute face. "You cannot go to Gretna Green with Gilroy!"

"I am, Penny, and nobody will stop me." Persephone pulled a dress from her wardrobe and laid it out on the bed, tapping her lip.

Penny groaned. "Please do not tell me you are making a Plan."

"Of course I am." Persephone paused in her Planning to throw a dark look at Penny. "Do not even consider telling anyone about this, Penny, or I shall . . . I shall . . . I shall tell Aunt Millicent it was your idea to write to His Grace in my stead and that you forced me to comply!"

"Uh!" Penny gasped at her sister in outrage. "That is just villainous, Persephone! And you cannot go, please. I need you here today. His Grace plans to inform Uncle Horace of his intention to court me—you."

Persephone looked at Penny with an assessing glance that raised the hairs on Penny's arms. "It seems to me, then, that I had best be on my way. You will continue to be me, and I will elope with Gilroy as you. I am leaving her a note she won't find until she readies for bed tonight. Nobody will be the wiser until it's too late, and until then, Millicent won't care one whit that you've disappeared."

What's in a Name?

Penny winced. "That is cruel, you know."

Persephone's gaze softened for a quick moment, but it was gone before Penny was certain she'd even seen it. "She's a ridiculous woman, Penny, and we both know it. I've not been a good sister to you at all since Mama died, and I believe the best thing I can do for you is leave. Today."

"Persephone." Penny's panic grew, and she plunked herself down on her sister's bed, feeling more like the dramatic twin since, well, ever. "He will not want me when he learns what I've done." Her eyes burned with tears yet again, and it made her angry. "Our whole relationship is based on a lie!"

Persephone studied her carefully as she folded an armful of undergarments and placed them into an open trunk at the foot of the bed. "Did you write to him in my voice? That is, did you say things you knew I would say, write about the things in which I have an interest?"

"Well, no, but—"

"Did you tell him you were the older of two twins, that we live with an irascible aunt who loves you the most because you're accomplished in the domestic arts and your sister can never measure up against you?"

"No, but I—"

"So, you wrote as yourself and did not pretend to be me other than signing my name at the bottom of your letters."

Penny paused. "Yes, however—"

Persephone plunked her hands down in the middle of the heap of frothy unmentionables and stockings. "Then what could possibly be the problem? Aunt Millicent? Do you believe she'll prevent your association with His Grace? Lock you in the attic? Have you shanghaied or shipped off to the colonies? Penny, I am going to marry Gilroy, and you are going to marry your duke, and she will have nothing to say in the matter."

Penny stared at her suddenly practical sister. "Then why are you eloping?"

Persephone shot her a wry glance and folded a blouse. "Do you honestly think she'll willingly allow me to marry Gilroy? Of course not. That is why I must do it this way. By the time she screeches her objections, the deed will be done and it will be too late."

Penny frowned. "Be certain you consummate it, then. She'll probably insist on an annulment and demand proof."

Persephone gaped at Penny before tipping her head back in laughter. "Penny, how wicked you are!" she said when she finally caught her breath. She set her clothing down and crossed to the other side of the bed. Her laughter still playing on her face, she reached down and put her arms around Penny. "I do love you, Pen. More than anything. And Millicent is an absolute beast."

Penny returned the embrace, closing her eyes until Persephone finally released her and straightened. "Now then, I must go in the next twenty minutes. Millicent will return from the milliner's in less than an hour, and I cannot be here. I need you to wear one of my dresses and pretend to be me one last time. It will serve you just as well when His Grace comes over to declare his intentions."

Penny smiled sadly at her sister. "At least one of us will be happy. I'm afraid to admit I don't know His Grace well enough to predict his reaction."

"You didn't lie to him about who you are at your core, Penny." Persephone smiled at her fondly before whirling around and pulling a pink dress from her wardrobe. "Here, wear this one. And for heaven's sake, fix your hair."

What's in a Name?

Millicent gaped at Penny, her eyes shining. "He is speaking with your uncle, Persephone! I knew you could do it! You are going to be a duchess, my girl, and we shall take the *ton* by storm."

Penny bared her teeth in what she hoped resembled a smile. Persephone had been gone for nearly two hours and should reach the border and cross into Gretna Green by nightfall. All Penny had to do was maintain the charade long enough to give her sister the time she needed to marry her love. And then consummate that love. Penny held back a snicker and smiled with narrowed eyes at her aunt instead. If it weren't for her own impending misery, she'd have relished the apoplexy Millicent would soon be experiencing.

Uncle Horace's study door opened, and Penny caught her breath. Henry wore a dark blue coat with buff-colored breeches and gleaming black boots. He was tall and majestic and so very handsome she couldn't help but rest her hand on her heart, the very vision of a smitten, idiotic ninny.

His lips quirked, and he dropped his gaze to her hand. She moved her hand and still his gaze lingered, which sent a rush of mortified, delightful heat rushing to her face. As though from far away she heard her uncle's hearty felicitations and her aunt's screeching delight. Her eyes remained glued to His Grace's fine physique, and she barely registered him asking Millicent if he and *Persephone* might have a moment to chat in the parlor. Alone.

"Of course!" Millicent gathered her stitchery in a flurry of movement. "I'll just check on some things in the kitchen and then return to chaperone. In a while." Her aunt and uncle left the room, the door opened barely a crack. Penny shook her head. When it came to Persephone, Millicent was willing to throw out the propriety rule book entirely in order to secure a match with the duke.

Henry crossed the room to the hearth where Penny stood, unconsciously wringing her hands together. He clasped her cold fingers in his own and brought her hands to his mouth, his eyes never leaving hers. He touched the tip of his tongue to her knuckle and the breath left her lungs in a shuddering sigh. Smug male satisfaction crossed his face, and he tugged her toward the settee.

"I've thought of nothing but you since last night." Henry kept hold of her hands, tracing his thumb along her skin.

Penelope swallowed, dropping her eyes to his expertly tied cravat. *If only . . . if only . . .*

"What are you thinking?"

She shrugged miserably, and he placed a finger beneath her chin, tipping her face up. He looked at her with a mixture of desire and tenderness, and his smile was nearly her undoing.

"Persephone, what is it? What are you trying not to say?"

Penny shook her head, thinking of Persephone on her way to Scotland but not nearly close enough yet. She and Gilroy rode in a carriage; Millicent could hire someone from town to chase them down on a swift horse and cut them off before they made Gretna Green.

"Will you be at the bonfire supper tonight in the village square?" she finally had the courage to ask.

"I had planned on being there with you, yes. I attended as a child; I seem to remember a suppertime picnic of sorts with multiple fires set around the square and the Ellshire village park."

Penny's lips quirked. "Yes. Controlled fires, though. And enough of them to keep everyone warm while they celebrate the ending of another harvest season." She paused and sighed. "There is something on my mind, Henry, and I shall tell you what it is tonight. Another's happiness is at stake, and I must wait until later."

His lips tightened fractionally. "You must wait and speak to this someone first?"

She frowned. "Speak to someone?" She shook her head. "No, I just have to wait for . . . well, I must wait." She lifted her shoulder in a miserable shrug.

He tipped his head, confusion clearly written on his face.

"It will make sense later, and if you still decide you want to court me, then, well, I shall be most happy."

He blinked at her, his head still held in the same position, and she gritted her teeth at the fact that, once again, Persephone had made a Plan that affected Penny.

Henry shook himself free of whatever he'd been thinking and smiled at her, squeezing her hands. "Will you show me your fossil creek bed? I've been anxious to see it."

Penny felt excitement bubble to the surface until she was so happy she wanted to float into the clouds. Finally! Another who would delight in her discoveries! "Yes! I'll grab my shawl and bonnet."

Millicent paused at the entryway where Henry was helping Penny adjust her blue shawl across her shoulders. Her aunt carried a tray of refreshments, and she now looked at Penny in some confusion. "You're going outside?"

"Well, yes, I thought I would show His Grace the beautiful meadow." Penny grasped desperately for her sister's mannerisms, her turn of phrase, her affectations. Regrettably, her mind drew nothing but a blank.

"The meadow?" Millicent blinked.

"Yes." Penny smiled brightly and tied the bow on her bonnet.

"Why are you wearing Penelope's wrap and bonnet, Persephone?" Millicent said with a sideways glance at His Grace. "Are you feeling well?"

Penny leaned close to her aunt and whispered in her ear. "I am so giddy with excitement I fear I've lost my mind!" She allowed the last to come out on a small squeal and was gratified when Millicent beamed at her conspiratorially.

"Very well, then, but do take care to avoid that dreadful creek bed in the woods where Penelope likes to sit."

Penny narrowed her eyes but squeezed out a smile. She didn't sit in the creek bed, for heaven's sake. Well, she didn't sit there merely for the sake of sitting there. She had a purpose, after all. But as she was skating on borrowed luck, she refrained from further comment, gave her aunt a delighted shrug and a bright smile, and pulled Henry from the house.

"Penelope also enjoys the creek bed, then?" he asked as Penny ushered him out of the small yard and around to the meadow and the woods.

She glanced at him, surprised to see amusement there, rather than confusion. "She does, on occasion." Penny figured she wasn't going to hell for all the lies and half-truths she'd implied; she was already there. But she was determined to enjoy every last drop of daylight she had with Henry, showing him her beloved creek bed and discussing the wonder of seashells and ancient rock formations. The night would come soon enough, and with it, her heart would break.

Nine

Henry watched the firelight play on Penelope's features as they sat on a warm blanket near one of several small bonfires in the village park. The festivities had grown since he was a boy, and he was surprised to see the same number of people around the park and village square as had been at the ball the night before. It seemed the Ellshire Autumn Masquerade Ball and Festival had become a draw for neighboring towns, as well. For his part, he was grateful. The more people there were milling around, the more anonymity he enjoyed.

Penelope caught him watching her, and she smiled. Their afternoon had been the best of his life. He had examined her beloved creek bed, impressed at the things she'd uncovered and the potential for more still hidden in the ground. They had walked a mile to the shore, where she showed him several caves she hoped to explore in search of more fossils. They'd broken the rock she'd nearly been run over for in the village street and discovered that it was, indeed, a beautiful geode with crystal formations on the inside. Her delight had warmed him up inside until he'd felt positively smitten and ridiculous. They'd eaten lunch at a small pub near the water and returned in time for her to change her clothes for the bonfire supper.

"Did you enjoy your day?" she asked, nibbling on a meat pie. He watched her lick a stray crumb from her finger and swallowed audibly. If too much more time passed before he kissed her again, he was likely to implode.

"Very much." He smiled and tucked an errant curl behind her ear.

She blushed. "I never can stay tidy for very long."

"I prefer it." He paused, knowing her well enough by now to recognize the telltale bobbing of her knee, even though they sat on the ground. Her skirts moved subtly with the movement, and he was desperate for her to put her anxiety behind them so they could move forward. "You said you would tell me what was on your mind tonight."

She exhaled softly and set her plate down on the blanket. She slowly wiped her fingers with a linen napkin, and he wanted to grab her by the shoulders and shake her confession out. "Henry." She looked at him with such longing in her gaze that it took everything he possessed to keep from shushing her, from telling her he already knew her terrible secret. He smiled. If that was the most terrible thing she ever did to him, he'd count himself a lucky man.

"Henry, I must confess something to you. My letters to you, that is, when we began . . ." She rubbed her forehead with fingers that trembled.

He reached for her hand and held it gently. He opened his mouth to end her misery when a flash of movement from the side cut him off, and he stared as a bony hand reached down and hauled Penelope up by the arm.

"You!" Millicent stood on the blanket, her furious visage inches from Penny's. Henry stood and pried the woman's vicious fingers from Penny's arm, inserting himself between the two women.

"Madam, I urge you to rethink whatever it is you have to say in the next few moments," he murmured to her in a deadly undertone.

She glared up at him, her eyes snapping. "That girl,"—she stabbed her finger around him—"is *not* Persephone!"

"I know."

"She—what did you say?"

Penny edged out from behind him. "You what?"

He placed an arm around Penny's shoulders and pulled her close against his side, his lips thinning in anger at the spectacle Millicent was making at Penny's expense.

"What have you done?" Millicent snarled at her niece. "You encouraged Persephone to run off with that doctor,"—she spat the word out—"so you could claim His Grace for yourself! Pretending to be your sister!"

"No." Penny shook her head and glanced at Henry. "I did not encourage Persephone to do anything. She makes her own choices, and I am not to blame."

"Where are they?" Millicent's face turned an alarming shade of purple.

"Gretna Green. They should be there by now." She glanced up at Henry. "Which is why I couldn't tell you . . . what I wanted to tell you until tonight. Now."

He closed his eyes. It was as he'd guessed after spending the afternoon with her and watching for little signs, small anecdotes that gave herself and the nature of her relationship with Persephone away. She had written to him for Persephone, so that Persephone could pursue her interest in Doctor Fitzroy. She had stood in her sister's place this weekend to protect Persephone's romance with the doctor, and even now, she put aside her own dismay and sadness, thinking she was risking her relationship with him to buy Persephone enough time to make it over the border.

"I hope they hurry and consummate it," he muttered as a quiet aside to Penny.

She nodded at him. "That's what I told her."

His lips twitched, and he fought back a laugh.

"This is not in the least amusing, nor is this the last of it!" Millicent leaned toward Penny, and to his surprise, Penny shifted her stance slightly, aggressively toward her aunt.

"This *is* the last of it, Aunt Millicent. Persephone will return to Ellshire a married woman, and you will have no say in the matter."

"You ungrateful wretch. If you think you're going to remain under my roof after this, you're mistaken!"

"That's just as well," Henry told the woman. "She won't need to. My mother has invited Penelope as her guest at Wilmington indefinitely. We will return to your home to pack Penny's things, and you will remain well out of the way until we are gone. I expect I've made myself clear."

Millicent took a deep breath and let it out. With one final, angry nod, she spun on her heel and left. Henry looked down at Penny, still nestled against his side, and tapped the end of her nose with his fingertip. "My lady, we must talk."

Penny avoided the stares of the gathering crowd and held onto Henry's hand as he led her to the edge of the park, leaving the people and the bonfires behind. He guided her through a small stand of trees away from prying eyes and put his hands on her shoulders before dropping them to his sides. She studied his face, bewildered, and felt cold without his arms around her.

She shook her head. "You know I'm not Persephone? How?"

He took a deep breath. "I've known since about thirty seconds after I saw you for the first time."

"Wha— How? How on earth did you know?" She searched his face, looking for signs of subterfuge on his part, wanting him to say something quickly that would make sense to her.

"I knew you only from the inside, Penny, from your letters." He lifted his shoulders in a small shrug and ran a hand through his hair. It was the first time she'd seen him agitated. Unsure of himself. "I knew your soul, and I also knew that the twin I met first wasn't quite . . . right. And then you came in from outside and I just,"—he spread his hands wide—"I just knew."

Her heart skipped at beat at the sound of her true name on his lips. "Why didn't you say something?"

"I was . . ." He muttered something she couldn't make out.

"You were what?"

Again, the mumble.

"Henry, what are you saying?"

He looked at her, the sheepish expression on his face giving him the appearance of a young boy caught with his hand in the cookie jar. "I was aroused."

Her head spun. "You were . . . aroused?" He wasn't making any sense. "What the devil does that even mean, you were aroused? At what? My lie?"

"No, Penny." Again, he ran his fingers through his hair and paced a small distance away from her, then returned back to the spot he'd just left. "The thought of you trying to put one over on me, as it were, I found it intriguing. Amazing. Interesting. I wanted to know what you were going to do, and I didn't want to spoil it. And by the time I realized it was causing you a fair amount of distress, I wanted to tell you I knew, but then I kissed you, and then I never wanted to stop kissing you. And the longer we went without talking about it, the harder it seemed to broach. I wanted you to tell me this morning, but you said you couldn't, and I thought maybe it was because you were in love with the doctor and had to tell him I was courting you . . ."

Her eyes widened, and she stared at him, unable to believe she'd heard him correctly. "You thought I was in love with a man named Gilroy Fitzroy?"

"Exactly!" He gestured in the air. "So you see my dilemma?"

Penny chewed on her lip. "I am so confused." And she was. Should she be angry at him? After all, he'd done nothing worse than she had.

"My darling Penelope." Henry placed his hands on her shoulders and then cupped her face. "Please forgive me for allowing it to go on as it did. Forgive me for not realizing until I was well into the mess that it was causing you pain. I know why you wrote to me as Persephone."

Drat. She felt the tears gather again. "You do?"

He nodded and thumbed away an escaped tear. "You've done everything for her. And in this one instance, I thank my lucky stars that you did. If she had written to me instead of you, I would have tossed the letter into the fire and never known you. Never fallen in love with you. Would never have been so desperate to meet you that it was all I could do to wait until this blasted festival to see your face, to kiss you."

"Henry, I'm so sorry for all the confusion, the half-truths." She sniffled, and he took a handkerchief from his pocket. He paused and reached in again to his coat pocket and pulled out a small object. He smiled at her and opened his hand, moving her to a small shaft of moonlight that shot through the trees.

She recognized it immediately and gasped, bringing her hand to her lips and then laughing through her tears. "You have a trilobite in your pocket!"

"That sounds slightly inappropriate."

She laughed again, harder. She carefully took it from his hand and clasped it in both of hers, turning her face to him and feeling so much joy she thought her heart would burst. "I can't believe you carry this around with you. I am utterly in love."

He chuckled and traced his fingers gently down her cheek. "With me or the fossil?"

She swatted at him. "With you. And the fossil."

"Then you'll marry me? Please, for the love of heaven, say you'll marry me. I'll never find another woman in the world who will go searching for ancient sea life with me. And incidentally, Wilmington lands stretch to the shore. The caves you showed me today—I own them."

She laughed so hard she actually fell into his chest. He promptly closed his arms around her and tipped her face up to meet his unrepentant grin.

"Yes, I will bribe you."

"Henry, dear man. Of course I'll marry you. But I warn you, I am not at all conventional." She felt a stab of insecurity. "I'm hardly duchess material."

"You're my perfect duchess. I don't want you to change even one thing. I love you, Penelope Timely."

"I love you too, Your Grace. My Henry."

Her last thought before his lips closed over hers was that she couldn't imagine a brighter spot of heaven on earth—to be kissing the man she adored and clutching a fossil at the same time. And then rational thought quite flew out the proverbial window as he kissed her senseless. For a deliciously long time.

ABOUT NANCY CAMPBELL ALLEN

Nancy Campbell Allen (N.C. Allen) is the author of 11 published novels, which encompass a variety of genres from contemporary romantic suspense to historical fiction. Her Civil War series, Faith of our Fathers, won the Utah Best of State award in 2005 and all three of her historicals featuring Isabelle Webb, Pinkerton spy, have been nominated for the Whitney Award. Her formal schooling includes a B.S. in Elementary Education from Weber State University and she has worked as a freelance editor, contributing to the recent release, We Knew Howard Hughes, by Jim Whetton.

Nancy served as the Teen Writers Conference chair in 2011 and 2012, and has presented at numerous conferences and events since her initial publication in 1999 with Covenant Communications. Her agent is Pam Van Hylckama Vlieg of Foreword Literary, and she is currently writing a series of Gothic Steampunk novels and other short novellas. Nancy loves to read, write, travel and research, and enjoys spending time laughing with family and friends. She and her husband have three children, and she lives in Ogden, Utah with her family and one very large Siberian Husky named Thor.

Visit Nancy's blog: NCAllen.blogspot.com
Twitter: @necallen

Dear Timeless Regency Collection Reader,

Thank you for reading *Autumn Masquerade*. We hoped you loved the sweet romance novellas! Each collection in the Timeless Regency Collection contains three novellas.

If you enjoyed this collection, please consider leaving a review on Goodreads or Amazon or any other online store you purchase through. Reviews and word-of-mouth is what helps us continue this fun project. For updates and notifications of sales and giveaways, please sign up for our monthly newsletter on our blog:

TimelessRomanceAnthologies.blogspot.com

Also, if you're interested in become a regular reviewer of these collections and would like access to advance copies, please email Heather Moore: heather@hbmoore.com

We also post our announcements to our Facebook page: Timeless Romance Anthologies

Thank you!
The Timeless Romance Authors

MORE TIMELESS REGENCY COLLECTIONS

Don't miss our TIMELESS ROMANCE ANTHOLGIES:
Six short romance novellas in each anthology

www.ingramcontent.com/pod-product-compliance
Lightning Source LLC
LaVergne TN
LVHW021801060526
838201LV00058B/3188